MEREDITH RESCE

Echoes in the Valley

Golden Grain Publishing

Acknowledgements

Thanks to the production team on this project:

Iola Goulton (editing), Rochelle Manners (layout design), Carmen Dougherty (cover design), Jennette Bishop, Angela Weeks, Karen Jones (first critique team), Chelsea Abrahams, Gavin Abrahams, Matthew Lister and Lisa Hendry (cover image models and production).

Judge not - These two words dominated my thoughts as I read, *Echoes in the Valley*. This story doesn't sugar-coat the ugly effects of sin. It shows how one mistake can have dire consequences, and how condemnation can destroy relationships. This story spoke to my heart. It made me contemplate Scripture, and gave me fresh insight into 'rebuke' vs 'judgment'. Although this book is part of the *Green Valley* series, it works well as a stand-alone novel. I look forward to reading more *Green Valley* stories.

Rose Dee

www.rosedee.com

Bookseller's Choice CALEB Awards 2012; Fiction Winner CALEB Awards 2013.

I've loved all Meredith Resce's books and am delighted she has revisited her great Australian *Green Valley* historical series. This 6th book highlights how individuals and small communities had to help each other with understanding, faith and love to try and recover from the grief and the disruptions caused by World War I. As with Meredith's other books, I found this hard to put down and, although this is a "stand alone" book, if you have not been privileged also to read the other books in this series, I highly recommend you do so.

Mary Hawkins

www.mary-hawkins.com

Best-selling inspirational romance author

For twenty years, Meredith Resce's *Green Valley* series has faithfully followed several generations of true blue Aussies. In *Echoes in the Valley*, main characters Grace and Alex face a sensitive situation which is made even more urgent because they live in the Great Depression era. It's good to experience the attitudes of times long past through the tension in these stories. For readers who have read previous Green Valley novels, we also get to catch up with other favourite characters. I congratulate Meredith for the authenticity of time and place she evokes.

Paula Vince

Award-winning author of *Picking up the Pieces*; co-author of *The Greenfield Legacy*.

A beautifully written and gripping love story set in the years of the Great Depression, about two people seeking forgiveness for the unforgivable. A must read.

Andrea Grigg

Author of *A Simple Mistake* and *Too Pretty*.

www.andreagrigg.com

Echoes in the Valley
Published by Golden Grain Publishing
PO Box 880 Unley SA 5061

© Meredith Resce, 2015

Cover Design by Book Whispers
Layout by Book Whispers: www.bookwhispers.com.au

National Library of Australia Cataloguing-in-Publication entry

Creator: Resce, Meredith, 1963- author.

Title: Echoes in the valley / Meredith Resce.

ISBN: 9780977592777 (paperback)

Series: Resce, Meredith, 1963- Heart of Green Valley ; 6

Dewey Number: A823.3

This is a work of fiction. Names, characters and incidents are either the product of the author's imagination or are used fictiously, and any resemblance to actual events or persons, living or dead, is entirely coincidental.

Author note

I started to write the first novel in the *Heart of Green Valley* series in 1993. It appeared first as a serial in the SACWA magazine (see my website for the full story www.meredithresce.com). Readers have engaged with the stories and characters for about twenty years now, and as we approach the twentieth anniversary of the first novel release, I wanted to celebrate with a new story. Echoes in the Valley is set about 14 years following the end of the Great War, and coincidentally, it is nearly 14 years since the last release of *Heart of Green Valley #5 – Beyond the Valley*.

This new story was a tough one to write, as I couldn't simply hide what happened with the characters, and I couldn't conveniently kill off the main obstacle character. I wanted to, but it would have read as an easy solution. So I embarked on a journey of staying with the drama and crisis that had been created, and would not resolve easily. The subject was highly controversial in the 1930s and is still, to a much lesser extent, within Christian circles today. I had no idea how I was going to get out of this without stirring up trouble and indeed, being insensitive to some very real current-day situations. In the end, one of my review readers came up with the solution – 'It's only by the Grace of God.' I was so relieved. I had to really investigate and embrace the Grace of God for myself to be able to really see how it would apply in this situation. I pray that you will also encounter His Grace as you read *Echoes in the Valley*.

Chapter One

Green Valley – Victoria Australia – 1932

Grace Shore heard the mournful tones of the bugle float out across the early morning air as the sun's golden-orange rays spilt over the eastern horizon. Warm tears spilled from her eyes. Her throat was tight from pent-up emotion, from this burden of grief which would always be with her. She joined her family on the 25th of April every year to remember those young men and women who had fallen during the Great War—especially Johnny Laslett. He had been the man she had loved, and the day she received news of his death, she had decided that she would never love again. Not in the way she had loved Johnny.

The poignant strains of the Last Post rang out, bringing back the gut-wrenching grief she had felt those years ago. When the bugler finished, the emotion was further heightened as a minute's silence ensued. Grace heard the birds' busy calling and wondered how they managed to continue with life, untouched by the tragedies of war. Then the bugle broke into the Reveille. The tune was animated and seemed to call for life to resume. Grace waited through the raising of the flag, not quite ready to let the grief go for another year. And then it was over. The folks around her began to murmur to each other. Grace didn't join in. It was mainly returned servicemen who were gathered, and now they had fallen out of rank and chatted quietly amongst themselves.

The impact of that dreadful time of tragedy and pain lived on, and enduring bonds had been formed between these men. Grace didn't speak, but simply observed.

Would the men ever get over their wartime experiences? She wouldn't. Johnny's death had marked her life forever. She would never get over it.

She didn't have the heart to engage in conversation with anyone. There were few women present and the returned soldiers seemed to share a camaraderie forged in the valley of death—something she didn't understand. She had only felt death's sting second-hand, in witnessing Johnny's name listed amongst those killed in action. There was something far deeper that she could see, but couldn't fully comprehend, drawing the returned servicemen together on this day of memorial.

Grace drew away from the assembly to walk back home in the fresh morning air. She'd come with her brother, Charlie, but he was talking to his mates. Charlie would more than likely pick her up before she reached home. They'd come out together in the horse-drawn two-seater sulky. They had a motorcar in the shed, but rarely used it these days. Times were hard, and petrol difficult to come by. Still, it was good to be alone with her thoughts in the quiet of the day, and she was no stranger to walking between one place and the next.

***

Alex Moreland was surprised at the sense of connection he felt with the other men who stood to attention during the minute's silence. These were not his comrades in the sense that he had not fought in their company. His wartime mates would be standing at the War Memorial in the park back home at Mitcham, a good 800 miles from Green Valley. He'd stood with them in years past, remembering his good mate and brother-in-law, Raymond Johnson, who'd been killed in action on the Western Front.

Alex had been in the habit of taking his other brother-in-law, Frank, to the Dawn Service. Frank had returned from the war whole in body, but he had lost his mind. The shell-shock had reduced him to a child-like state, and Alex's wife, Nancy, had pleaded with him to look after her invalid brother. Alex shook the thoughts of his in-laws from his mind. That was in the past now. He had moved on.

'You're new to the district?' A gentleman of about his own age spoke to him.

'Yes. Just passing through. Looking for work.'

The man held out his hand. 'Name's Charlie Shore. Fought with the 12th Light Horse in North Africa. You?'

'10th Infantry Battalion, AIF. Started out at Gallipoli, ended up in France.'

'Where you from?' Charlie asked.

'Small town a bit south of Adelaide.'

'South Australia. That's a bit of a hike.'

Alex nodded. He didn't know how much he wanted to share with this stranger, but something about having served in the forces gave them an automatic connection.

'You travelling on your own?'

'I've got my kids with me.'

Charlie raised his eyebrows. It looked like he wanted to ask a hundred more questions, but something seemed to hold him back.

'Well, if you're up for it, the fellows here will be meeting at the Green Valley pub around ten. We do that every Anzac Day. Share a beer, and play a round or three of two-up.'

Alex allowed a ghost of a smile.

'Used to do that with the boys back in Adelaide, though I was never much one for the drink.'

'Me neither,' Charlie said. 'I used to drink a bit before the war, but I got into a heap of trouble. I just have the one to remember my brother-in-law.'

'I lost a good mate as well,' Alex said. 'I married his sister after the war.'

Charlie smiled. 'Must have been the thing to do. I married Johnny's sister too, after I sorted myself out.'

Alex nodded. He was surprised at how much he had told this relative stranger. *All the emotion of the ceremony has made me soft.*

'Anyway,' Charlie continued, 'I'd be pleased to have you come to eat breakfast at my place, unless you've somewhere else you're expected.'

Alex took a deep breath. 'I've got three children with me. I don't want to impose.'

'No trouble at all. I've got a house full already. Four more are hardly going to make any difference.'

'Thanks. I appreciate the offer.'

'I've only got the sulky with me,' Charlie said. 'Do you have transport?'

'We've been walking.'

'All the way from Adelaide?'

'We've stopped at places along the way, where I could find work.'

'And your missus?'

Alex paused for a long moment. 'She passed away about seven years ago.'

'I'm sorry. Tough times.'

Alex nodded.

'Well, it's doubtful we'll be able to squeeze six of us into a two-seater, so I'll get Grace to drive the sulky home, and I'll walk with you. She can take a couple of your children if you like.'

'Will your wife mind you lobbing in with four extras for breakfast?'

Charlie laughed. 'My wife is a missionary. She is used to working in difficult situations with nothing to hand.'

***

Grace had only walked a couple of hundred yards before she came across three children sitting on a fallen branch beneath a tree.

'Hello,' she said in a friendly tone. 'Are you waiting for someone?'

'Our daddy is at the Dawn Service.'

The smallest of the three children volunteered the information, a young girl who looked to be about ten or eleven. Her older brother drew himself up to his full height.

'We're not supposed to be talking to strangers,' he said, his voice breaking as he spoke.

'Of course not. I'm sorry.' Grace could see the boy was taking his duty of care seriously. The three children looked to be about the same ages as Charlie's three youngest, her two nephews and niece.

'Well, I hope your parents return soon.'

'Our mother is dead.' The youngest girl seemed eager to share information.

'Shush, Jean! Keep your mouth closed.' Her brother scolded.

'She seems like a nice lady,' Jean said. 'I was just being polite.'

'She doesn't need to know about our family affairs.'

'It's all right, Jean,' Grace said. 'Your brother is right. It isn't wise to tell strangers all your family information.'

'But she doesn't look like a stranger.' Jean turned back to Grace. 'I like the look of your face. You seem to be a good lady.'

Grace smiled. 'Thank you. It is nice of you to say so.'

'Now shush, will you, Jean, for goodness sake,' her brother said.

'It was nice to meet you,' Grace said, and turned to continue walking.

'I hope I meet you again soon,' Jean called after her.

'Jean!' Both her brother and sister scolded her this time.

Grace couldn't help but laugh. The child was charming and irrepressible. As she walked away she could hear the two older children lecturing their little sister. They sounded just like her nieces and nephews, especially Charlie and Meg's four. They could be a handful, but she loved her job as their housekeeper and nanny. It was her mother who couldn't quite accept her unmarried state, and continued to orchestrate meetings with potential suitors. Grace was not interested. Thankfully her younger brother, CJ, also remained unmarried, though at thirty-two he was sought after as a most eligible bachelor. She, at thirty-four had reached old-maid status. Sometimes it stung, but not today. Johnny was her one and only love. There wouldn't be anybody else.

***

'My kids are sat under a tree back down the road a bit.' Alex waved his hand in the general direction.

'I'll get the horse and sulky, and meet you there in a few minutes,' Charlie said.

Alex turned and walked away from the war memorial and flag pole where the dawn service had been held. He hadn't stopped to read the eight names of the fallen inscribed there, like he would have back in Mitcham. If he'd been at home, he would have taken some minutes to reflect. Of the names inscribed on the Mitcham Park memorial, he'd known most of them, including his best friend, Ray. Fourteen years had dulled the pain, but never the memory.

They shall grow not old, as we that are left grow old. He recited the line from The Ode of Remembrance that had now become part of the Anzac Day service.

Alex didn't feel particularly old at thirty-five, at least, not in body. He was fit and healthy but he had seen too much tragedy, and there had been more loss and betrayal added to his life since the war. He wondered if he had the heart of an old man, even if his body was young.

'Daddy!' Jean came running down the road to meet him. 'We met a really nice lady.'

'I told her not to talk to strangers,' Jimmy said, as he and Irene followed behind.

'Jeanie. If you do not know who you're talking to, then you should keep quiet.' Alex hated scolding her. Her sunny disposition was just like her mother's, but he'd learned about betrayal the hard way. He wasn't going to make the same mistake again.

Once they'd shouldered their swags and each picked up a bag, the three children fell in step with their father and began to walk along the road. They were all quiet. Alex knew that Jean took being scolded hard, but he didn't have the heart to cheer her up. Jimmy and Irene had already learned the tough lessons of life. They didn't have the cheerful, outgoing personality their sister did.

'I can see the lady.' Jean pointed in front of her. 'See up the road there. She was walking, too.'

Alex didn't answer. He could see the woman walking ahead of them.

'Can you see her, Daddy?'

'Yes, darlin'. I can see her, but remember what we discussed about strangers.'

'I think you might be wrong this time. The lady had a very nice face, and was very kind to us.'

'Why didn't you keep your sister away from talking to strangers?' Alex frowned at his son. 'I left you in charge.'

'I tried, Dad. But you know how she is.'

'He did try,' Irene said. 'But Jean never listens to us.'

Alex recognised the fury that burned in his gut. He remembered another time all too well, and he wasn't going to let that happen again.

'Just make sure you keep an eye on her next time.'

Jimmy sighed, and Alex sensed his son's anger. He knew it wasn't fair to put that responsibility on a thirteen-year-old, but Alex had to work. He couldn't be watching Jean every moment of the day, and he didn't trust anybody else.

The tense silence was broken as Charlie Shore approached, driving his horse and sulky. He pulled up next to the family and got down from the vehicle.

'Sorry I took so long,' he said. 'I got caught up talking to my neighbour.'

'That's fine,' Alex replied. 'These are my children: Jimmy, Irene and Jean.' He pointed to each one in turn, and watched as they bobbed their head in acknowledgement. 'Children, this is Mr Shore. He has kindly invited us to breakfast.'

Alex watched as Jean's face lit up with a smile. She was such a social child, so different to the rest of them.

'I can see Grace on the road up ahead. Give me a moment and I'll bring her back. She can drive the horse home, and perhaps give one or two of you a lift.'

'It's the lady who stopped to talk to us. She isn't a stranger after all.' Jean was beaming, and Alex couldn't help but smile in return.

He watched as Charlie trotted the horse down to catch up with his wife. He felt a little relieved that Jean could meet the lady properly and that she was not going to be a threat to them after all.

'Can I ride with the lady back to her house, Daddy? Please?'

'Just be patient, Jean. Let Mr Shore organise things first. He hasn't even told his wife that he's invited us yet. She might not be prepared to have so many extras for breakfast.'

'She will. She is a really nice lady.'

Alex looked across to his son and other daughter. Jimmy just shrugged his shoulders. 'Don't ask me. I'm no judge of strangers.'

Charlie only took a couple of minutes to pick his wife up, and return.

'Would you like the girls to ride back to the farm with Grace?' Charlie asked Alex.

'If it isn't too much trouble,' Alex replied.

Straight away Jean moved to the side of the sulky and put her foot on the step to climb up.

'I'm so glad to see you again,' she said to the woman in the cart.

'I'm pleased to see you again too,' Grace replied.

Irene put her foot on the step to climb up as well.

'Now Jeanie, don't you talk Mrs Shore's ear off. Do you hear me?'

'I won't.' She gave a wide smile.

'Actually, it's Miss Shore,' Grace said gently. 'I'm Charlie's sister. Meg is Mrs Shore.'

Alex felt his head spin and stomach clench. He wouldn't fall for this a second time.

'Jeanie, Irene, come down from the cart – now please.'

'Daddy, why?' Jean complained.

'Do as you're told. I said to get down.'

Irene climbed down as ordered, but Jean hesitated.

'Jeanie.' Alex's tone was steely.

'I'm sorry, Miss Shore,' Jean said, giving a sigh of resignation. 'Daddy gets all funny around ladies.'

Alex reached up and grabbed his daughter around the waist, whisking her to the ground.

He knew that Charlie was frowning at him. He regretted that he had just lost a free meal for his family, and most likely the opportunity to look for work in the district. But he was not going to put himself in that position again. He'd been there once, and once was enough.

***

'What on earth was that?' Grace asked her brother, once he'd seen the family off.

'I have no idea, Gracie, but there's more to it than meets the eye.'

'So you don't think he is just a rude obnoxious man, then?'

'He was certainly very rude to you just now, but he's a war veteran. You can't always understand a man by the way he appears to be.'

'He was fine while he thought I was your wife, but as soon as he realised I was your sister, he turned hostile. Why? Do you suppose he is afraid of women?'

'He's been married, obviously. He told me his wife died years ago. There must be something else. That was a strange way to act for no reason.'

'Mmm.' Grace wasn't ready to give him the benefit of the doubt. 'His youngest child shows something different, I suppose. Perhaps you are right. She does tend to let family information out when perhaps she shouldn't.'

'What did she say?'

'That daddy gets all funny around ladies.'

'Not all ladies—like you said, he was fine when he thought you were my wife. I think he gets funny around single ladies.'

Grace blushed. 'What do you mean? Do you think he thought I ...'

Charlie shrugged. 'I don't know, but he has trust issues.'

'He seemed to trust you and your wife all right.'

'He's had women troubles in the past. I'd put a quid on it.'

'And he'll have more women troubles in the future if he continues to behave like that. I've never been so insulted.'

'I wouldn't take it to heart, Gracie. I don't think it was you. I think it was your status.'

'What? My status as an old maid—desperate, and ready to entrap any hapless male that crosses my path?'

Charlie laughed.

'Well, rest assured, brother dearest, I have no intention of trying to trap that man or any other. You have my word on that.'

Charlie covered her hand with his. She knew what he meant. He, like her mother, made no secret about the fact that they hoped she would find love again one day.

'Johnny Laslett was the only man I will ever love, Charlie. That won't change.'

Charlie didn't say anything.

Chapter Two

'I'm hungry,' Jean said yet again.

Alex heard her well enough, this time and every other time she'd mentioned it in the last hour. The only thing he was thankful for was that Irene and Jimmy seemed to realise that complaining didn't help the situation.

'If you apologised to Mr Shore, he'd probably forgive you and let us eat with them.'

'Jeanie, please. You need to be patient. I will get us some food as soon as I can. In the meantime, you can drink some more water from your canteen.'

He saw her open her mouth to complain again, but at his stern look she closed it and grabbed for the water canteen hanging from her swag.

Alex knew he had overreacted to the situation with the woman in the sulky, but it was too late now. He'd been looking for a farmhouse that might offer opportunity for a meal in exchange for some labour, but the three doors he knocked on all yielded the same answer. There was nothing to be had. Alex hoped that the folks at this next door would be more helpful.

'I don't have any work, I'm sorry,' the woman who answered the door said. 'My husband has gone into the town to meet with some of the other men at the pub. It's Anzac Day, you know.'

Alex nodded.

'If you wander in there, someone will know if there's any work to be had in the district.'

Alex tipped his hat and began to turn away from the door.

'Do you think you could give us something to eat?'

'Jeanie. Don't be rude,' Alex said.

'There are some apples on the tree in the back yard that have moth in them. If you're careful, you can cut around the grubs, and get plenty of fruit from it. Help yourself.'

'Thank you soooo much,' Jean said. 'I'm starving.'

'Jeanie.' Alex frowned at her again. 'Thank you.' He turned back to the woman at the door and tipped his hat again.

As they walked around the side of the house, Alex knew he should scold Jean again, but he couldn't bring himself to do it.

'You see, Daddy. Not all ladies are horrible. I don't know why you get so funny about it.'

'Leave Dad alone,' Jimmy spoke up on his father's behalf. 'You talk too much, and sometimes you get on our nerves.'

'Well, it's better than being an old grump like you!' Jean's anger flashed on her face. 'I don't know what's the matter with you all, treating people like they are monsters or something.'

Alex ignored the bickering. He didn't have the mental or emotional energy to deal with it. At the moment, he was too caught up with worrying about how he was going to feed his kids.

'You'd better only pick the ones that have moth, if you can tell the difference,' Irene said.

'Do you think the lady would mind if we picked a good apple?' Jean asked.

'I really don't know,' Irene replied, 'but she said we could have the ones with moth. We'd better not start out leaving a bad impression, just in case we get to stay around this area.'

Alex heard Irene's comment and wondered if she was having an indirect dig at him for his aggressive behaviour earlier. Too late. It was done now, and there was nothing he could do to change it.

'After we've had our breakfast of mothy apples, we'll go into the town and I will go into the hotel to see if anyone there knows where I might get some work for a day or two,' Alex said.

'And this time, Jean, if a stranger comes by, just nod and keep your mouth shut. Please.' Jimmy gave Jean a fierce look.

***

Charlie was surprised to see Alex Moreland come into the hotel bar. After their odd encounter earlier, he'd thought that would be the last he'd see of him. He had felt offended at the way Alex had behaved towards Grace, so didn't make any effort to move away from the men he was talking to in order to greet him.

There was a rowdy game of two-up in full swing in the corner, and several other fellows sitting at the bar making their way through their third or fourth schooner of beer. They'd had their moments of sombre reflection at the Dawn Service; now they relived those years of comradeship, of shared trial and pain. Some drank, some gambled, and some just talked. Charlie drank his one beer for Johnny, and then set himself in a place where he could talk through the dark days with others who'd shared the journey. As fate would have it, he was now talking to Johnny's father, the Reverend John Laslett. The minister looked like a fish out of water in the pub, but he came every year just the same.

'Excuse me, Charlie,' John said, as he pushed back from the table where they were seated. 'There's a stranger just come in. He looks a bit lost. I'll just go and say hello.'

Charlie didn't bother to stop the minister. He was so much like his deceased son in personality and compassion, it hurt Charlie to see. He missed Johnny, particularly on days like today. Johnny Laslett had tried with all his might to keep Charlie on the straight and narrow when they were younger, but it had taken a sniper's bullet to get Charlie's attention–the bullet that both killed his friend and sent Charlie home injured.

'Charlie, can I introduce you to someone?'

Charlie looked to see John with Alex Moreland in tow. The look on Alex's face was hard to read, but as Charlie had said to Grace earlier in the day, you couldn't always tell what was going on inside a man.

'Alex Moreland, this is Charlie Shore. I'm sure he'll be able to tell you if there's work available in the valley or not.'

Charlie stood up and extended his hand in greeting. Alex grasped it in return and looked him in the eye.

'I must apologise for my outburst this morning,' Alex said.

'It's all right, mate,' Charlie said. 'Sit down with us a bit, and let's talk about work.'

As Alex pulled another chair up to the small table, Charlie could see John was confused, so he explained.

'I met Alex this morning at the Dawn Service. I had invited him and his family to share breakfast with us, but something came up to upset the plans.'

'So you have family with you?' John asked.

'Just my three kids.'

'His wife passed on several years ago,' Charlie offered quietly.

'I'm sorry to hear that,' John said. 'Where have you travelled from?'

'South Australia,' Alex replied. 'With these tough economic times, the family business was under too much pressure to support all of us, and so I took to the road to find work.'

Charlie could tell John was preparing to launch into a full investigation, but sensed that Alex wasn't the sort of man to be sharing every detail on first meeting.

'I think I have a bit of work that might see you for a day or two,' Charlie said. 'I can speak to my father. His place is much bigger than mine, and there was some talk of my younger brother going up country for a while. He might be in need of a hand then.'

'Where's CJ going?' John asked, looking surprised.

'Uncle Harry's place, up near Bendigo. Since Auntie Alice's father passed away, Uncle Harry has been struggling to keep up with both properties. He's asked CJ if he'd like to look at James Park, with an eye perhaps to managing it.'

'How will your father manage Wallace Hill?'

'Well, that's just it. Having Alex come by at this time might be just the thing—if he works through the trial period ok.'

Charlie was careful to include the word trial. He couldn't make out whether Alex Moreland was a man to be trusted or not. The one factor that was in his favour at present was his engaging youngest daughter, Jean.

***

Grace was surprised to see Charlie come home with Mr Moreland. She had been certain that they wouldn't see him again, and had been thankful. But here he was, being shown into Meg's lounge room.

'Do you want a cup of tea?' Charlie asked Mr Moreland as he invited him to sit down.

'No, thank you,' Alex replied. 'I'd better be quick settling the business. The kids will be getting hungry and I'll have to sort something out for their tea.'

'I'll make them some sandwiches.' Grace couldn't help offering to feed the children, despite her resolve to fade into the background.

'No. That won't be necessary.'

Grace felt the sting of rejection in his tone.

What on earth have I done to warrant such hostility? And why on earth has Charlie invited him in to have another crack at me?

She moved out of the lounge room and into the kitchen. Charlie must have his reasons, she supposed. Still, she found it incredibly difficult not to put together a wholesome picnic for the three children she saw sitting on the low stone fence outside the kitchen window.

Poor mites.

The little one, Jean, spotted her staring out of the window. Grace felt guilty. She felt she should pull away and hide, but how could she ignore the wave and beaming smile the child sent her way?

Bother the man, she thought. *He can just be all out of sorts.*

Decision made, Grace made up a plate of cupcakes she'd baked yesterday, and filled a jug with the special lemon cordial her nieces and nephews loved so much. She walked out the back door, tray of goodies in hand. The man had no right to let his children starve because of his own stupid pride.

'Hello again,' she said. 'Are you children hungry?'

'Are we ever?' Jean answered.

Even though Jimmy and Irene didn't answer, Grace could see the hunger in the longing looks they cast at the cupcakes.

'Well, I'd be pleased if you would finish up these cupcakes for me. They are yesterday's batch, and I'll need to make a fresh batch for tomorrow's school lunches.'

'Do you have children?' Jean asked, already peeling the patty-pan from her cake and stuffing it into her mouth.

Grace offered the tray to Jimmy and Irene, and was pleased to see them each take a cake, though they were more cautious than their sister.

'I don't have any children of my own,' Grace said, 'though I do have four nieces and three nephews. They're all visiting with their grandparents today, as it is a school holiday.'

Grace could see Jean was dying to say something else, but her mouth was full of cake. She took the opportunity to place the tray on the top of the stone wall, and began to pour glasses of cordial. She had just set the jug down when Charlie and Alex came around from the front of the house. Guilt hit Grace as she looked to the children's father, though she knew she had no reason to feel that way. For a moment, she thought his look of thunder would convert into harsh words, but he didn't say anything.

'Do you have somewhere to stay tonight?' Charlie asked, once they'd joined the children.

Alex nodded.

'We usually sleep under the stars.' Jean's mouth was finally free of cake, so she was able to continue her usual stream of information.

Grace hid a smile. She could see Alex was upset with her, but he and Charlie must have had words, because he kept his thoughts to himself.

'That sounds like an exciting adventure,' Grace said, defying the tension she could feel.

'It's not such a great adventure when it rains.'

Grace was surprised to hear Jimmy speak freely for a change. She glanced at his father and could see he was surprised too, and embarrassed.

'Hurry up and drink your cordial,' Alex said. 'We need to sort out somewhere to stay.'

'Alex, I would prefer it if you would take up my offer. Stay for tea with the family, and you can roll out your swags in our shearer's hut. You have to be here early tomorrow anyway, so you may as well stay.'

Alex still seemed reluctant.

'Do you have a better offer?' Charlie challenged him.

'Thank you.'

Grace noted the deep breath he took as he spoke and guessed he had struggled to accept.

'I'll take the children over to your hut and set up their bedding. What time does your family sit down to tea?'

'We may be a little later than usual,' Grace answered. 'Charlie has to go over to our parents' place to collect Meg and the children. They've been spending the holiday together.'

'I'd think we will be ready to eat by about half-past six. We'll see you then,' Charlie said.

Alex nodded, turned and herded the children away towards the shearers' quarters. Jean turned and waved to Grace.

'Bless her heart,' Grace said. 'What a bright child.'

'Will you be all right fixing tea for all the extras?' Charlie asked.

'That is what we had arranged.'

'Actually, we had arranged that we'd all spend the afternoon over at Wallace Hill.'

'Charlie, I'm not going to go over this again. You know that I just want to be alone on Anzac Day. You go over with your family and enjoy the holiday together.'

'You're part of my family, Grace.'

'I know. But not today.'

'What happens if they all decide to stay at Wallace Hill for tea?'

'Charlie, don't you dare. That man is so hostile towards me. You make sure you're back here by six o'clock. No later.'

'He's not as hostile as you think.' Charlie grinned. 'He's troubled about something, but I have a strong feeling he's a good man.'

'Don't you go getting any ideas,' Grace warned.

'As if that would be likely. I don't think even mother could get him to show any interest in you, Grace. I think you are quite safe from Alex Moreland.'

***

Alex had ordered the children to take a bar of soap over to the animal trough near the windmill.

'Make sure you clean your face and hands properly.'

'How come you've decided to eat with them?' Jimmy asked.

'Because I did.'

'But you're always telling us to keep away from people.'

'I'm not asking you to make friends with them. They've offered us a meal, and at this stage, I've decided to accept the offer.'

'We don't have any other way to eat,' Irene said to her brother. 'It can't do any harm.'

'Except if Jean keeps blabbing on and on,' Jimmy said.

'You kids understand why I want to keep things private, don't you?'

'I do,' Jimmy said. 'Don't ever put me in a situation like that again.'

'It's Jean,' Irene said in her quietest voice. 'Norma didn't abuse her the way she did Jimmy.'

'Or you,' Jimmy added.

'She was always taking a switch to you. She never whipped me like that.'

'But she made you pay for standing up for me. Don't think I didn't see it.'

Alex cut them off. 'I don't want to talk about it. I made a mistake leaving you with her, and I won't do it again. I promise.'

'Well, I don't know what you're going to do about Jean. She's got no sense when it comes to telling everybody everything.'

Alex sighed as he heard his son's assessment. He knew that Jean had no fear of strangers. She didn't understand how people could take advantage of a situation, use and abuse with no scruples. But he also

18

knew that Jean was a sunny and social child. Even with Norma, she always saw the bright side. She'd actually cried when they'd left.

'Look, just be polite to Mr and Mrs Shore. There's no need to be dragging out our dirty laundry.'

'What about Miss Shore?' Jimmy asked. 'She seems to be just like Jean.'

'I'd prefer it if you kids kept your distance from Miss Shore.'

'Why, Daddy?' Jean had just returned from the water trough and joined in the conversation.

'Because I said so, Jean. You need to do as you are told. You may be polite, but I don't want you telling her things that are private family matters.'

'You're always so grumpy,' Jean complained. 'No wonder people don't want to give you work.'

'That's not fair, Jean.' Jimmy flared at his sister. 'Dad is always polite, and he works hard.'

'He wasn't polite to Miss Shore. He's always rude every time he sees her.'

'That's because she is single, and he doesn't want her getting any ideas,' Irene said.

'Ideas about what?' Jean asked.

'That's enough!' Alex stood up from the log he'd been sitting on.

This conversation was completely out of control, and he had no idea how to negotiate the complexities of it. If he wasn't so desperate for work—if it had just been him who had to go hungry—he'd have high-tailed it out of Green Valley before sunset. But the kids needed to eat, and he had no money in reserve. He'd have to figure out how to deal with the situation between Miss Shore and his children.

***

It wasn't unusual for Meg to arrange two tables when another family visited for a meal. The children would sit around the wooden table in the kitchen, while the adults used the formal carved and polished table in the dining room. Grace had spent the rest of the afternoon making fresh bread to go with the soup, and frying some mutton chops to be served with boiled vegetables. It wasn't a fancy meal, but no one had been expecting guests, and she was lucky that Meg actually had enough mutton chops in the cellar cool-safe to go around.

Once the Moreland family had come inside and been introduced to the rest of the family, Grace disappeared into the kitchen. She wished that she could have sat down with the children and avoided Mr Grumpy Moreland, but that would have seemed odd, especially since there were already six children to be seated in the kitchen, and only four adults in the dining room.

'Auntie Grace, can I help you dish up tea?'

'Thanks, Aimee. That will be a great help.'

Charlie's nineteen-year-old daughter came across to the work bench and helped lay the plates out ready for serving.

'So what do you think of Mr Moreland?' Aimee asked.

Grace was caught. What she thought was she didn't wish to discuss the man at all, but she could tell her niece was ready to discuss all manner of possibilities.

'He's rather good looking, don't you think?' Aimee said.

'Mmm.' Grace refused to commit to the subject. She couldn't deny the man was darkly handsome, but handsome is as handsome does, so she'd always understood. 'Drain the potatoes for me, will you love?'

Aimee picked up two padded pot holders and lifted the heavy saucepan from the wood-stove, bringing it across to empty the boiling water away from the cooked potatoes.

'I heard Dad tell Marmie he's a widower. What do you think about that?'

'I think it's very sad for his children to be without their mother.'

'Exactly,' Aimee said. 'I remember when Dad adopted me, then finally married Marmie. It was wonderful to have a real family.'

'Yes, I remember. You were such a dear child, and I remember you helped meddle to get your father and mother together.'

'I'm not ashamed of that one bit,' Aimee said, as she began to mash melting butter into the hot potatoes. 'I think I did rather a good job. Don't you?'

Grace laughed. 'I do. I love having Meg as a sister-in-law, and now you have a sister and two brothers. It was a job well done.'

'So what about Mr Moreland?'

'Aimee! You're not six years old now. You know better than to meddle in other people's affairs.'

'Perhaps.'

She banged the potato masher against the edge of the pot, then took a large serving spoon and began to dish out mounds of potatoes onto each plate.

'But, you know, Auntie Grace, at your age you could use a little encouragement in love.'

'Love! Aimee, what on earth are you talking about?'

'I'm talking about Mr Moreland.'

'I can assure you that Mr Moreland is no more interested in love than I am, and I advise that you don't go on talking about it, especially in front of him or his children.'

Aimee went across to the stove and took the saucepan full of boiled broad beans off next. 'I just want to see you happy, Auntie Grace. It must be so lonely without someone to love.'

'For goodness sake,' Grace said. 'You haven't got a boyfriend, Aimee. Are you lonely?'

'Who said I didn't have a boyfriend?'

Grace paused from scooping thick gravy onto her chops and raised her eyebrows at her niece.

'Does your father know?'

Aimee grinned. 'Not yet. It's not like I want to get married yet. It's just somebody I like at this stage.'

'And does this somebody like you back?' Grace asked.

Aimee nodded and gave a coy smile.

'Well, I advise you to concentrate on your own love life, and let me worry about mine.'

'Of course, if you want. I just want to add my opinion.'

'Which is …?'

'Mr Moreland is very handsome and available.'

'And obnoxious.' Grace shook her head. 'I don't think he's a suitable possibility at all. Besides, I loved your uncle Johnny, and I won't ever love anyone else.'

'You told me, but time heals. I think you should consider it, at least.'

'Well, thank you for your advice. My advice to you is to make sure that you discuss your secret love with your mother, at least, before making any rash decisions. All right?'

Aimee nodded, and kissed her aunt on the cheek.

'I'll call the children to sit up at the table, and then I'll help you take the plates into the dining room.'

'We need to put these in the warming oven, and serve the soup first,' Grace said. 'But you call the children in. It won't take me a moment to get the soup ladled into the bowls.

***

Alex felt insecure sitting at the fancy, formal dining table with the elegant Mrs Shore. He knew his children were in the kitchen with the Shore children, and while he was thankful for the food that was provided, he worried about what Jean might say to Miss Grace Shore, who was obviously in charge of the kitchen this evening.

'So, Mr Moreland, do you expect to be in Green Valley for long?'

Alex's attention was drawn back to Mrs Shore's question.

'I'm not sure,' he replied. 'Times are hard right across the country, and work is hard to find. If I can find something stable, it would certainly be an incentive to stay longer.'

'I spoke to my father this afternoon.' Charlie joined the conversation. 'He's not sure, but it seems fairly certain that my younger brother, CJ, will take Uncle Harry's offer to manage James Park. That's some distance from here, and Dad will need help.'

'I would have thought you needed help too,' Meg said to her husband. 'At least during the busy times.'

Charlie nodded. 'We can try you for a couple of weeks, Alex. Two days a week with me, and three over at Wallace Hill. If you work well, we can probably give you some form of security for the immediate future, at least.'

'I appreciate it,' Alex said, dipping his head. 'It's been hard having to drag the kids from place to place, with nowhere permanent for them to settle.'

'I hope you don't mind me asking,' Meg said, 'but why did you come away from your home in Adelaide?'

'My father-in-law's business used to support all of us—he owns a general store—but with the onset of the Depression, it became obvious I'd have to find other work to support my kids. He didn't want us to leave, of course, but he just couldn't make ends meet.'

Alex was pleased when Charlie changed the subject, and invited them all to give thanks for the food, but the reprieve was only short lived.

'Jean was telling the children that you had been working in the outback?'

Grace sat down with the rest of the adults.

'Yes.' Alex didn't want to elaborate, especially not now Grace was here.

'Did you have the children out there with you?'

'No. There wasn't any accommodation for family. I left them in the care of a woman.' The questioning was getting too personal, and Alex kept his head down and concentrated on eating. He breathed a sigh of relief when Charlie broke into the conversation again.

'Enough of this interrogation, ladies. Let the poor man eat in peace.'

Meg laughed. 'I'm sorry, Mr Moreland.'

'Call him Alex. That's all right, isn't it?' Charlie asked.

Alex nodded.

'Excuse me.' Alex sensed more than saw Grace push back from the table and head into the kitchen. He wished that the children weren't there unsupervised, especially with Jean's habit of saying whatever came into her head.

'My sister-in-law is such a help to me,' Meg said, as Grace left the dining room.

'Your husband said you had been a missionary.' Alex steered the conversation away from the available spinster in the house.

'Yes. During the war, mainly. I was stationed in India.'

'We went back in 1925 for a few months,' Charlie said.

'Had you served as a missionary as well?' Alex asked, surprised.

Charlie and Meg both laughed.

'Hardly,' Charlie said. 'Meg is the angel. I spent most of the war years as far away from God as I could possibly get.'

'Except that God has his ways of staying close to you, even when you're trying to be distant.' Meg smiled at Alex. 'Charlie wanted to visit the mission with me to see where my heart had been.'

'And how was that?' Alex asked, glad the topic had shifted away from him.

'It's hard to describe, because it's so different to what we know here in Australia,' Charlie said. 'All I can say is the work folks at the Leprosy Mission do is such a wonderful thing. Meg still works for them, only by organising support for them here.'

'Yes, sometimes I get dreadfully busy, between working with mission aid and helping my father with his parish work. If it weren't for Grace, this family would probably fall apart.'

And back to Grace again, Alex thought ungraciously.

'She's been with us since the war. My brother was killed in North Africa, and Grace was very attached to him.'

Alex nodded. He hated to seem ungrateful, but he wasn't interested in Grace, and he could tell Mrs Shore was calculating possibilities.

'Will you be sending your children to the school while you're in Green Valley?' Charlie asked.

Alex paused for a bit before answering. He knew these people were just being friendly, and had already been very kind, but he wished they weren't so interested in his personal life.

'Not at this stage.'

He kept his eyes down, but could see from his peripheral vision Mrs Shore was about to launch into another spiel. Charlie forestalled it by placing his hand on her arm.

'Well, if you ever feel you'd like to enrol them, we can introduce you to the headmistress.'

'Thank you.' Alex was thankful that his stomach was full and the children were well fed, but he couldn't wait to get out of the house.

Chapter Three

'The Morelands will be staying on with us for the foreseeable future.' Charlie made the announcement over dinner a week later. 'He's a hard worker. Dad wants him up at Wallace Hill half of the time, and he'll be here with us the rest of the time.'

'Where will they be staying?' Grace asked.

'For the time being, they're using one of the rooms in the servants' quarters out the back of Wallace Hill. The problem is there's only one room available, and it's too cramped for the four of them. I've been thinking we need to organise proper workers' quarters here. Those old shearers' huts are close to falling down, and I think we can afford to repair at least two of them. That way, the Morelands can have their own private accommodation with a bit more room.'

'But there are no kitchen facilities in the shearers' huts,' Grace said, 'even if you do fix them up.'

'Dad's got an old wood oven sitting out behind the stables at Wallace Hill. It was left over after they put in the new stove several years ago. We'll bring it over and fit it in.'

'Besides,' Meg said, 'they're welcome to eat with us, if it comes to that.'

'I doubt that would be an option Alex would be happy with,' Charlie said. 'He's a good worker, but a bit funny about privacy.'

'A bit funny! That's an understatement.' Grace raised her eyebrows. 'He's a totally closed book, and he wants to keep those children all wrapped up as well.'

'He's had a bad experience with the kids recently,' Charlie said.

'Mmm.'

Grace went on eating. She wasn't convinced. She hadn't been convinced from the first day she'd met the Morelands on the road. But the rest of the family seemed willing to overlook Alex Moreland's "funny" ways and give him a place and position.

***

Grace was used to being at home alone. Meg's parents relied on her help where the parish was concerned. The Reverend Laslett and his wife were really too old to still be the parish ministers, but there wasn't enough money in the offering plate each Sunday to lure a younger minister to replace them. Meg's brother, Johnny had been dedicated to serving the Lord, and people had expected he would take over the ministry from his father, but he was gone. Meg, with her missionary training, had been dedicated to the ministry too, but it wasn't seemly for a woman to be in charge of a congregation. In truth, she did most of the work, but the authority lay with her father and always would.

Grace relished the quiet times at the farm house. Aimee worked as an assistant teacher at the school where her younger brothers and sister went, so was gone for the day. Meg was out on church business, and Charlie was busy with farm work. They would be shearing soon, so they would be bringing the sheep back to the home property. Come shearing time, Meg would stay at home with her, and her mother would also come to lend a hand. Feeding shearers was a mammoth task, and Grace could never accomplish it on her own.

With the weather turning towards winter, Grace often went out to the woodpile to bring in wood for both the wood oven and the fire place in the lounge room. Both wood boxes were currently low, so she set out to refill them.

'Hello, children,' she said to the Moreland children, who were sitting just inside the car shed.

'Hello, Miss Shore.' Jean was eager to answer, and got up off the ground the moment she'd seen her. 'Can I help you?'

Grace looked to Jimmy and Irene for a cue. She knew Alex didn't want his children interacting with her. Of course, he'd hadn't said it like that. He'd said they weren't to bother her, but Grace could read between the lines.

'I need to bring some wood inside for the fires,' Grace said. 'I can manage, as I'm sure you children have something you should be doing.'

This was a complete lie. Grace could see they had nothing to do, except shiver in the cold.

'Why don't you light a fire for your sisters, Jimmy? You're welcome to use wood from the woodpile, or go collect some of your own.'

'Better not,' Jimmy replied. 'Dad's scared we'll burn ourselves or chop our fingers off or something.'

'Well, you'll likely freeze to death if you keep this up. The temperatures are only going to get colder from now on.'

'Can we come inside with you for a while?' Jean asked. 'It is very cold, and I might be coming down with something.' With this, she gave a well-performed cough.

Grace knew she was putting it on, but she couldn't deny them the basic necessity of warmth.

'I won't have you coming down with some terrible sickness when you can be inside by the fire, drinking some warm broth. I'll explain it to your father, Irene. Don't you worry.'

There wasn't much resistance. The three children helped fill the wheelbarrow full of chopped wood, and Jimmy offered to wheel it to the back door. Jean chattered the whole time, and even though Irene and Jimmy didn't say much, Grace could tell they were pleased to be doing something other than waiting around for their father to come back.

'You fill the woodbox in the lounge room, Jimmy. Irene, you and Jean can fill the woodbox here in the kitchen. I'll warm up some broth for you. It looks like you could use something hot to drink to bring some colour back into your cheeks.'

It didn't take long to get the job done, and then the children sat down at the kitchen table and accepted the enamel mugs with steam rising from their warm contents. While they sipped at their drinks, Grace began to plan.

'I'm going to make some toasted sandwiches for your lunch,' she said. 'I know your father would prefer you didn't bother me, but I will work much better knowing you're inside out of the cold, and you're getting properly fed.'

'Can we do something to help you?' Irene asked.

'Perhaps a little later—if you're still here—but at the moment, my nephews and niece have a number of books that might be of interest to you. Can you read?'

'We can,' Jimmy said, 'but Jean can't. Not really.'

'I can so,' Jean objected.

'She can read a little bit,' Irene said. 'But she hasn't been in school for over a year, and she's forgotten a lot of what she learned.'

'Well, there you go.' Grace smiled at them. 'Irene, you and Jimmy can help your father out by coaching your sister with her reading. That will be good practice for both of you.'

Grace was both pleased as well as apprehensive about the children coming into the house to eat and read. She spent the rest of the day going through the excuses she would use when Alex came home and demanded an explanation.

He is such a bothersome man. There is nothing wrong with them coming in out of the cold.

However, she knew that Alex would be unhappy, and so when he appeared, she was somewhat prepared for the outburst.

'You children get your coats on, and go sit in Mr Shore's dray.'

'Thank you for a lovely day,' Jean said as she picked up her coat from the chair.

'Yes, thank you.' Irene sounded almost defiant when she spoke to Grace before leaving the room.

'I do not wish you to have anything to do with my children.' The door had no sooner closed before Alex began his tirade. 'I thought I had made that clear.'

'Oh, you made yourself abundantly clear.' Grace raised her chin.

'I know what you're doing.' Alex went on as if she hadn't spoken. 'And you need to know, it won't work.'

'What am I doing?'

'You're trying to get to me through the children.'

'Get to you? Why would I try to get to you? I have no reason to wish you harm.'

'Then leave my children alone!'

'Your children are shivering in the cold, with nothing warm to eat, and nothing to do, and you expect me to just ignore that?'

'They'll be fine.'

'Will they? Jean had a cough earlier.'

'That's none of your concern.'

'If a child falls ill in sight of my kitchen window, then it is my concern.'

'I don't want to have anything to do with you. I'm not available for marriage.'

Grace paused at this. She swallowed her breath and fury for a moment while she recalibrated her thinking.

He thinks I want to marry him? No! Surely he's not that arrogant.

'So now that you understand, you will see that trying to lure the children won't do you any good.'

Finally Grace found her voice again, with a new surge of outrage.

'You honestly think I'm out to capture you?'

'Of course. I can see what you're doing.'

'I'm being friendly and concerned about three young children. Their father, however, I'd like to see the back end of. You are the most irritating person I have ever met, and if you think I'm even slightly interested in you as a marriage partner, then you have the completely wrong end of the stick. You have no money, no position, and you're dragging your family around the country like a bunch of urchins. What possible allure do you think you have?'

Alex looked abashed, perhaps even hurt. Maybe she had been a tad harsh and unkind, but he had her dander up, and she had no intention of apologising.

'I don't want them spending any time with you.'

'I don't want them hanging around my kitchen window freezing and starving where I can see them. If you intend to neglect them, leave them somewhere else.'

Alex turned from the kitchen and stamped out of the room, closing the door with more force than was necessary.

'Exasperating man!' She hoped he heard her.

***

'I think I may have offended Mr Moreland.' Grace made the statement in the middle of tea time.

'Alex?' Charlie asked, once he'd finished his mouthful. 'Why, what did you say?'

'I can't remember all of it, but I may have used the word irritating.'

'Goodness, Grace, what on earth did he do to warrant such a description?' Meg asked.

'Well, he is irritating,' Grace said, 'but I'm afraid that wasn't the worst of it.'

'Auntie Grace,' Aimee complained. 'I had such hopes for you.'

'And that is the problem,' Grace snapped at her niece. 'He has it in his thick head that I am out to trap him into marriage.'

'Surely not,' Meg said. 'You haven't given him any reason to think...'

'None at all. Quite the opposite, I assure you.'

'Then why would he think such a thing?'

'Because he is an arrogant—'

'Grace!' Charlie cut her off. 'Don't speak too quickly.'

'I'm afraid it's too late,' Grace said. 'He provoked me with his implication that I was using the children to trick him into marriage, and I just spouted out all sorts of unkind things.'

'Grace, how could you?' Meg asked.

'Because he is an arrogant—'

'Grace!' Charlie raised his voice.

'What, Charlie? I know you and Dad think he's a wonderful

30

worker, but he had this ridiculous notion that I was after him. As if I would ever consider such a thing. He's got no money and he drags those children all around the countryside, neglecting them.'

'You didn't say that, did you?' Aimee asked.

'I'm afraid I did.' Grace's tone diminished. 'I'm sorry, Charlie. I would never have said such nasty things—even though they are true—if he hadn't been so abominably rude and presumptuous.'

Grace looked toward her brother for his assurance, but she couldn't tell whether he was about to laugh or explode in a temper.

'I couldn't help it. Really. It was out of my mouth before I knew what was happening.'

Finally, Charlie laughed. Meg looked uncertain and Aimee looked aggrieved.

'I'm not sure it's really that funny,' Grace said. 'When I think about it, I think he looked quite hurt as he stomped out of the house.'

Charlie laughed harder.

'Charlie.' Meg obviously found her husband's laughter inappropriate. 'Poor Alex.'

'Poor Alex!' Grace burst out. 'What about poor *me*? He was absolutely rude and I don't know what else ...'

'She's right, Meg,' Charlie said. 'Alex has a thing about single women being after him. I picked something up from what the kids said about the woman who used to look after them while he was working in the outback. She must have done a number on them, as they're apparently glad to have escaped her.'

'Well, I'm not that woman, and I resent the inference that because I'm single, I must be so desperate that I would resort to underhanded, dishonest tactics to trap him. For goodness sake, he's no great catch even if I was interested.'

'He's very good looking, Auntie Grace,' Aimee reminded her. 'You're not going to deny that.'

'Handsome is as—'

'Handsome does,' Aimee finished for her. 'I know. So you've said a thousand times.'

'There's no need to be disrespectful to your aunt,' Charlie said.

'I'm just pointing out the fact that he is handsome.'

'Which is hardly relevant from your point of view,' Meg said to her daughter.

'I can make an observation, can't I?' Aimee asked.

'Yes, thank you. Your observation is noted.'

'And not denied, so I notice.'

'Aimee, please.' Grace turned pleading eyes towards her niece. 'Yes, Mr Moreland is handsome, but he is so wound up about this woman they've run away from, he's a little soft in the head.'

'I think that might be an exaggeration,' Charlie said, having returned to his meal. 'He's a sensible fellow, and is doing the best he can in difficult circumstances. I'm sorry he got his wires crossed in regard to your intentions, Grace, and I'm even more sorry you blew your top at him, but I really don't think he's that bad.'

'Well, I was just letting you know what happened, so if he picks up the children in the night and disappears, you'll know why.'

***

Alex couldn't understand why the Shore's eldest girl was grinning at him when he walked into the schoolroom.

'Mr Moreland,' she said in a cheerful voice. 'I'm so glad to see you.'

'Thank you,' he said. 'I'm wondering if I could talk to the headmaster about enrolling my children?'

'We have a headmistress, but I'm certain she will be happy to include them in classes. I'm so glad you've brought them along.'

Alex watched as Aimee Shore went off in search of the headmistress. *What was she so happy about? Had Grace Shore told them about the heated exchange?* He felt a wave of embarrassment flush his face. He had allowed Norma to get to him to such an extent that he'd behaved like a fool. If Nancy had still been alive, she would have been so angry with him for being so presumptuous, and stupid.

Of course Grace Shore wasn't out to trap him. He didn't have any money, not like before when Norma thought he would inherit the General Store from his parents-in-law. He didn't have a house, like he had before he'd left to work in the outback open-cut mine. Grace was right: he had nothing, and there was nothing to induce any woman to be interested in him—even if he had wanted female attention. He'd been so rude to Grace that if he were ever to change his mind, she wouldn't give him the time of day.

So why was Aimee Shore smiling like the Cheshire Cat? Surely she wasn't interested in him? No. Aimee was only just out of childhood. He was in his mid-thirties, with three children in tow. He shook his head. He wasn't going to bark up that tree a second time.

He could almost hear Nancy's voice: *you think you're that handsome Alex Moreland, do you?*

Nancy had always told him he was handsome, and he'd loved her compliments. Perhaps he'd got everything out of balance. Grace Shore's lambasting last evening had caused him to sit down and have a long think. That, and the argument he'd had with Irene on their way home.

'You are so rude to Miss Shore,' Irene had said. Alex had been surprised because out of all his children, Irene was the least likely to be opinionated.

'You know what I told you,' Alex had excused.

'We know, Dad,' Jimmy said, 'but it is unreasonable.'

'Unreasonable?'

'All she did was allow us into the warm, give us some hot food, and allow us to read some books. There is nothing wrong with that, and you are being unreasonable.'

It wasn't like Irene to stand up to him. But Jimmy had said she used to stand up to Norma on his behalf, and got whipped for it.

That cursed woman.

'Mr Moreland.' A silver-haired, bespectacled woman strode into the room, a large book in her hand. 'Miss Shore tells me you wish to enrol your three children in our school.'

'If it is not too late for them to start.'

'Earlier in the year would have been better, but better late than never.'

Alex couldn't feel pleased leaving the children behind at the schoolhouse. They were happy enough, especially Jean, who he had left chattering to Aimee Shore. It was more that he felt the rebuke that had been delivered to him like a shot from both barrels. He had neglected his children when he'd had opportunity to do better for them, and all because he couldn't let go of his hurt and mistrust.

'How are you?' When Charlie asked the question, Alex heard genuine concern in his tone. He met Charlie's gaze.

'She told you then?'

'Grace?'

Alex sighed. 'I'd rather not talk about it.'

'That may as well be, but it would appear that you've got the weight of the world on your shoulders, and I fancy a cup of tea, so why don't we just sit down and get it off your chest, before we get on with the day's work.'

'I hate wasting time,' Alex said.

'So do I, so let's not dilly-dally. Grace has gone out with Meg, if that makes it any easier for you.'

Alex sighed again and followed his employer inside the house.

'So you've decided to stay then, after Grace's outburst.'

'She didn't say anything that wasn't true.'

'No?'

'I feel like an idiot, Charlie. I know exactly why I got into that frame of mind, but it doesn't really excuse the behaviour, does it?'

'I don't know. I haven't heard the story behind it.'

'A woman by the name of Norma. When my father-in-law's business could no longer support all of us, I had to find work. One of my army buddies told me there was plenty of work to be found out at Iron-Knob, in South Australia's outback. I went out and found work straight away, but there was no accommodation for the children, so I made arrangements, and left the children with Norma. She had been all sweet as sugar to the children, but once she came to live in my house, she turned nasty.'

'She lived with you in your house?'

'I wasn't there. I didn't know about it for a long time. I came back to visit every three months or so, but she somehow managed to intimidate the children into putting on a performance. I'd been gone nearly two years before I found out what really had been going on. I came home without warning, and found Jimmy sleeping outside in the chook shed, half starved, and marked from constant whippings.'

'You got rid of her, I hope?'

'She wasn't that easy to get rid of. For some reason, Jean thought the sun shone out of her, and Norma made all sorts of excuses about how Jimmy was a difficult child. In the end, I just took the children and left. I didn't have any work there anyway.'

'How long have you been on the road?'

'A little over a year. Your sister managed to put the fear of God into me yesterday. I realised I've been caught up with the Norma nonsense, and haven't really been doing what's best for the children.'

'She feels she might have been too harsh.'

'Yes, well … I don't suppose kind suggestion would have done the job. Anyway, I took the children into Green Valley this morning and enrolled them in school. At least they will be warm and cared for during the day.'

'I would take it as a great favour if you would allow school lunches to be prepared for them from my kitchen. Then you can be sure that all their needs are met for the day.'

Alex dropped his head. He felt ashamed of himself.

'You said it yourself, Alex. We need to do what is best for the children.'

Chapter Four

Grace felt embarrassed by her behaviour after the confrontation with Alex. She wasn't usually a short-tempered person, nor was she ungenerous. Her cutting words must have hurt him. It was only his own appalling behaviour that prevented her from going cap in hand to beg his forgiveness. The best she could do was make sure that she made three additional nutritious school lunches to send with his children when they went off to school each day. Usually Charlie let them take the old horse and dray, with Johnny driving. When it had only been the Shore children travelling, on wet days one of the adults would bring the Model T out of the car shed and drive them.

It was raining for the second day in a row and Charlie had packed all six children and Aimee in—one sitting on top of the other—to transport them by motor car to the school house.

'Grace.' Charlie called out to her when he got back from taking the children to school.

Grace brushed baking flour from her hands and went out to the hallway to meet her brother. He still had his hat and coat on, and his boots were wet, so she was glad he had waited by the door.

'Would you have time to drive Meg over to the manse, and then drive me up to Brinsford station?'

'Where are you going?' Grace asked.

'I'm off to Melbourne. I've got some business in the city, but I'll be back on tomorrow night's train.'

'It's very wet.'

'That's an understatement,' Charlie said. 'It's worked out well, actually. We can't get on with shearing, and it's too wet to do anything else. It seems like a perfect time to attend to business.'

'When do you have to be at the station?' Grace asked.

'The train will arrive at 11.15, so we've got plenty of time if we leave soon.'

'Do you mind if I get this batch of scones in the oven? They'll only take twenty minutes to bake.'

'That will be perfect. Gives me time to talk to Alex about what I want him to do today.'

Grace went back to finish cutting her scones into rounds and putting them into the oven. Just as she opened the oven door, Meg came in, her hat on her head and coat ready to put on.

'It's awful weather,' Meg said. 'If it's still raining like this in the afternoon, you'll have to drive in to pick the children up from school.'

'How will you get home?' Grace asked. 'Do you want me to come a bit earlier and pick you up, then make the second trip?'

Meg sighed. 'I'll telephone and let you know. Mum has been unwell, and Dad just doesn't cope well on his own, anymore. I might have to stay overnight.'

'So I'll have the children all to myself tonight?' Grace asked.

'Aimee will help you with tea and cleaning up.'

'Of course. She usually does.'

'Good. Do we have time for a quick cup of tea before we leave?'

Grace nodded. 'Actually, you do, but I better go and get my coat and boots. Can you keep an eye on those scones for a few minutes?'

Meg nodded as she poured herself a cup of tea from the cosy-covered teapot.

Grace had just enough time to brush her hair, fetch her winter woollies, and pull the golden-brown scones from the oven before Charlie called her from the front door again.

'Are you girls ready?'

'I really don't like him shouting through the house like that,' Meg said as she put her coat on. 'Sounds like he was bought up in the bush.'

Grace smiled. She loved her family.

Once outside, Grace was a little concerned. Heavy rain was still falling. It had been raining like this all night, and the ground had rivulets of water everywhere, feeding into large mud puddles. She wanted to run to the car shed, but was concerned she would slip and end up backside in the mud. Instead, she walked as briskly and carefully as she could.

'I better drive,' Charlie said, when they got to the car.

'Why? I have to drive home, so I may as well start out now.'

Charlie conceded. Grace slid into the driver's seat, and allowed Charlie the privilege of turning the crank handle at the front of the car to get the engine started.

'Do we have enough petrol?' Meg asked, once the engine jolted to life.

'Filled her up this morning,' Charlie said. 'Used just about the full month's ration. Hope this rain stops soon.'

The round trip was not without incident. They got Meg to the manse without mishap, and the drive to Brinsford was on good road. Even so, Grace drove slower than usual, and was attentive to the conditions. As she drove down the short road that led to their farm house, she was more careful. It was very muddy and the tyres were slipping, as though they were losing traction. When she came to the wooden bridge over the creek, she noticed the water had risen a lot, and was flowing only inches below the wooden structure. She managed to reach the farmyard without mishap, but didn't bother to back the car into the carshed. Instead, she drove over to the work shed, hoping she'd find Alex there.

'Mr Moreland.' She called out to him the minute she saw him. He was working at the grinder, sharpening shears in preparation for the shearing that would happen when the weather cleared.

'Miss Shore.'

Grace felt ridiculous, with the pair of them clinging to formal names when everyone else was on a first-name basis. The stupid misunderstanding stood between them like an unclimbable wall. She shook her head. Now was not the time to be worrying about that.

'I think I will go back into Green Valley and pick up the children from school early,' she said.

'You worried about the creek?'

Grace nodded. 'The water is already up to the bottom of the bridge, and the rain doesn't seem to show any sign of letting up. Another two hours, and I think it will be impassable.'

'Do you want me to come with you?' Alex asked.

Grace shook her head. 'There's hardly room for all of them to squeeze in as it is. Just keep a look out for us. These roads are awful at the moment, and I could easily run off the road and get bogged.'

'Is it safe for you to go?' Grace heard genuine concern in his tone.

'I will drive slowly. I've been out to Brinsford this morning already. It's ugly weather, but if I'm careful it should be all right.'

Alex didn't say anything. He had a frown on his face. She was used to seeing his face with a frown. It was usually to show how much he disapproved of her.

'I will be careful, but I think I'd better go now.' Grace injected firmness into her tone. She didn't want him to start lecturing her or issuing nasty words based on his strange presumptuous ideas.

'If it looks too dangerous after you've got the children, I'd prefer it if you just stayed in Green Valley. I don't want them involved in an accident.'

I don't suppose you'd mind if I was involved in an accident. That might be what it sounded like, but she knew better than to say it. She was making an extra effort to curb her tongue and not launch into a verbal attack. She turned to go back out into the rain.

'I'll crank the car for you,' Alex offered, following her out.

'Thank you.' Grace was glad she hadn't said what she'd thought. Perhaps he was just concerned for the children, and not trying to be nasty to her.

It didn't take long for her to get the car running, and she had to wrestle with the gear stick before the car lurched forward. The creek was only a couple of hundred yards from the house, and as she approached, she could see the water had already started to flow over the top of the bridge. Judging from the side rail posts, it looked to be about three or four inches deep, which should still be passable, so she changed back to first gear and moved forward.

The water had begun to flow over the banks and was already running across the road leading up to the bridge. Once again, it seemed to be only a few inches deep, and Grace felt sure the vehicle would make it through. The wheels of the car ploughed through the water as Grace guided the car slowly forward. All went well until she reached the middle of the bridge, where the car stalled.

'Oh, not now!'

She tried to restart the engine by stepping on the starter and adjusting the throttle lever, but the engine coughed and died. Grace tried again, with no success. She was feeling anxious—the sound of the rushing water was loud, and told her that even if she got to the other side, she wouldn't be bringing the children back. The water was definitely rising, and at a rapid pace.

She opened the car door and stepped into knee-deep water. It was already at the level of the door and beginning to run into the car.

Now Grace was afraid. She needed to get off this bridge and away from the fast flowing water. She gave up the idea of trying to crank start the car again, and was about to begin wading back across the bridge when it shifted beneath her, the wood groaning under the pressure.

Oh Lord! Help!

It took a few moments for her to gather her wits, and she took hold of the railing and began to inch her way back towards the farmhouse.

***

Alex hadn't wanted to tell Grace she shouldn't attempt to cross over the bridge, not after their previous interaction. She'd sounded confident enough, so despite his concerns, he kept his thoughts to himself. Still, he put his hat and raincoat on, and followed the car around the house to make sure she crossed over all right. But as he watched from the corner of the house, he saw the car stalled, and then she got out of the car.

Just come back out of the water. It looked as if she were considering another crank start. *Just leave it.*

As he watched, the bridge began to give way under the force of the fast flowing water. He raced back to the work shed, grabbed a long rope, and ran through the mud towards the bridge. He was thankful his strong leather boots had good tread. He hoped that by the time he'd got to the edge of the water, Grace would already be wading through to the bank, but the situation had changed quickly.

The whole bridge was completely skewed and the railings were broken. The car was hanging precariously off the side, half submerged, and Grace was covered up to her chest in a fast-rushing torrent, clinging to one of the bridge posts. A quick assessment told him the post wouldn't hold much longer.

Alex took the rope and fastened one end around a gum tree some yards from the creek and tied the other end around his waist. Although he was a strong swimmer, he guessed that even he would find it difficult to make it through this water without being washed away.

He was right.

The water was quickly up to his armpits, and he struggled to stay on his feet. He used his arms in some semblance of breast-stroke to help propel him through the water. He wanted to call out to Grace, but the roar of the water was so loud that he doubted she would hear even if he tried. It seemed to take an age, but he was soon close enough to call out to her.

'Grace!' He had to shout to be heard above the din. She turned, and the look of relief on her face made him feel like a hero. But the feeling was temporary as the force of the flood waters pulled at him, making it difficult even to stand.

'I've got a rope around my waist. We can pull ourselves back. Grab a hold of my hand.' He held his hand out and she gradually pried herself from her grip on the precarious looking post.

As he closed his grip around her arm, the rest of the bridge gave way. Alex lost his footing, and they were washed under the churning brown water. It was a shock at first, then a struggle, but Alex didn't let go of Grace's arm.

Eventually he surfaced, and pulled her up with him, but they were caught in the fast-moving flow. They couldn't go far, as the rope wasn't that long. Sure enough, he felt the tightening of the rope and the pressure as it bit into his flesh. It took a minute or two, but Alex managed to find solid footing again, the water now up to his chin. Grace was shorter than him, so he moved his arm to support her under her arms, and help keep her head above water.

'If you put your arms around me and hold on, I'll haul us back in with the rope.'

Grace nodded. She put both her arms around his shoulders and manoeuvred herself so she was behind him, almost like a piggy-back ride. The tree where the rope was anchored was up stream so it took all of Alex's strength to haul the pair of them back against the rushing force. He was finally able to get good purchase on the soggy ground beneath, and wade the last ten yards or so, in thigh-deep water. Grace also got her footing, and though she supported her own weight, she didn't let him go. Alex couldn't help feeling relief, and a secret surge of heroism.

He'd just saved her life, and by the strength of her grip, he got the feeling she might not have realised that they were now safe.

***

Grace's heart rate thundered. She'd offered her last prayer to God several times in the last few minutes, asking Him to take her safely to heaven. Then she found she was on her own two feet, ankle deep in water, still clinging to her rescuer.

'Are you all right?' he asked, and Grace heard genuine concern in his tone. She couldn't have answered him if she tried, but turned into his embrace and allowed a few moments of fear to dissolve in tears. Eventually she realised who it was she was clinging too, and gathered her wits. Pulling back from him, she stood upright and lifted her chin.

'Thank you, Mr Moreland. Thank you for saving my life.'

He took a deep breath and didn't appear to have anything to say. Instead he turned his attention to untying the rope around his middle. Grace felt awkward, but this was not the time to be focussing on an emotional issue, especially since the water was still rising even now around their ankles. They needed to get free of the rope and back to the farmhouse.

She went to the tree and tried to loosen the knot that was on that end, but the rope was wet, and the knot had been pulled tight with the pressure.

'Leave it,' Alex said. 'I'll come back and get it once the water recedes.'

Grace nodded. He'd used his pocket knife to cut himself free, and now held his hand out to help her back to the road.

'Your head is bleeding,' she said, as they made their way.

'It hurts. I think I hit it on something underwater when the bridge gave way.'

'Thank you for taking the risk. I couldn't have swum out against that.'

'It's all right. Not sure your brother is going to be happy to learn he's lost his motorcar though.'

'Luckily it wasn't full of children,' Grace said. 'You were right to be concerned.'

'I didn't realise the water was rising that fast, or I would have insisted.'

By this time, they'd reached the farm house.

'I'll go down to my quarters and get changed. You'd better telephone your father and let him know what's happened,' Alex said.

'Yes,' Grace replied. 'He can collect the children from school and take them to Wallace Hill. Obviously we're not going to make it through to them today.'

Alex nodded and began to walk away.

'Mr Moreland,' Grace called after him. He turned back to face her. 'The cut on your head is quite nasty. I can clean it up for you after, if you like.'

'Thanks.'

He trudged away, obviously no longer worried about the rain that was still falling. He couldn't get any wetter than he already was.

***

By the time Alex had got out of his wet clothes and put on a clean shirt and trousers, his head was aching furiously. He looked in his small shaving mirror—the cut was still bleeding. He pressed a clean handkerchief against it for a few seconds.

The muscles around his middle also hurt. There was probably some rope burn and bruising. He didn't have a first aid kit—he would have to swallow his pride and ask Grace Shore for some Aspirin and something to put over the cut on his forehead.

He was sore and tender as he shrugged into his spare woollen jumper. His one coat was sopping wet, so he hung it over the hook on the back of the door. He didn't have anything else to protect him against the weather, but he wanted to inspect the water line again. He decided to see if Charlie had a spare waterproof coat he could borrow before going out in the rain again.

When he got to the front door of the main house he stood on the veranda and knocked on the door. When there was no answer, he began to worry.

Perhaps she took a blow while under water as well. He could well imagine that she was lying on the couch in a state of unconsciousness. With these thoughts foremost, he turned the front door knob and opened the door.

'Miss Shore,' he called out. 'Are you all right?'

'Stop!' Her voice came from the direction of the kitchen. 'Don't come in. I'm taking a bath.'

Now what was he supposed to do? He didn't have another set of dry clothes to be going back out in the rain, but he didn't want to intrude either.

'Is it all right if I just wait on the veranda?'

'You can sit in the lounge room. I won't be too much longer.'

Alex moved inside and took a seat in one of the lounge chairs. It would be better if Charlie was here; or the children. Anyone, really. He could hear Grace was obviously bathing in front of the kitchen fire.

His mind went back to his days of being married to Nancy. She would always pull the tin bath out in front of the kitchen fire in the winter months. Before they'd had children, he'd not been shy of sharing moments with her as she bathed.

Alex wanted to close his thoughts down, but the sound and the memories kept prompting unwanted images in his mind's eye. It seemed like forever before she finally emerged from the kitchen, fully clothed, her hair wrapped in a towel.

'I'm sorry, Mr Moreland,' she said. 'I was chilled through, and was beginning to feel all aches and pains from being wrenched about. I felt a soak in hot water would help remedy everything at once.'

Alex nodded.

'Are you aching as well?' she asked.

Alex nodded again. 'Actually, I was going to ask if I could beg some Aspirin from you. Truth be told, I'm aching all over.'

Grace turned back to the kitchen. 'Come in next to the fire. You could probably use a soak in the tub too. Do you want me to heat some more water for you?'

The idea of soaking in hot water was tempting, but the situation was too awkward. He shook his head.

'I'll be all right for now. Just some Aspirin, and perhaps a sticky plaster over this cut.'

Grace pulled bits and pieces out of the medicine cupboard. She opened an Aspirin bottle and handed him a tablet with a glass of water. Alex swallowed it with half the water.

'Sit down and let me take a look at that cut,' Grace said, pulling a chair out for him. 'It's already swollen and bruised.'

Alex sat down and tilted his head back. Grace carefully brushed his long dark fringe back. 'It is quite a cut, but it has stopped bleeding. I'll put some Dettol on it, and put a plaster over it to keep it clean.'

Alex submitted to the ministrations, trying desperately to forget the memories of Nancy and the intimacy they used to share. Grace was not Nancy. But that was where his argument ended. Like Nancy, Grace was attractive, shapely, kind. Alex couldn't understand where his aggressive objection to her had gone. He needed it right now, more than he could say.

He didn't want to be attracted to Grace. It was impossible. The situation with Norma was at the back of his mind to remind him that he should run a hundred miles away from her. Except he was trapped by the swollen creek and he couldn't run anywhere. He felt the intimacy of the situation, but she didn't appear to be affected in the same way. *Thank goodness.*

'Are you sure you don't want to sit in the water for a while?' Grace asked, once she'd fixed a sticking plaster over the cut. 'I can go into another part of the house and keep out of the kitchen for a while.'

'No, that's fine,' Alex said. 'Did you ring your father?'

Grace nodded. 'He didn't even know Charlie had gone up to Melbourne.'

'What did he say?'

'What could he say? He's just glad we weren't severely hurt. A motor car can be replaced, he said.'

'Not in today's economy,' Alex said.

'I must thank you again for acting so quickly. I would have drowned if you hadn't.'

Alex shrugged off the compliment. 'Listen, I'm going to go back down to the creek behind my place and see how the water level is. It's still raining, and at the rate it was rising before, I'm … well, I'm a bit worried.'

'I'll ring Dad again and see what he thinks.'

Alex got up to go. 'Does Charlie have a waterproof coat I can borrow? All my wet weather gear is sopping.'

Grace went out to the laundry and found him a heavy oilskin raincoat.

'Can you let me know what you think after you've assessed the situation?' Grace asked. 'I have to admit, I'm a bit nervous myself.'

Alex let himself out the front door to face the still-falling rain. He didn't know what was worse—the rain, the rising floodwaters, or the emotional storm he'd just faced in Grace Shore's presence. *Thank goodness she can't read my mind.*

Chapter Five

'I couldn't believe how fast the water rose.' Grace spoke to her father through the handpiece attached to the box telephone.

'Remember we constructed that extra bank that runs between the creek and all the buildings? That was to ensure against rising flood waters. It should direct the waters away from the house.'

'It's just it's still raining, and doesn't look like it will let up any time soon.'

'I haven't ever seen water rise any further than where that bank is, Grace. I think it should be all right, but if you're worried, get Alex to fill some sugar bags with soil and stack them near the gate entrance. There is the stone garden wall around the house as well.'

Grace sighed. She wanted to accept her father's reassurance, but she had never seen water rise so fast as when she was stranded on the bridge.

'Can you call Meg and let her know what is going on, please? The bridge didn't hold firm in this water. If it gets around the telephone poles, they could go down as well, and then there won't be any communication.'

'I'll take care of the children and Meg. I'm sure the rain will stop soon, Grace. It will be all right.'

Grace hung up the handpiece, but talking to her father hadn't eased her alarm. She went to get her own raincoat and hat and stepped out into the weather. Walking around the house to the garden on the side where the creek ran, she was alarmed at what she saw. The flood waters were only inches from the top of the bank, and that was about fifty yards from where she stood. The sound of rushing water was all around, and the rain kept falling. She looked around to see if she could locate Alex and saw him coming back from down near the shearer's quarters.

'What do you think?' she called out to him.

He just shook his head. 'The water is already lapping around my place. That bank which is supposed to protect the house is holding at the moment, but the water is still rising. If it breaks, the water will rush straight up to the main house.'

'Dad said we should sandbag the gates and let the garden walls keep the water out.'

'That would've been my next idea. Do you have some flour or sugar bags I can use?'

'In the laundry. Come with me.' Grace walked back towards the main house. They saved these sorts of bags. There were always uses for them. 'The trouble is, the ground is so saturated it's going to be difficult to fill the bags.'

'I was thinking of digging soil from under the hayshed canopy. That shouldn't be quite as waterlogged.'

'Good idea. I'll help you.'

Alex nodded. There was no sign of his former aggression or animosity. Grace sensed that he was just as worried as she was, which wasn't really a comfort.

***

It was already getting dark by the time they'd finished sandbagging the garden gates, and now Alex was really aching. He wished he'd been able to take up the offer of a long soak in front of the fire, but feared they had still more work to do yet. Water had begun to pour over the top of the bank, and Alex was of the opinion that it wouldn't hold.

'I'll go and make something hot for us to eat,' Grace said. 'We're going to have to get changed all over again.'

'This is my only spare set of clothes,' Alex said. 'Do you think Charlie would mind if I borrowed something of his to wear?'

'Of course not. Let's get ourselves inside,' Grace said.

As they stomped the mud off their boots on the veranda, Alex struggled to dismiss the idea of relaxing in the warm. He couldn't just drink tea and ignore the threat, so continued to make more emergency plans in his head.

Grace got him some clean trousers, shirt and jumper to wear.

'Thanks,' he said.

She disappeared into her bedroom, and he hurriedly changed from his wet things. When she re-emerged in the kitchen in dry clothes, he decided he needed to talk his worries through.

'Miss Shore—' She held up her hand, stopping him.

'Do you think we could drop these ridiculous formal titles?'

He gave a short nod and started again. 'Grace, I'm almost certain that bank will break, and the sandbags will only hold if the water doesn't continue to rise. The trouble is—'

'It's still raining,' she finished for him.

'We can't get out of here, and I'm afraid this house is going to be flooded.'

He watched her face to see how she would take his assessment. He saw her worry, but nothing more than he was feeling himself. Thankfully, she didn't panic.

'We should try to rescue precious things and store them up in the roof space above the ceiling.'

'Where is the manhole into the ceiling space?' Alex asked.

'It's in the hallway. There's a ladder out in the work shed, if you are up to going to get it.'

Alex nodded. 'Why don't you go around the house and see what you think is irreplaceable and bring those things into the hall to start. We can get other things later.'

'Do you think we are overreacting?' Grace asked.

'I wish we were, however, listen to the rain. It's still falling, and you saw the water. I think it will be in the house before the night's over.'

Grace didn't say anything else but moved out of the room to start getting things together. Alex found the oilskin coat, even though it was still wet, and put it on for one more trip out into the rain.

Grace retrieved the wicker washing basket and the trolley it sat in, and wheeled it around the house. Into the basket went family photographs, the children's favourite books, and knickknacks she knew Meg valued. To protect the fragile pieces, she wrapped towels and pillowcases around each of them. Once the basket was full, she wheeled it into the hallway and parked it beneath the manhole. Alex had already returned, with a ladder leaned up against the wall, and the manhole cover removed.

'What have you got?' His head appeared from out of the ceiling. It was a long way up, twelve feet, and the ladder hadn't reached the whole way.

'What about we bring the kitchen table into the hall? It's solid. I can put a chair on top, and pass things up to you.'

As an answer, Alex manoeuvred himself out of the manhole, placing his feet on the rungs of the ladder, and climbed down. He didn't appear to be a man of many words, and Grace followed him into the kitchen to help move the table. It didn't take long to build the platform she'd suggested.

'Before I get back up there, let's go around the house and get some more stuff. Useful things that will be more helpful dry if we need to clean up later,' Alex suggested.

'Good idea.'

She emptied the wicker basket and took the trolley out to the laundry to fetch brooms, buckets, dry rags, soap, and other bits and pieces. As she wheeled the second load back into the hallway, she wondered if they were completely overreacting to the threat at hand. But then she allowed her imagination to conjure pictures of dirty muddy water up to her waist, flowing through the house. She emptied that load and went around the house again, this time gathering pillows, cushions, sheets, quilts and blankets.

'I'll start to store some of this in the ceiling,' Alex said, when they met back in the hallway. 'You never know if we might have to sit up there ourselves for a bit. It might be smart to have some food.'

Grace nodded. She went back to the kitchen and collected the full cake and biscuit tins, and the bread crock. She had some jars of preserved fruit, but wondered if that might be going too far. She put two jars in anyway. By the time she had it back in the hallway, Alex was balancing precariously on the ladder, shoving things over his head into the ceiling cavity.

'If you climb up into the ceiling, I'll pass things up to you,' Grace said.

Alex put his hands either side of the manhole and hoisted himself up. Grace had begun to put things onto the table, and then she climbed up as well.

'Be careful,' Alex said from above.

'I've already had an afternoon of dicing with death. I think I can manage.' Grace gave a wry smile as she passed up her bread crock.

They worked mostly in silence, speaking only when necessary. After about an hour, Grace rested her hands on her hips.

'I think we've put half the house up there,' she said. 'I hope it wasn't all for nothing.'

'Actually, I hope it is for nothing. Far better to pass a few things up and down again than have to clean up a flood-damaged house.'

'Have you done that before?' Grace asked.

'Yes, once before. My parents used to live on a flood plain. Back in 1921, there was a terrible flood that nearly destroyed a number of houses.'

'Destroyed? Like you mean mud and water damage?'

'Like a couple of them had severe structural damage and had to be pulled down.'

'But they withstood the flood waters?'

'On that occasion, yes.'

'Alex, you're making me nervous. This house will be able to withstand the force of the floodwater, won't it?'

'It's a weatherboard house, Grace. I don't know how strong the structure is, or how strong the force of the water will be if the bank breaks.'

Grace felt upset and went to the door to look outside again, but it was now too dark to see anything.

'We'd better get a lamp and put up in the ceiling as well,' she said as she came back indoors. They had a 32-volt windmill electric generator that supplied a couple of light and power sockets in the house, but with the threat of flood water, it was likely they would lose power as well. Grace retrieved a kerosene lamp from the sideboard in the lounge room.

'What about the sheep in the shed?' The idea of the sheep being caught in a flooded shearing shed suddenly came to Grace.

'I let them out earlier,' Alex said. 'I opened the gate to the back paddock for all the stock. They'll make their way up into the bush on the ridge, no doubt.'

'Do you think we should try to climb up onto higher ground as well?'

'Is there any shelter up in the hills?'

Grace shook her head.

'It's up to you. There is a small chance the bank will hold, but if not, the ceiling cavity is dry and is stocked up with food and water. How well do you think we'd fare out in the weather with nothing at hand?'

'I think we're better trying our luck here.'

Alex nodded.

Now that they were finished squirreling things up into the ceiling, Grace was overcome with weariness.

'Do you think we should go to sleep?'

'If I let my eyes close, I'll be out to it for the night,' Alex said. 'If we're going to sleep, we'd be better off in the space above the ceiling in case we're caught by a rush of water.'

'Do you really think?'

Alex took the lamp from her hand, fumbled with some matches and lit it. He took it back to the front door and looked outside again, this time holding the lamp up high to give them some view of the yard. The entire garden was a couple of inches under water.

'Do you think the bank has already burst?' Grace asked.

'No, this is just from the rainfall. You can still hear the roar of the water. If it had burst, it would be over the garden wall and into the house.'

'It's still raining.'

'I'm not going to take the chance. You can sleep in your room if you like, but I wouldn't.'

Grace nodded. She was too anxious to worry about being trapped in a confined space with Alex Moreland.

'Do you think there's time for a cup of tea?' she asked.

Alex smiled. 'Why not? If we are alert, we can get up to safety if something happens.'

***

The sweetness of the tea was fortifying in the face of the tumultuous day they'd had. Alex's body was bone tired and still aching, but he knew he wasn't going to have a great night's rest.

'What about we throw a couple of lounge chair cushions up into the ceiling?' he said over a sip.

Grace seemed to understand what he was thinking.

'Yes, and I'll bring that bottle of Aspirin too, I think.'

'It's been one ugly day, hasn't it?' Alex said.

'Just five minutes of drinking tea like civilised people can't hurt.'

Alex had already finished his cup. He decided to have another quick one while he had the opportunity, and he swallowed the Aspirin that Grace gave him.

'All right, I guess I'm ready,' she finally said.

Alex stood, and turned off the electric lights. 'You hold the lamp while I climb up, then hand it up.'

Alex used the ladder, as it got him closer to the manhole. He used the strength of his arms to pull himself up. Once inside, he lay flat on his stomach and leaned out. Grace placed the lamp on the chair while she climbed up, then handed him the lamp. He found a flat spot in their makeshift space to set it down.

As he made sure the lamp was secure, he heard the roar that he knew was the bank breaking, and within seconds the loud thunderous sound of water hitting the side of the house.

'Alex!' Grace cried out. She was halfway up the ladder when the front door burst open under the pressure of the crashing wave.

'Quick, grab my hands.' Alex watched, helpless as Grace overbalanced in her panic and the ladder began to come away from the wall. He leaned further forward and caught hold of one of her hands. He was able to steady her and get hold of both hands, but then the rush of water washed the ladder out from beneath her. With an almighty effort, he got her to finally get a grip on the edge of the manhole, her feet dangling in mid-air, a couple of feet above the water.

'Hold tight,' he said, and let go of her.

'Alex!'

He got himself up into a squat position and took hold of her forearms again. This time, with the added use of his leg and back muscles, he drew Grace up into the ceiling, away from the angry brown water that was quickly submerging the household furniture.

Grace fell into the space. She lay on her front for a few moments, hiding her face in her arms. Alex watched her to see if she was all right. The shuddering of her shoulders told him she was crying. He gently placed his hand on her shoulder.

'It's all right, Grace. You're safe now.'

Eventually she calmed down and pulled herself up into a sitting position, wiping at the moisture on her face.

'That's twice in one day,' Alex said, offering her a tentative smile.

'In a moment, you'll be wanting me to call you my hero.'

Alex laughed. 'I haven't had so many opportunities to be a hero in a long time.'

'A little out of practise, are you?'

Alex couldn't tell whether Grace was being light-hearted or not. She sounded like she was teasing, but she was rubbing her arms as if to ease pain.

'Did I hurt you?'

'You and that flood water, which seems mighty determined to take me under today.'

'I'm sorry.'

Grace shook her head. 'The hazards of being rescued, I imagine.'

***

Now that she was actually in their safe spot and there was some light from the lamp, Grace took stock of the surroundings. They could stand, if necessary, where the roof pitch was the highest, but the rest of the space was for bending or crawling only. Still, it would do—she didn't imagine they would be involved in any great exercise.

She could hear the sound of water below, but it was completely dark down there now, so she had no idea how high the water had risen.

'I guess we'd better make ourselves comfortable,' she said.

Alex nodded.

'Do you think it would be excessive if I swept the space here in the centre?'

'It will create a cloud of dust.'

'After all the water today, dust might be a nice change.'

Alex smiled. 'If you must. There is a heap of mouse or rat droppings too, so I guess it might be nice to have a cleaner space.'

'As it happens, I packed a hand brush and dustpan.'

'I'll organise some of this stuff into a better place out of the way while you sweep.'

Grace tried to block out all the troubling thoughts demanding her attention while she applied herself to the task, but she was only mildly successful. Was the house structurally sound enough to withstand the water that was battering it? That was the first worry. Then there was the elephant in the room. She and Alex were thrust into close quarters, and prior to this day they had not enjoyed a very cordial relationship. It was going to have to be discussed. They were going to have to sleep right next to each other, for goodness sake. After his earlier presumptions, she felt she was going to have to make some clear statements.

By the time they'd finished, they had arranged a reasonably comfortable place to sit and large enough for them to lie down when they finally chose to sleep.

'Grace...'

'Alex...'

They both started at the same time, and Grace wondered if he had been churning things over in his mind as much as she had. He didn't talk much.

'Go on,' Grace said. 'You go first.'

'I need to apologise for the way I treated you when we first met.'

Grace didn't say anything, but she did engage him by looking him straight in the eye, almost insisting he elaborate.

'I wasn't in a very good state of mind.' He swallowed hard, and seemed to be dry in the mouth. 'I know it's not an excuse for my unforgivable behaviour. You might not believe it, but I've never been known to be a rude or angry man.'

'Well, perhaps we just need to talk about it, and get it all out in the open so that there can be no more misunderstandings.'

'Given the circumstances, I think that would be best.'

'First things first,' she said. 'I'm not married, and I have no wish to marry. I've already covered this ground numerous times with my mother during her many attempts to match-make.'

'Charlie said you were committed to the memory of your fiancé?'

Grace was silent for a bit, then she spoke. 'Johnny and I were never engaged.'

'I wasn't formally engaged to Nancy either, when I enlisted, but we both understood that we'd marry if I came back. The thought of her waiting for me was a huge comfort in the trenches.'

Grace listened, and suddenly felt the urge to be honest.

'Mr Moreland...'

'I thought we were going with first names.'

'Alex. I was madly in love with Johnny Laslett, but he and I never went together. I was only sixteen at the time, and didn't really want to see it. But I'm thirty-four now, and I know the passion was all on my side.'

'He didn't care about you?'

'No. He cared about me. He even loved me, I think, but only like a sister.' She gave a small sad laugh. 'You see, Charlie and I were equally in love with those two from the manse, and while they were both kind, they weren't interested in marriage.'

'But Charlie and Meg are married.'

'That's a long story. At first, she wouldn't have him, though he nearly turned himself inside out to win her.'

'Why?'

'Charlie was going through his "atheist" phase, and Meg was devoted to becoming a Christian missionary.'

'That would have been awkward.'

'Charlie couldn't see there was any problem until Meg refused him outright. She chose God over him, and he became so bitter, he enlisted. By the way he tells it, he became hell-bent on the battlefield. It was a miracle he survived.'

'And Johnny?'

'He died saving Charlie's life during a sniper attack.'

'Oh!'

They fell silent for a few moments.

'I like to think that if Johnny had come back he would have seen me as a woman, not just a friend.'

'But he didn't come back.'

'No.'

'I'm sorry.'

Grace gave a wry smile. 'Well, it's what I've held onto these years since he was killed. I told my parents and my interfering relatives I was happy single, that I would never love anyone else.'

'Is that how you still feel?'

Grace took a deep breath. That question was way too personal and she had never considered that the answer would ever change.

'In light of where we are, and the close proximity that we currently share, I think I'd better say: yes that is how I still feel.'

Alex nodded. 'Yes, I think that is wise. I'm sorry for prying.'

'Well, it is my turn now. Tell me about Nancy.'

'We were childhood sweethearts, but there was never any question as to what we both felt. She told me she loved me, and I told her I loved her. The moment I got back from Europe, we got married.'

'The moment?'

'Figuratively speaking.' Alex smiled. 'Jimmy was born the year after.'

'You really loved her then?'

Alex gave a small sigh. 'Those early years with the children and me working with her father in his store—they were the best years of my life.'

'How old was she when she died?'

'She was twenty-seven. Died giving birth to our fourth child.'

'I'm sorry.' Grace could feel tears welling in her eyes. She didn't feel as if she could say anything else for the present.

They sat in companionable silence for a few minutes.

'It was Norma who practically destroyed me.' Alex suddenly broke the silence. 'She was working for my parents-in-law as a shop assistant, and when Nancy died, she began to help care for the children. Doris, my mother-in-law, wanted to look after them, but she suffered too much from arthritis, so Norma shifted her responsibilities into the house and began to look after the kids to help their grandmother.'

'Didn't the children like her?'

'Oh, they liked her. You might be surprised to know that was the very reason I reacted so badly to you at first. I saw the way the girls took to you, and all I could see was Norma.'

'What did she do?'

'Once the Depression made it impossible for Johnson and Sons to support all of us, I had to go way out from the city to find work.'

'You didn't take the children?'

'It was open cut mining in the outback. There was no family accommodation, so I set Norma up with the children in my house.'

'And?'

'For two years, I had no idea that she was physically abusing Jimmy. I think about it now and get so angry.'

'Why just Jimmy?'

'I don't know. I don't understand the woman at all. She kept telling his grandparents that he was a difficult child, and that his sullenness was rebellion.'

'But?'

'Irene told me she wouldn't let him in the house, wouldn't give him any food, and whipped him often.'

'But he came inside to sleep.'

'No, he slept in the chook shed.'

'Oh, Alex, that's awful.'

'I took the kids and went on the road for the simple reason that if I'd stayed around, I'm afraid I might have tried to kill her.'

'You wouldn't have.'

'No, that's why I went on the road. But the anger is still there, like a pit of acid. When I saw you being so kind and friendly to the children, that's what bubbled up again. I'm sorry.'

'Now that I've heard the story, I completely understand.'

'I just wish there was a way I could get the memory of her out of my head. Every time I think of her, I boil with anger.'

'Well, we could talk about the worry of the water gushing around beneath us. Do you want to take a look and see how high the water level is?'

Alex got up from his cushioned seat, took the lamp across to the manhole and looked down. Grace moved across next to him. Neither one said anything. The water was only about four feet below them.

'Are we going to be all right?' Grace asked.

'I hope so. Perhaps Meg and her parents are praying for us.'

'They will be. She'll have them all praying, the children included.'

Chapter Six

They talked for another hour or so. Alex was tired, but he was still anxious, and knew sleeping would be difficult. Eventually Grace suggested they turn the lamp down and try to sleep. Thankful they'd had the foresight to put pillows, blankets and quilts up in the ceiling, they managed to construct a bed that was reasonably comfortable. The winter air was cold, and they had been wrapped in blankets while they'd talked. Now he tried to adjust himself to a position where sleep would come. But the rain continued to fall, and he could hear the water.

'Are you asleep?' Grace's voice came through the darkness.

'No.'

'Are you worried?'

'Yes.' It wasn't exactly words of comfort and reassurance. 'I'm sorry, Grace. I don't know how this is going to turn out.'

Silence fell again for another few minutes, but Alex could tell she was still awake. Then came the sound of something heavy bashing up against the side of the house. He imagined it was a large branch or something being carried along by the swift-flowing water.

'Alex. I'm afraid.'

Alex didn't know what else to do. He shuffled closer to her and manoeuvred the blankets until he was able to wrap her in his embrace. Far from being offended, she turned into him and grabbed hold as if he were a lifebuoy.

'I'm sorry, Alex.'

'What for?' he asked.

'I don't think we're going to make it.'

'That's not your fault.'

'But I feel so badly for your children. They love you and need you.'

Alex hadn't allowed his mind to go that far, but when she mentioned it, he realised how much he wished to be with his children right now.

'We don't know how this will turn out, Grace. We should remain hopeful.'

He felt her nod against his shoulder.

Just feeling the warmth of another human being, and the beat of her heart against his, made Alex feel as if he could sleep. His mind began to fade out and he allowed himself to relax into unconsciousness. He didn't know how long, but he was jarred awake again by more heavy thumping sounds against the house, as if something was hitting the iron roofing. He felt Grace cling tighter to him and then could tell she had begun to cry by her shuddering shoulders.

'It's only something hitting the house.' He hoped he sounded positive.

'But the water is so high it's hit the roof.'

'It was probably only the veranda roof. Let me go and have another look.'

It seemed like she was reluctant to let him go, but he got up anyway, lit the lamp and took it over to the manhole.

'How far?' Grace asked.

'It's about a foot down.'

Alex turned back and saw her looking totally forlorn. Something moved deep in him, dulling his sense of reason and logic. He moved back to their makeshift bed, took her in his arms and kissed her hair. Grace turned her face up to his and whatever sensible barriers of morality that should have been in place were washed away, just as the bridge had been washed away. While the world outside was being flooded and brown muddy water flowed in places it shouldn't go, Alex's emotions broke their banks and flowed into dangerous territory. And Grace didn't do anything to prevent it.

Grace gradually woke from a deep sleep. Several things assaulted her mind at once. Firstly, she was aware that the rain had finally stopped. This moment of relief was quickly arrested by other thoughts. She realised she was still firmly ensconced in Alex's embrace, and neither of them were clothed. She felt a wave of conflicting emotions. What she had experienced with him hours ago had been deep and passionate, and she had yielded completely to the pleasure of it. But she also knew on a foundational level their intimate physical exchange outside of marriage was wrong.

She had never considered she would ever be in such a position. In fact, she had held a rather harsh opinion of girls who got themselves into such trouble. Yesterday, she would have said there was no excuse for such behaviour. Today, as the dim light of day filtered in through gaps in the structure, she had to consider what she had done, and what she would now do in response to it.

Alex was still fast asleep, his chest rising and falling with even breaths. Grace knew she should get up, get dressed and get away from him as fast as was possible, but she couldn't. They were still stuck together in their safe haven for a start, but even so, she didn't want to hurt him. He hadn't taken advantage of her any more than she had of him. Something had moved in her on a deeper level than she had ever thought would happen. In the gray light she suddenly realised that Johnny was long gone, and the affections she thought she had reserved only for him had transferred without warning.

Eventually she moved away from Alex. As she rolled away he woke up. She saw him look at her and there were a thousand thoughts in her mind, but she couldn't articulate any of them. It seemed as if he understood, as he rolled over and looked the other way. Grace took the opportunity to retrieve her clothes and make herself decent again. But she didn't feel decent even with her clothes back in place.

'The rain has stopped.' It was the only thing she could think to say.

'I heard. Looks like we're going to make it after all.'

Grace moved away from the bedding and looked out of the manhole, giving him time to find his clothes.

'The water has gone down a bit,' she said.

'Hopefully the rain has moved on, and now all we have to do is wait for the waters to recede.'

Grace came back and began to rummage through the food supplies. 'Do you want something to eat?' She resisted the desire to look at Alex, aware that he was still bare-chested and finding his shirt.

'No.' Alex sounded firm. 'Grace, we need to talk.'

Grace wanted to talk, but she also didn't want to talk. Her feelings were all over the place and she didn't know what on earth she was supposed to say.

'Please,' Alex said. 'Come back and sit down for a bit.'

Grace let out a sigh and seeing that he was fully clothed, she stepped back into the circle of bedding. It appeared as if Alex was struggling with words as much as she was. Eventually she took the initiative.

'You know you asked me last night if I still felt as if I would never love anyone other than Johnny? Well …'

'Grace, stop.'

Grace was confused by his abrupt command, and she frowned at him.

'What happened last night …' He paused, as if struggling for words.

'Yes?'

'I'm sorry. It shouldn't have happened.'

She gave a short laugh. 'I know that. What sort of woman do you think I am?'

'I took advantage of you. I'm sorry.'

'No, Alex, I took as much advantage of you. I don't blame you for it.'

He took a deep breath and tilted his head as if he was searching the roof for answers he couldn't find. 'I had no right.'

'Yes, Alex, I understand all that. The point is, what happens now?'

'That's the point,' he said. 'Nothing happens now.'

Grace heard what he said and took a moment to process it.

'What do you mean?' she asked.

'I mean that despite what happened last night, there can't be anything between us.'

She paused again, her brow creased with her thoughts. 'I don't understand what you mean.'

'Look, I'm aware that you could reasonably expect that I should do the honourable thing and marry you.'

'The thought had crossed my mind.' She fidgeted with her sleeve, feeling the awkwardness of this conversation. 'I'm getting the feeling that your dislike of me was real right from the start, and still is real now.'

'No.' He shook his head. 'No, I don't dislike you. I was afraid of what you represented at first, but I so find you attractive and that's the problem. Far from dislike, Grace. I'm growing to really like you.'

'I don't see how that is a problem. You couldn't go another step to love and commitment, considering what just happened?'

'Is that what you want?'

Grace paused to consider. 'If not for last night, I wouldn't have thought of it, no.'

'Can we just pretend that last night didn't happen?'

'I don't understand,' she said again. 'What is there about me that makes you determined not to do the honourable thing?'

'It's not you; it's Norma.'

'Alex, I'm not Norma.'

'I know that, but Norma still rules in this situation.'

'You've got to get over what she did to you and the children. You can't let her control you forever.'

Alex paused, let out another deep sigh, and dropped his head.

'Alex? What is it?'

'I married Norma.'

'Norma was your wife?' Grace could almost feel her eyes open as large as could be.

'Not was my wife—she is my wife.'

Grace felt nauseous. Then she felt angry, and then dirty.

'How could you?' she shouted at him. 'How could you do that to me … to her?'

Alex shook his head.

If there had been somewhere to run and slam a door, Grace would have done it. But there was nowhere to go. Throwing something would have been good, or perhaps launching at him with her fists to beat his chest. But none of these actions were options.

'I understand that you are angry—'

'That's an understatement!'

'When we get out of here, I'll take the children and leave.'

That statement took the wind out of Grace's sails. 'Where will you go?' Her tone immediately changed.

'I need to go back to South Australia and sort out the situation with Norma.'

'Go back to her, you mean?'

'There's no way I would ever put my children anywhere near her again,' he said. 'She is a vicious cruel woman, and I don't want anything to do with her.'

'But she's your wife.'

'Look, Grace, you might have a low opinion of me because I have abandoned my so-called wife, but you don't really understand.'

'Tell me then.'

'I didn't really want to marry her in the first place. I didn't love her.'

'Then why did you marry her?'

'Because of the children. She put on this show of being a wonderful kind motherly figure. The children all liked her, to start with. They needed a mother. Doris wasn't able to care for them. I needed someone to take care of my home.'

'Did she know that was all you wanted?'

'I don't know what she thought. I was wrong to enter into the marriage in the first place, but my heart was still broken from the loss of Nancy. I just thought it was the best thing for the kids.'

'How long were you together?' Grace asked.

'Well, I married her in 1928—four years.'

'But how long did you live with her? You know, as husband and wife?'

'Never. I never saw her as my wife.'

'So you were never intimate with her?'

Alex pursed his lips as if in resignation.

'If you're asking if I consummated the marriage, the answer is yes. She wanted to—'

'Never mind. I don't think I want to know.'

'Well, I only lived in the house with her for about a month before I got the work out north.'

'It doesn't really matter though, does it Alex? She is still your legally wedded wife.'

'Yes, she is.'

'Which means you have no business courting another woman.'

'No, I don't.'

'Well I wished you had said that …'

'I did say that, remember, Grace. I told you that I didn't want to have anything to do with you, and that you wouldn't trap me into marriage.'

'Yes I remember, but I didn't realise that was because you were *already* married. I just thought that was because you were an arrogant beast.'

'Thank you.'

'Well, that leaves me in a difficult position, doesn't it?'

'As I said before. I'm sorry.'

'Well, just for your information, Mr Alex Moreland, you nearly managed to break through to this icy heart. For a few short hours I almost believed that I could fall in love with a real live man.'

Alex sat, stony faced.

'I won't say anything to anybody,' she said. 'I know it was as much my fault as yours.'

'Just for your information, Miss Grace Shore, you did manage to break through to this broken heart. I only wish it was mine to give you.'

Grace turned her head away from him and allowed warm tears to flow down her cheeks. This was too much. To find the hope of love after all these years of being alone, and to have it snatched away before it had a chance to form. It was more painful than she had expected.

Chapter Seven

Grace couldn't bring herself to engage in small talk. She was hurt by this sudden loss. She was also angry, not just with Alex, but with herself as well. She couldn't understand how she had allowed herself to succumb to temptation. Thinking about it, she couldn't even call it temptation. She hadn't sat around and thought about Alex for hours, like she used to do about Johnny. It was only when she came into his embrace that her body responded to his strength and warmth. Then when he'd kissed her hair, it was like a natural response. In terms of logical thought, there hadn't been any.

She was aware that Alex was just as miserable, but there wasn't anything she could say to relieve the tension.

'I'm going to try to get some more sleep,' she said.

Alex nodded. Grace felt bad for him.

'You may as well try, too. The damage has already been done. Lying down together now isn't going to make any difference.'

'You sound very practical.'

'I have to, don't I? I'm tired. It might be hours before the water recedes, and I'm cold and stiff. I just want to lie down and try to forget everything.'

She didn't say anything else, but arranged herself under the quilts. She was aware that Alex resumed a sleeping position as well, but this time, he made sure there was a safe distance between them. Angry, she repressed the desire to turn back into his embrace.

Why do I still want him? I can't have him. It's wrong.

***

'Grace.' Alex's voice broke through her heavy sleep. 'Grace, wake up.'

She took a few seconds to gather her thoughts and fully wake up. Stretching, she sat up.

'What is it?'

'The water has gone right down now.'

Grace's head was still a little foggy, so she was slow about getting up and moving over to the manhole to look.

'There's still a few inches on the floor,' she observed.

'Yes, but we could probably clear it out with brooms and buckets. At least we could make a start.'

Grace nodded. Though she was still stiff, sore, and felt sluggish, she was glad that they could at least move about and do something useful. She hoped it would beat this terrible thing growing in her. She wanted Alex, and couldn't seem to shake it. On one hand she felt like a brazen hussy, and on the other, she didn't care.

She employed every fibre of self-control to make sure she didn't give him any indication of how she was feeling, adopting the cold-hearted approach. Hardly speaking to him, never looking at him. She hoped he would stick to his end of the bargain. He had a wife, and he needed to remember that. If he should so much as speak kindly to her, she felt her facade would crumble and she would rush into his arms again.

Alex had to jump down, as the ladder had been washed away, and the water had pushed the table and chair further down the hallway. Grace didn't watch. She was worried he would hurt himself, and then she'd be back to square one. But he managed to land without mishap in a splash of water. It didn't take him long to retrieve the ladder and put it back into place.

'Can you make it down all right?' he asked.

Grace nodded. She was determined. Alex stood beneath the manhole and gave instructions as to how far the top rung was from where her foot dangled in mid-air. Finally she felt it and began to feel for the next one down.

'I've got the ladder,' he called.

Great! I'm going to climb right down into his arms again. And she wanted to, but by the time she was at the bottom, he carefully moved away from her. She felt bereft.

Alex sprang into action. They moved the soggy kitchen table into position, and he climbed up into the ceiling again. Grace knew he was going to pass down the cleaning things. The operation went smoothly enough, and before long, they were sweeping mud and water out of the house. The more they worked, the more Grace was able to concentrate on the task at hand. The water damage to the furniture was terrible. She didn't know how much of it would be salvageable, but the first job was to get the water out of the house. One thing was certain: there was more hope for restoring the house than there was for restoring her heart.

***

Alex threw all of his frustration and anger into physical work. He was all too well aware of Grace working within the vicinity. He tried to find the antagonism he'd had towards her when they'd first met, but it just wasn't there. His current anger was towards Norma and his own idiocy in marrying her. Still, he saw the walls had gone up between himself and Grace, and his sensible mind told him it was just as well. *How could this have happened?*

He had known all along that nothing could ever come of a relationship with Grace, or any other woman. Norma legally had him and there was nothing he could do about it. He wasn't the sort of man to take marriage lightly, and though he had known people who had obtained a divorce, there had to be cause—usually unfaithfulness. As far as he was aware, Norma had been faithful to him.

But I haven't been faithful to her. He gave a huff. It was ironic. The whole situation had been wrong since the day he'd asked her to enter into a marriage. *What was I thinking?*

The thing was, he hadn't been thinking. Not about marriage, only about his children and how he was going to manage a family without their mother. He hadn't been thinking last night either. Yet something about it had seemed so right, even though he knew it was completely wrong. The timing, the level of intimacy, the exchange—it had all been wrong. But Grace: she had been right.

'Blast!'

Grace looked around to see what had happened. 'What's wrong?'

'Nothing,' he answered. 'Excuse my language.' *Nothing except the fact I married the wrong woman, and now I've found the right one, I can't have you.* 'I'm going to go outside for a while for some air.' He propped his broom against the wall.

Grace nodded. It was on the tip of his tongue to ask her to come with him, but he swallowed the words. There was nothing to be gained by trying to cultivate an impossible friendship.

It was late afternoon and although the water level had gone down considerably, inches of water still lay over the land around the house. He could see where the bank had broken, and the water in the creek was still high and flowing fast.

Thankfully, the cloud cover had cleared a little and the sun had shone through several times. He had high hopes the water would have receded even further by tomorrow, although the ground was going to be soggy for days. Alex didn't want to go back into the house, so he walked around the puddles and water-filled depressions towards the bridge. It was gone, but he knew there was a ford for the animals to cross. He stopped and considered the rushing waters. It would be dicey to try and get a horse across today, but there would be a good chance tomorrow. With this in mind, he made a new plan.

***

Grace had decided to concentrate on one room at a time, and had chosen the kitchen first to see if she could make anything functional. So far, she had beaten the mud and water, but not the dampness that had been absorbed into everything. She wanted to find some wood and get the cook stove alight. This would give them some warmth, and possibly help dry, at least, that room out. With this in mind, she went outside to see what she could find.

'I'm going to walk up to the back paddock and see if I can find some wood we might be able to burn,' she said to Alex as he came stepping his way through the water towards her.

'I'll come with you,' he said. 'I was going to see if I can catch one of the horses. We should be able to swim a horse through the water tomorrow.'

Grace didn't answer but fell into step beside him. She had ignored the possibility of having to spend another night with him. Now it seemed it would be inevitable. She took a deep breath and decided to deal with one problem at a time. Right now, her mission was to find some wood. She hadn't been able to locate her rubber boots, which was hardly surprising as they usually sat outside the house on the back veranda. Now she had to put up with water squelching inside her work shoes. Her feet were wet and cold, but she had hopes of warming them up in front of a roaring fire.

'Did you find a halter or bridle to catch the horse with?' Grace asked.

'The saddle room was washed over by the water. No such luck.'

'How are you going to catch a horse?'

'My braces.'

Though Grace had determined she wasn't going to engage in friendly conversation, she couldn't help it. 'What will keep your trousers up?'

'I'll hoist when necessary.'

She exchanged a look with him. They laughed.

Then Alex sighed. 'This is such a rubbish situation, Grace.'

'I assume you mean the state of the property.'

'You know I mean the state of affairs between us.'

She didn't reply.

'Now I can't even form a friendship with you, and despite our shaky start, I have a feeling that we would have got on quite well together.'

'Do you think it's helpful talking about this when we both know we have to avoid it?'

'Probably not, but it's rubbish. That's all I'm saying.'

'Hopefully it will only be one more day.'

'You think we'll feel differently just because we are back in company? From my point of view, I'll still think it's rubbish.'

'Me too, Alex, but that's just the way it is, isn't it?'

Chapter Eight

Grace was relieved to find that they had managed to endure another night without mishap. They had warmed themselves in front of the kitchen cook stove, but the house was too damp to set up their bedding. They returned to the ceiling cavity, but only after they had worked themselves into such a state of exhaustion that sleep was all they could possibly manage once they lay down.

This morning, Alex had gone outdoors again to see if he could scavenge something that resembled a halter or bridle. Grace continued to work in the house. It was going to be days, if not weeks, before it was truly habitable again. Charlie would probably have to repaint the house, and the peeling wallpaper in the lounge room and bedrooms would all need to be replaced. Still, there was the ever-present mud to be got out, one room at a time. Grace dedicated herself to this task.

'Grace!'

She put her scrub brush down and rushed out. It was Charlie.

'Thank God you're safe!' Charlie jumped down from his horse and rushed over to his sister, wrapping her in a warm hug. 'We were all so afraid that you'd drowned.'

'Safe and sound,' she said, though inwardly she felt as if she had been battered beyond repair.

'Have you seen Alex? Did he make it?'

'Yes, he's been with me the whole time. He went out this morning to try to find a bridle. He was hoping to ride through the waters. I see you've made it across.'

Charlie returned and picked up the reins of his horse and patted its neck. 'It was quite deep, but the old girl swam through.'

'I'm surprised you took the risk.'

'We were going mad over at Wallace Hill, not knowing if you were alive or not.'

'I'm glad you're here now. I'm sorry to say the house hasn't fared very well.'

'The house we can fix, Grace. But I would hate to have lost you.'

'And Alex.'

'His kids are beside themselves. Poor little things. Imagine losing their father as well as their mother.'

Grace nodded. 'Why don't you go and see if you can find Alex, and I'll make a cup of tea.'

'I thought by the look of it the house had been flooded.'

'It was. We managed to rescue a lot of stuff before the bank broke. Stored it up in the ceiling.'

'Is that where you stayed during the flood?'

'We nearly didn't make it. Alex managed to rescue me as the water washed the ladder from beneath me.'

Charlie gave a low whistle and shook his head. 'Dad told me Alex had rescued you from the creek earlier in the day.'

'Yes, twice in one day. But we lost the motor car. I'm sorry.'

'I don't care about the car. I'm just glad you're all right.'

'Go and find Alex. I'll make the tea.'

***

Alex made the decision. 'I want to swim the horse across today,' he said. 'I need to see my kids.'

'Of course,' Charlie said. 'I'll stay here with Grace.'

'Why can't I ride double behind you?' Grace asked her brother.

'I guess,' Charlie said. 'This place is a mess.'

'You should have seen it before we started the clean-up,' Grace said. 'We've made huge progress.'

'If you're going to come as well, I'll go and get the horses ready. You bank the fire and close up the windows.'

Grace went about shutting all the windows she'd opened before to let air through to dry the place. But things already smelt musty. The air outside was still too damp to dry anything. It was going to take forever to get the house liveable again.

She eventually emerged to find the two men with the horses. She hadn't brought anything with her. There was nothing in a clean state even if there had been room. She put her foot in the stirrup while Charlie hauled her up behind him. Alex was riding the other horse bareback. They'd made a makeshift halter from some rope they'd obviously found lying around. The ride through the creek was quite hair-raising, and Grace clung tightly to her brother, closing her eyes against the memory of her near-drowning. The water came right up to her knees as the faithful horse swam its way through to the other side. They emerged on the other embankment dripping wet, and rode the three miles to Wallace Hill.

***

As they neared Wallace Hill, the dogs barked at their approach. Alex saw the front doors open and the family pour out, including his children. They ran across the gravel drive towards the horses. Alex slid off the horse and moved straight across to them. He caught Jean as she threw herself at him for a hug.

'Daddy,' she cried. 'I thought you were drowned.'

'I'm all right, Jeanie. Safe and sound.'

Irene moved in to hug him as well. She didn't say anything, but Alex knew she was close to tears. 'It's all right darlin'. I'm here now.'

'I'm glad you're safe, Dad,' Jimmy said. He didn't rush in for a hug, like his sisters, but stood back. Alex didn't care for the unemotional manly image his son was trying to uphold. He grabbed him and gave him a strong hug. 'I'm glad you're all safe too.'

'Where were you?' Jean asked. 'We thought you drowned.'

'We were trapped by the floodwaters,' Alex said. 'We couldn't get across the creek to you.'

'Did you stay with Miss Shore in her house?'

Alex knew that question would come out sooner or later. Jean would keep asking until she had all the details.

'Our little house was washed away, so I helped Miss Shore rescue some of Mrs Shore's precious things. We stored them in the roof space above the ceiling of the farmhouse.'

'Why did you put them in the ceiling?' Irene asked.

'The farmhouse was flooded too.'

'Well, where did you stay?' Even Jimmy wanted details.

'In the ceiling cavity of the farmhouse,' Alex answered.

'With Miss Shore?' Jimmy asked.

Alex nodded.

'Daddy, I hope you weren't mean to Miss Shore. I know you don't like her very much.' Jean's words were like a bullet in Alex's gut. He looked across to Grace. She had been watching the whole exchange as if she wished she could have been a part of it.

'Was he mean to you, Miss Shore?' Irene asked.

'No need to worry, girls,' Grace answered. 'He was very kind. He even saved my life twice.'

'Really, Dad?' Jimmy turned his full attention to Alex as if he was really proud of him.

'Well, I guess I did.' Alex cast a glance toward Grace. Something in her eyes disturbed him, as if she didn't want their time together to end. He didn't either, but he knew he had to go. But he was going to leave all talk about returning to South Australia for another time. Tonight he was going to be thankful that he was alive and back with his family.

Charlie's parents made no fuss over having two families move in with them. It was a huge house with plenty of bedrooms, as well as the spare room in the servants' quarters out the back. Everyone pitched in to help put the flooded farm back in order. Alex found the situation difficult. It was easy enough being over on Charlie's property, working with him to repair fences and burn dead animals that had been unable to escape the flood waters. But when Grace and Meg returned with their mother to continue the cleaning and airing of the house, Alex baulked. To say he hated seeing Grace was not true. He longed to see her, but was in torment when he did. He knew he should leave soon. He worked for a week before he took the opportunity to talk to Charlie.

'I'll need to be moving on in the next week or so,' he said to Charlie as they worked together putting in new fence posts.

Charlie stopped what he was doing and looked at his worker. 'Why?'

'I need to sort some things out back home, things I've let go for too long.'

Charlie didn't look convinced, but Alex didn't have any other excuse to offer. They continued to work for a few minutes before Charlie spoke again.

'Did something happen between you and Grace during the flood?'

Alex paused before asking a question in place of answering. 'Why do you ask that?'

'I'm not blind,' Charlie said. 'I've seen you two look at each other as if you're communicating, but you never talk. Did something happen?'

Alex nodded.

'Good or bad?'

'It depends on how you look at it.'

'How do *you* look at it?' Charlie asked.

'It was the best thing that could have happened—and the worst.'

'Would you mind explaining?' Charlie had stopped digging and was now leaning on his tall crowbar.

'I don't think you really want to know.'

'Grace is my sister. Of course I want to know, if it affects her.'

Alex hung his head, but couldn't seem to put what happened into words. Charlie was watching him closely and obviously drew his own conclusions from the silence.

'I hope you intend to do the honourable thing.' There was a steel edge to his voice.

'I can't,' Alex said.

'Because …?'

'Because of my wife.'

'I beg your pardon? I thought your wife had passed away.'

'The children's mother, my first wife, died, yes, but my second wife …'

'Norma? You married Norma?'

Alex nodded. He waited, sure that Charlie would become all big-brother aggression in defence of his sister's honour, but he didn't. Instead he blew out a loud breath that seemed to indicate a sense of heavy concern.

'I intend to take the children and leave,' Alex said. 'I can't stay here watching her all the time. It's killing me.'

'Killing you?' Charlie said with eyebrows raised. 'Do you know how she feels about it?'

'Yeah, I do.'

'You've talked about it? To her?'

'We were stuck in a tiny place for nearly three days. I know how she feels about it.'

'But you can't marry her?'

'Bigamy is a criminal offence, Charlie. Otherwise, I'd be glad to.'

Charlie blew out another breath and shook his head. Alex was still waiting for a physical explosion of anger from him. Again it didn't come.

'I'm sorry,' Alex said. 'If I could make it right, I would.'

'I suppose you think I'm angry with you.'

'Well, I'm angry with myself.'

'But you did warn her that there could never be anything, didn't you?'

'Don't remind me.'

'I'm not going to judge you, Alex. I've done stupid things in my time too, you know.'

Alex raised his eyebrows in question.

'Meg is my second wife.'

'Really?'

'My first wife … well, let's just say she would be good competition for Norma in many ways.'

'Why did you marry her?'

'Why did you marry Norma?'

'Because I wasn't thinking, and I needed someone for the children.'

'Better than me. I met Janielle one day, married her the next, and shipped out for North Africa the one after. And I only did it to aggravate my mother —I wanted to show her that I didn't need her self-righteous judgement.'

'Did you divorce her?' Alex asked.

'No, she eventually died of alcohol poisoning. She was Aimee's mother.'

'So you had a child with her?'

'No, I adopted Aimee to rescue her from neglect and abuse.'

'So you know what I'm talking about when I talk about Norma's treatment of my children?'

'Of course I do. You can't let a woman like that have care of your children.'

'That is the only reason I ran. I believe that marriage is sacred.'

'Not sacred enough, apparently.'

Alex sighed. 'We both thought we were going to die, to be honest. We just clung to each other, and then …'

'I get it. Doesn't make it right, however.'

'Yeah, I know.'

'What will you do when you get back to Mitcham?'

'I hope to get a divorce.'

'Well she has grounds for divorce now, doesn't she?'

'I hope she'll take the opportunity.'

'And then what will you do?'

'I'd like to think that perhaps I may come back and court Grace properly.'

'That might not work out as well as you'd like.'

'Because?'

'Because, whatever else she is, Grace is a stickler for morality.'

'Meaning she wouldn't marry a divorced man.'

'That's what I mean.'

'That might be a bit hypocritical considering what has passed between us. Is it about how it appears to others?'

'I don't know, mate. You'll have to talk to her about it.'

'How do you feel about it?'

'It's not up to me, is it? As I said, I've already made a bunch of mistakes in my life that could have ended up a lot worse than they have. This is about you and Grace, and what she will accept. She may just want to let you go and continue pretending that she's happy in her singleness.'

'You think she was pretending?'

'Not at first, she wasn't. Since she met you? I think it would be a huge act if she pretends she doesn't care.'

'I know she cares. We've already discussed it.'

'Well, my friend, you are going to have to go back to your wife and see what can be sorted.'

'So you won't condemn me for seeking a divorce?'

'It's not my life. You have to make your own decisions according to your own beliefs.'

'I don't believe in divorce, but …'

'But that was before Norma nearly destroyed your family.'

Alex nodded.

'Aimee's mother did her best to destroy us as well. I do understand.'

'So I have your support?'

'I said I wouldn't judge you, and I won't, but I am not sure how I feel about Grace marrying a divorced man.'

Alex raised his eyebrows. 'That sounds like a judgement to me.'

'Yeah, well, it's not something I ever considered I'd have to deal with. You'd better talk with her before making any plans. I've a feeling it won't go any further than that anyway.'

***

Grace didn't want to face it. Charlie told her Alex wanted to talk to her, but she didn't have anything to say to him. She was physically attracted to him, she really liked his children, she even felt as if they might get along together—but none of that was relevant. Alex was married, and there was an end to it. *I refuse to be involved with him in any way. One mistake is enough.*

'He's planning on leaving tomorrow,' Charlie said. 'Don't you think you owe him a few minutes?'

'How do you figure that?' she asked. 'I don't owe him anything. He told me up front he wasn't going to marry me, and apparently there was a good reason for that. So let's just leave it at that, shall we?'

'So you won't give him a chance?'

'Chance for what? He's married, Charlie. I'm not a home-wrecker.'

'What about if he—'

'No, Charlie! Not in any circumstance. Alex Moreland can go back to where he came from. He doesn't mean anything to me, and I don't want to discuss it anymore.'

Thankfully Charlie let the subject drop. Grace kept her "couldn't-care-less" pretence up for another fifteen minutes before she excused herself. Then she retreated to the room she was sharing with Aimee, and burst into tears.

What a liar I am.

She couldn't get *that* night out of her mind. She hadn't just responded to him physically, but had, for the first time in her life, opened her heart and soul to a man. Alex would leave tomorrow with his children, and he would take her heart with him. There was no way, however, she would let him or anyone else know that. She loved him and hated him all at once. He'd stolen her happy delusion. She couldn't even resurrect Johnny's image in her mind any more. The story she'd told herself for the last fourteen years—that she would never love anyone but Johnny Laslett—had turned out to be an unsatisfying fairy tale. Now the story that had taken its place had Alex Moreland in the middle of it, and real love hurt. Grace cried herself to sleep.

Chapter Nine

Alex didn't know how to feel when the train pulled into the Mitcham railway station. He ushered the children out onto the platform.

'Irene, watch Jean while Jimmy and I go and get our things from the baggage car.'

They really didn't have much by the way of luggage, but it gave him something to think about to keep his conflicting emotions at bay.

'Do Grandma and Grandpa Johnson know we're coming?' Jean asked, once they'd begun to walk along Belair Road.

'I sent them a letter last week, but I didn't tell them what day we'd arrive,' Alex replied. 'I'm sure they'll be happy to see us, no matter what time we get there.'

'Will we go back to our house?' Jimmy asked the question, and Alex heard the underlying anxiety that was in his son's question.

'No.'

'Does Norma still live in our house?' Irene asked.

'As far as I know.'

'Oh, can we go and see her?' Jean asked.

'No.' Alex clamped down his emotions. He knew he would go and see Norma, eventually, but he had no intentions of letting the children anywhere near her.

'Why not?' Jean complained.

'Because, silly,' Irene said. 'Just leave it, Jean. Dad said so, that's all.'

'Dad is always so mean to ladies.'

Alex tried to shut his mind to his daughter's talk. He wondered briefly if he should try to explain it to Jean. Nancy probably would have. But then, if Nancy had been here, he wouldn't have been in this predicament.

Even as he thought about her, he walked past the park where he and Nancy used to sit of an evening before the war. Beautiful memories that stabbed with the pain of loss. Alex shook his head, trying to think of something else. Then he saw the war memorial. More painful memories of mates lost in the terrible war gutted him. He'd barely thought about these things while he'd been on the road. And not at all while he'd been in Green Valley.

Grace. Alex wanted very much to swear, but restrained himself in front of the children. Every way his mind turned, there was pain and regret.

'I can see Grandpa's house from here,' Jean called. 'Can we run ahead?'

'Only if Irene or Jimmy go with you.'

'Come on,' Irene said, breaking into a run. 'I'll race you there.'

As the girls moved out of earshot, Jimmy nervously cleared his throat. 'You won't go back to Norma, will you Dad?'

'No, son. Not ever.'

Jimmy released a sigh of relief.

'I'm sorry I ever left you with her,' Alex said. 'I didn't know she would treat you that way.'

'Did you ever love her?' Jimmy asked.

'No. I appreciated it when she seemed to care for you children.'

'But she didn't care for us.'

'But I thought she did. That was the way she acted before I asked her to marry me.'

'Why did you marry her? How could you forget Mum so quickly?'

'I've never forgotten your mother. I loved her with all my heart.'

'Well, why did you marry Norma?'

Alex shook his head and sighed. 'I was confused. I needed help. I thought Norma would be good to you.'

'I wish you hadn't.'

'So do I. Believe me, it was the biggest mistake of my life.'

'What will you do now?'

'I'm not sure. I need to work something out for her. She *is* legally my wife.'

'But you won't move back in?'

Alex could hear the insecurity in his son's voice.

'I said I wouldn't. I won't, Jimmy. Trust me.'

'Because I think Jean would, in a flash.'

'Norma didn't treat Jean like she did you.'

'I don't know what I did wrong. I don't know why she did that to me.'

Alex put Jean's swag in his left hand with his own, and put his free arm around his son's shoulders. 'I'm so sorry, Jimmy. I hope one day I can make it right.'

'Just don't make us go back.'

By the time he and Jimmy mounted the front steps of his parents-in-laws' house, the girls had already alerted Samuel and Doris of their arrival. Samuel came out onto the veranda and grasped his son-in-law in a genuinely affectionate hug.

'I'm so glad to see you back, Alex,' he said.

Alex just nodded. He couldn't say he was glad to be back. There was nothing here for him but conflict and pain.

'Come inside,' Samuel said. 'Doris was thrilled when she received your letter. She hasn't been very well of late.'

Samuel then placed his strong arm around his grandson's shoulder. 'You've grown, my boy,' he said. 'How old are you now?'

'I'll be fourteen in December,' Jimmy said.

'Almost a man. Your Uncle Frank will be able to use some help from you in the storeroom.'

Alex watched as Jimmy walked inside with his grandfather. He knew it was good for his kids to be in a real family home. But the house held ghosts of their mother, and Alex couldn't enter without feeling that sense of loss rising in him again.

'Alexander. It is so good to see you, dear.' Doris Johnson didn't get up from her wheelchair, but opened her arms to her son-in-law. Alex responded and bent low, allowing her to give him a hug.

She was the only person who ever called him by his full name. His own mother used to use it when he was in trouble, but she had been gone many years now.

'Thank you for bringing Nancy's children back to us. I've missed them so much.'

Alex nodded in acknowledgement. He didn't have words to offer.

'Will you be going back to your place to stay?' Samuel asked.

Alex was immediately aware of the tension that Jimmy displayed, waiting for his answer.

'No,' Alex answered. 'I was hoping you wouldn't mind if we stayed here with you for a while.'

An uncomfortable silence seemed to descend as the difficult question was out in the open between them.

'Jimmy, will you take the girls out to the garden and see if you can find your Uncle Frank? I think he is hoeing some weeds in the vegetable patch.' Samuel gave the instructions, and the children didn't offer any protest.

'Uncle Frank is a bit funny, isn't he?' Jean said as they went out of the room. Nobody bothered to shush her on this occasion.

'We'll have to talk about it, Alex,' Samuel said. 'I know it's hard, but we need to lay all the cards on the table.'

'I don't know if you're aware of the extent of her abuse toward Jimmy.' He didn't mention Norma's name. He knew they were all talking about the same thing. 'Once I discovered it, I pretty much took off.'

'We were aware she wasn't fond of him, and suspected that she was very unfair to the boy,' Doris said.

'If she had been a man I would have taken my fists to her, and then reported her to the police for physical assault.'

'That bad?' Samuel said. 'Surely not.'

'I don't really want them to have to talk about it again, but you should have heard the things Irene told me.'

'But it was just Jimmy you said, she treated badly?' Doris said.

'I don't care if she treated the girls like queens. She abused my son, and I won't have her anywhere near them again.'

Alex was fuming with anger again, his breathing fast and body tense. After a few moments of tension he saw that Doris and Samuel were watching him anxiously.

'I'm sorry,' he breathed. 'I still get so furious. I wouldn't trust myself around her, to be honest.'

'She is your wife, however,' Samuel said. 'You are responsible for her, and yet you've left her to fend for herself these last couple of years.'

Alex hung his head in shame. He knew he'd abandoned his responsibility, and during his time away he hadn't given her a second thought. He'd barely made enough money to feed the children, let alone send anything home to a woman he resented with the fury of an injured bull.

'We gave her some credit,' Samuel said.

'And charity,' Doris added.

Alex ran his hand through his hair and looked around the room—anywhere but squarely in his in-laws' eyes.

'I don't know what to do. I've tried not to think about her for months.'

'If you were in the home, surely she wouldn't treat them badly.'

Alex felt nauseous at Samuel's suggestion, but instead of gagging as he felt like doing, he made an excuse. 'There wasn't any work for me around here before I left. I don't suppose that has changed.'

Samuel nodded in confirmation.

'Has your business picked up?' Alex asked, glad to push the conversation onto a different track.

'If we didn't have freehold on the business and house, it's doubtful we would survive.'

'It's not that people don't need groceries,' Doris said. 'It's just that no one has the money to buy anything but the absolute necessities.'

'So it hasn't changed. The store can't support me and the children as well as you and Frank.'

Samuel shook his head, looking grim.

'Then I can't stay. I have a job in Victoria, but I've come back to sort things out with Norma.'

'So you'll take her with you?'

Alex ground his teeth.

'You can't leave her to fend for herself,' Doris said. 'As much as I dislike the woman, it's such a dishonourable thing to do.'

'I mean to give her the opportunity to divorce me.' Alex felt the tension rise as he said the words out loud. He knew what divorce meant to a family's reputation. It wasn't hard to read Doris's disapproval.

'I can't live with her again. I didn't love her in the beginning, and now my feelings are not just indifferent, they are plain aggressive.'

Alex saw the hardness in Samuel's face and was frustrated by it.

'What other option do you suggest?' he asked.

Samuel took a deep breath. 'I wish you hadn't married her in the first place,' he said.

'So do I,' Alex said. 'I wish you had said something to me back then. Made me see sense.'

'She didn't strike me as an abusive woman,' Doris said. 'While I didn't really warm to the idea of anyone taking the place of my Nancy, I thought she would at least take care of the children. You know I couldn't do it.'

'I'm not blaming you,' Alex said. 'But Norma deceived us all. She pretended to care for the children, and then once she had taken charge of my house, she allowed her true character to come out.'

'And you're sure there is no hope of redemption for her? She may have reformed…'

Alex gave Samuel a look of disbelief.

'…Well, she might have thought about it while you were away, and changed her ways.'

'Do you really believe that?' Alex asked.

Samuel shrugged his shoulders. 'I don't like the idea of divorce in my family, Alex. I have to be honest.'

'It's not something I ever thought I'd be involved with either,'

Alex answered. 'I know what it means for your reputation—for my reputation. But I can't think of another answer.'

'Couldn't you just live separately?' Doris asked.

'And remain married and responsible for her?' Alex asked.

Doris nodded.

'I can hardly afford to feed the children, without having to support an estranged wife. And then there's ...' He broke off.

'There's what?' Samuel asked.

'If Norma had been what she pretended to be in the beginning, I'd never think of divorcing her. The children need a mother figure. I'm not blind to that. Even though I don't love her, I would live with her for the sake of the children.' He paused and saw the hopeful looks on their faces. 'But it's for the children's sake that I want to be fully divorced from her. She is an abusive woman, and I hope they will have a stepmother who truly loves them.'

'You are thinking of marrying yet again?' Doris sounded scandalised.

Alex didn't say anything.

'Have you met someone in Victoria?' Samuel asked.

For a moment Alex wondered if he could avoid this question, but knew he couldn't.

'I did. A woman of very good standing, in a strong and stable family. They are my employers.'

Doris tsked her disapproval and Samuel looked disappointed.

'I'm not taking Norma back,' Alex said. 'Divorce or not, I don't want her in my life.'

Alex felt as if he was involved in a Mexican standoff for a while. No one spoke for some minutes, but the tension was so thick you could have cut it with a knife.

'Well, you can't just obtain a divorce without grounds,' Samuel said after a long pause. 'There is no evidence of unfaithfulness that I'm aware of.'

'Not on her side,' Alex said. He let the words slide out without thinking, and then saw that Doris's shock had registered another few notches on the scale.

'Oh Alexander,' she said sadly, shaking her head. 'Not in front of the children?'

'Of course not' he blazed. 'It was a one-off occurrence. We were trapped together in a flood for several days. I didn't plan it, and if you're thinking she is a tramp, you couldn't be further from the truth. She and her family are upstanding Christian citizens. It was just something that happened.'

'But you knew you were married, and that nothing could come of it,' Samuel said.

'I also thought I'd die that night. We took comfort in each other's arms, certain that we wouldn't see the morning.'

'Alexander. That doesn't make it right.'

'I know that, Doris. I'm not stupid. But it is done, and now I mean to try to right the situation.'

'By divorcing your wife?'

'I don't see Norma as my wife. She has never been a wife to me, and she has been a nightmare for the children.'

Samuel issued another heavy sigh. 'All right, Alex. I don't think there is anything to be gained by canvassing the subject further today. You're going to have to work this one through on your own.'

'Do you mean to tell me we are not welcome to stay here?'

'Of course you're welcome,' Doris said. 'Whatever trouble you've gotten yourself into, I still love you, and of course the children.'

Alex gave a nod. This discussion hadn't gone well. He didn't anticipate that any other discussions on the subject would go any better. He was in an impossible situation.

Chapter Ten

Alex had left the children involved in a hive of activity. Doris had promised the girls she would teach them how to bake. They hadn't had any domestic input since being on the road with him, and though Doris was almost immobile, she could certainly give instruction from her wheelchair. Samuel had taken Jimmy with him to the general store. Both grandparents were alive with enthusiasm at having the children there. Alex wasn't sure if they were happy to have the children to help, or if they were thrilled to be able to include the children in their lives again. Probably both, he decided.

As Alex walked towards the property that used to belong to his parents, he felt anything but enthusiasm. This house with its small acreage was his childhood home. It should have held many fond memories from the years before the war, when he, Frank, and Ray used to kick around on the property, building tree houses, tadpoling in the creek, or running a billycart down the hill on their road out front.

But Ray was killed in action, Frank was reduced to a childlike state from his war trauma, Nancy was gone, and Norma was in the house. The fond memories struggled to come to the forefront. Norma always seemed to find her way to front and centre. Alex knew he couldn't break free and move on until he had confronted her and made some arrangement.

As he approached, he was pleased to see the garden looked to be well tended. The vegetable patch looked fruitful, and the grass under the fruit trees had been kept down. He saw she had kept the two milking cows, and the chook shed still had healthy-looking chickens scratching about in the ground.

She knows how to make the most of a property. He begrudgingly acknowledged that she was a capable and responsible worker.

But not a mother. He shook his head. He hated going over and over the abuses she had inflicted on Jimmy. He just wanted to forget and move on.

He opened the gate that let him into the side garden. This was his property, and he had abandoned it along with her. The place looked as if it could use a little attention. The gutters were looking a little worse for wear, and the paintwork was tired. Alex dismissed any ideas of painting. There was no money for that kind of extravagance, not with the Depression and work hard to find. As he climbed the two front veranda steps, his heart hammered. He didn't want to face her. He would prefer to let her have the whole property and just disappear forever, but he knew he couldn't.

'So, you've come back home.' The woman at the door looked like a stranger. Her face was hard and she appeared to have lost weight. 'Well, what have you got to say for yourself?' Norma asked.

'Can I come in for a while?'

'It's your house. I'd expect you to come back and stay permanently.'

Alex didn't bother to argue on the doorstep. He needed to gather his thoughts. Norma stood aside while he walked inside. She was right—it was his house, his furniture, and his heritage, but he didn't want it to be. Not while she was there.

'Well, are you going to explain yourself, or not?' Norma asked once they'd reached the kitchen.

'Can we have tea?' Alex was stalling.

'Of course, what sort of wife would I be if I didn't meet your majesty's demands?'

'Stop it, Norma.'

'Stop what, Alex? You want tea; I'll make you tea.'

'You know why I left.'

'Do I? Do I know why you left me without means or support?'

'You have the house, the animals, the garden. It's not like you're on the street, starving.'

'But I don't have my husband and children here, do I? Do you know how difficult that is to explain to people?'

'So you didn't tell them the truth then? How you physically and emotionally abused my children?'

'Don't be so dramatic, Alex. You know Jimmy is a difficult child. You couldn't expect I would put up with his attitude.'

'You didn't feed him, clothe him, or allow him in the house. *My* house.'

'Who told you that?'

'Irene told me exactly how you used to treat him.'

'Irene! She's always been a liar. I wouldn't believe anything she told you.'

Alex sprung up from the table, the fury right back at the surface again. He knew he couldn't say the words he wanted to say, and there was nothing else. His hands clenched into tight fists. He wanted to punch something.

'Get off your high horse.' Norma continued speaking as though he hadn't moved. 'If you want me to look after your children, then you have to allow me to discipline them when they need it.'

'I don't want you anywhere near my children,' he said through clenched teeth.

'Well, I want you back here where you're supposed to be.'

Alex glared at her. 'What for, Norma? You can't think …'

'You are my husband. I want to have children of my own. I need a man around the place.'

'You think I'd have children with you?'

'Why not? You're my husband.'

'After the way you've treated my children?'

'As I said before—'

'No! No way. I wouldn't trust you with children.'

Norma's face set in a mask of granite.

'I want a divorce,' Alex said.

Norma laughed. 'You don't have any evidence of unfaithfulness,' she said.

'What does that mean?' Alex asked. 'Are you saying there is evidence if I searched for it?'

Norma didn't answer.

'Well, I want to officially end our marriage.'

'You don't have any grounds.'

'No, but you do.'

Norma looked at him. Alex looked for a sign of hurt but didn't see any. Only hardness.

'I had an affair,' he said, just to make sure she understood.

Something crossed Norma's face, but it wasn't hurt. It was panic. She didn't say anything for a moment.

'Do you understand what I'm telling you?'

'You have a fancy woman somewhere, do you?'

Alex didn't rise to the bait. He didn't try to defend his position.

'Well, it's lucky I'm a forgiving woman. I'll take you back, even though you've shown no responsibility to your marriage vows.'

'I don't want you to take me back. I want you to divorce me.'

'Alex Moreland, I could have divorced you a year ago if I'd wanted.'

'On what grounds?'

'Desertion and neglect.'

'Then why didn't you?'

'Let's face it Alex, you need me.'

Alex gave a harsh laugh. 'What, to see if you can terrorise my children some more?'

She sneered at him. 'When the Johnsons are gone, who is going to help you run that general store?'

Alex paused to process what she was saying. 'What do you mean?'

'That general store won't run on its own, and I have grand visions for the place when we inherit it.'

'We won't be inheriting anything.'

'I know you're the executor of their will,' Norma said. 'I know you have power of attorney over Frank. You'll have full control of the store when they die.'

Alex was incredulous. Since the time that Samuel had shown him his will, and asked his permission to act as executor and trustee to the estate, he'd barely thought about it. But that had been before Nancy had died.

'How did you know about that?' he asked.

'You have the paperwork in your office.'

'You've gone through my paperwork in my office?'

'*Our* paperwork, Alex; *our* office.'

'You had no right.'

'You might have been dead on the road, for all I knew. Of course I went through your papers.'

Alex was silenced. Cutting off all communication from her had its price. She was correct. She would have needed to know how things stood legally if he was gone. He thought briefly of the night he thought he would die in the flood, and that thought was followed quickly by the idea of Grace Shore. Another stab in his gut.

'Well, I don't actually stand to inherit any of the Johnson's property.' Alex deliberately forced his thoughts away from Grace.

'The children inherit, I know that, but we are their parents. We will control it.'

'You are not their parent, Norma, and you won't be controlling anything.'

'You will be though. Let's face it, Alex, you don't have a head for business.'

'Stop, Norma. This is not going to happen. That business belongs to Frank.'

'Pfft!' Norma laughed. 'Frank is a child. He doesn't know what day it is. I know you have power of attorney over his affairs.'

'So this is why you don't want a divorce?'

'Well, you don't suppose it was because of the deep love we share, do you?'

Alex glared at her.

'Don't look so hurt,' she said. 'It's not like you ever loved me. I'm not that stupid.'

'Why won't you let me go?' he asked.

'Because you're worth too much. I'd be stupid to let all that go.'

Alex sighed in defeat. He eventually got up from the kitchen chair and turned to leave.

'I'd prefer it if you shifted the family back into the home. I don't like what the neighbours say about us,' Norma said.

Alex shook his head. He didn't like what the neighbours said about them either, but they didn't know the half of it.

'I'll expect you for dinner then?' Norma asked.

'No. Not today, not ever. I'm not coming back, Norma. I wish you'd understand that. Take my unfaithfulness and use it. Divorce me. The law will see you are provided for.'

'I think I'll hold out for the lot, Alex. Who knows, in time you might be desperate enough even to want me.'

Alex left, allowing the front screen door to slam behind him. The situation was like a millstone around his neck.

Once the children had gone to bed, Alex asked to speak privately with Samuel.

'How did your meeting with Norma go?' Samuel asked.

'Not good.'

'You didn't expect that she would be happy being a deserted wife, did you?'

Alex shook his head.

'Did you suggest divorce?'

'She's not interested.'

'Still in love with you, then?'

Alex gave a dry laugh. 'She was never in love with me. But she has an eye for opportunity.'

'Well, every young woman looks for a husband and security.'

'Actually, she has her eye set squarely on your business,' Alex said.

'My business?' Samuel sounded surprised.

'Johnson and Sons, yes.'

'She isn't in any position to ever get anything from us, other than the charity we've already given her.'

'She figures she'll control it once the children inherit.'

Samuel scoffed. 'Over my dead body.'

'Well that is what she plans, yes.'

'That business was supposed to go to Ray and Frank.'

'I know,' Alex said.

'I had a sum to settle on Nancy too, of course, but it was Johnson and Sons.'

'I know.'

'She has no right to think she'll take control of it.'

'I did try to tell her that, but she figures that as my wife, she will simply take the reins of running the business once I'm in control.'

'Is that what you plan?' Samuel asked.

'I hadn't even thought about it.' Alex sighed. 'You're fit and healthy, and I wouldn't have expected to think about it for another twenty years.'

'I'm slowing down a bit, Alex,' Samuel said. 'I might not die for another twenty years, but I'd really love to have one of my sons here right now.'

Alex could have mentioned Frank, but they both knew he was little use in running the business.

'I was hoping Jimmy might step into it in a few years.'

Alex had been running away so much, he hadn't considered his son's future; that he would one day be part-owner of a business. He dropped his head in shame.

A few moments silence descended. Alex couldn't seem to find an answer, but was aware that Samuel was thinking hard.

'Would you be offended if I changed my will?' Samuel asked.

Alex lifted his head and searched his father-in-law's face.

'I don't want to cut you out, Alex, but my property was meant for my children—Frank, and now Nancy's children. I don't want Norma getting ideas that it will be hers, and from what you've told us, I can imagine her using questionable means to control the girls.'

Alex nodded.

'If I asked Frank's cousin to act as executor and trustee instead of you, would you be offended?'

'No. Not at all. You trust him to take care of the property until the children come of age?'

'I do. He is honest and his own situation is quite stable.'

'I do feel bad about Frank,' Alex said. 'He'll need someone to look after him.'

'As I said, that might be another twenty years from now. By that time Jimmy and Irene, perhaps even Jean, will hopefully be around.'

'Do what you need to do,' Alex said. 'Once it's changed, I'll let Norma know that she can let go of that part of her ambition and see if she's still desperate to hold on to me.'

'I'm sorry, Alex. This is so ugly.'

Ugly was an understatement from Alex's point of view. If he'd only been in a better state of mind back when Norma was playing up to him, he wouldn't have asked her to marry him. But his grief had made him numb and careless.

Chapter Eleven

Grace knew that she couldn't hide it any longer. She had been praying for three months, ever since she realised that she was with child. She had hoped God would forgive her lapse with Alex and that she would simply lose the child she was carrying, but it seemed God was determined to make her sin known to the world. She wasn't going to miscarry, and the child was already moving around inside her.

On one hand she loved the child with her whole heart, and she loved the child's father. But on the other, she knew this child was conceived out of wedlock, even if she should suddenly marry. Marriage, however, was out of the question. Alex was not free to marry her; to give their child his name and protection. It was time to get help. She would have to go somewhere to hide the truth from the folks of Green Valley. She wished she had the means to get away without telling any of them, but did not. In the end, she decided that Meg was the best person to act as confidant.

Grace waited until everyone else had gone out for the day before she spoke to her sister-in-law.

'What's the matter?' Meg asked.

'I'm in trouble,' Grace said, failing to hide the tears brimming in her eyes.

'What kind of trouble?' Grace could hear that Meg was concerned. She wished she didn't have to spell it out, that Meg would just know. It was difficult to speak the truth out loud.

'What kind of trouble, Grace?'

Grace lifted tear-filled eyes to her sister-in-law, and willed Meg to guess the truth.

'Grace, you're frightening me,' Meg said. 'Tell me.'

'I can't,' Grace said, as months of pent-up tension and emotion bubbled over in a wave of tears.

Grace felt Meg put her arms around her shoulders, and heard her soothing tones. 'Shhh, Grace. Whatever it is, it can't be that bad.'

'It is worse than bad,' Grace said in a wobbly voice.

'What have you done?' Meg asked.

Grace waited another few moments, then just blurted it out. 'I'm pregnant.'

Meg pulled back and Grace saw the picture of shock that was painted all over her face.

'How could you be pregnant?' Meg asked after a silence that seemed to last an age. 'You've never been with a man …'

'Alex,' Grace whispered. 'When we were trapped during the flood.'

'Oh my goodness.'

Grace waited. She needed Meg to share her burden, to help her make a decision, to find a way to make this right. She hoped Meg was the right person to speak to.

'Did he force himself on you?' Meg asked. 'Is that why he left so quickly after the flood?'

'He left because of me, but he didn't force me. I was as much to blame.'

'But you and he … you had hardly spoken a civil word to each other in all that time. How could you have …?'

'I thought we were going to die. I was afraid; he comforted me. It just snowballed from there.'

'Oh dear. That was months ago, Grace.'

'Four months,' Grace said. 'I'm beginning to show. I have to do something, but I don't know what to do.'

'Have you told anyone else?

Grace shook her head.

'I'll have to talk to Charlie,' Meg said. 'Whatever we decide, he will have to help us.'

'Do you have to?' Grace teared up again. 'I can't bear the thought of everyone knowing.'

'I think we must at least talk to Charlie, if not your parents.'

'No,' Grace said. 'No, I don't want them to know.'

'Grace, they love you. They're not going to throw you out of the family because of one mistake.'

'This is not just a mistake. This is …' Her voice trailed off.

'What?' Meg said. 'What is this?'

'I don't know.' Grace broke down again. 'It's huge. It could destroy all of us.'

'A baby? Destroy a family? I don't think so, Grace. Don't you remember Charlie's misbegotten youth with Janielle and Aimee?'

'Yes, but—'

'Yes, but nothing. He made a proper mess of that, and yet look at Aimee today. You love her, don't you? She's a beautiful young woman, and she is part of our family, despite the mess Charlie made of the whole situation.'

'But this is such a disgrace. Mum and Dad will be so ashamed in front of all their friends and neighbours.'

'Perhaps,' Meg said. 'But I don't think that's the key issue here. What is more important is you, your health, and the health of your little one.'

Grace cried again. As Meg spoke her child moved within her, as if to remind her that he was listening, and part of what was going on.

'We'll talk to Charlie,' Meg said. 'I'll talk to him first, so that if he's going to be all upset about it, he can blow off his steam before he speaks to you.'

Grace nodded, miserable. She knew there was no other choice. She had to do something.

***

'What do you mean, you knew?' Meg asked her husband. She had struggled for hours about how she was going to tell him about Grace, and now he calmly said that he knew.

'Alex told me what happened.'

'I hope you told him he should do the honourable thing and marry our Grace.'

'Of course! But Grace knows he can't—not at the moment, anyway.'

'Why?'

'Because he's married.'

'Charlie, why on earth didn't you tell me all this?'

'Because, up until this point, there wasn't any need for anyone to know.'

'There's a need now, isn't there? And it's just a little bit desperate. Grace is beginning to show. She doesn't want anyone to know about what happened.'

Charlie pursed his lips.

'We need to find a place she can go to have the baby quietly, and then come back later,' Meg said.

Charlie shook his head.

'Why are you shaking your head?' Meg asked.

'Alex needs to know.'

'Alex doesn't have any say at this point. He's a married man who took advantage of our Grace, and got her into trouble. I don't think he deserves any consideration.'

'That's not what happened, Meg,' Charlie said. 'Did Grace say he forced her?'

Meg shook her head. 'No, she said it was as much her fault as his.'

'Alex is a good father. He'll want to know about his child.'

Meg wasn't convinced, but Charlie seemed adamant.

'What could he do about it in any case, if he's already married?'

'He was planning on getting a divorce.'

'Charlie, two wrongs don't make a right!'

'Look, Meg, the situation was complicated from the start. There are a whole lot of things you don't know about his family, about him. I'm not saying I like the idea of Grace marrying a divorcee, but it is a whole lot better than having an illegitimate child.'

'Grace feels it would be best to give the child up for adoption.'

'Don't you think we should at least give Alex the option to take responsibility? I talked to him, Meg. He cares about Grace, and he would definitely care about the baby.'

'He doesn't have any right to care about Grace.'

'You saw how he was when he first got here,' Charlie argued. 'He was aggressive, dismissive, aloof—downright unpleasant to her. All because he was married, and he knew he had no business thinking of another woman.'

'Then why did he sleep with her?'

'Shut together in a small place for days, afraid they would drown? Things happened, Meg. Give the bloke the benefit of the doubt.'

Meg shook her head. 'I think it is wrong.'

'Of course it's wrong, but it's done now, isn't it? If there was even a small chance that Alex was able to marry Grace, and she could keep the baby, wouldn't that be the better option than tearing the child away from her? You don't want the poor little thing being put in an orphanage or worse.'

'It would probably be adopted out.'

'But it is Grace's baby. He belongs to us, to our family.'

'But do our family want to admit they have an illegitimate child?'

Charlie shook his head. 'We need to talk to Alex. Get Grace to pack up for a trip. We'll go to Adelaide and see him in person. If that fails, we'll find a place there for her to stay for the duration of her confinement.'

***

'What has Charlie told Mum and Dad?' Grace asked Meg.

'That we've decided to take a trip to Adelaide, I think.'

'What excuse did he give?' Grace asked. 'We're in the middle of an economic depression. People don't just up and go on an interstate holiday.'

'They guessed you were attached to Alex, and wanted to go and see him.'

Grace groaned. 'How could Charlie let them think that? Alex is married. I'm not chasing him.'

'For a start, Mum and Dad don't know Alex is married. They think he's a widower. And secondly, if our meeting with Alex comes to nothing, then they'll believe that you were heartbroken and just needed to get away for a while. We'll find a baby home in Adelaide where you can stay until after.'

Grace dropped her head into her hands. 'That is such a lie,' she said. 'I hate lying.'

'It won't be a lie, Grace,' Meg said. 'You will be heartbroken, believe me.'

'Not because of Alex.'

'You can make all the protestations you like, but if he'd been free you would have taken him in a heartbeat. Don't deny it.'

Grace put her head in her hands again. She wasn't going to deny it. But marrying Alex was an impossible thought, one she hadn't even allowed herself to think. If she believed that pining after Johnny Laslett was hopeless, this was a hundred times worse. She would be heartbroken. She had to give her baby away, and already she was dreading the day.

'Come on, Gracie.' Charlie used her childhood nickname. 'We need to take one step at a time, and not be borrowing trouble.'

Grace could not arouse any positivity in her outlook at all. Even if she came face-to-face with Alex, and even if he was now divorced, she still couldn't marry him. She hadn't told Meg or Charlie yet, but she was sure it was impossible.

'Mum and Dad think we will be gone just for ten days or so. CJ is coming down from Bendigo to help out while we're away.'

Grace nodded. 'Who's taking us to the station?'

'We will take the children over to Wallace Hill to stay while we're away, and we'll go with Dad in his motorcar to Brinsford to catch the train.'

'I don't think I can face Mum and Dad. They'll know.'

'They won't know, Grace. There is nothing to suggest anything is out of the ordinary,' Meg said.

'Except us taking an unnecessary trip to Adelaide.'

'Your mother is happy you've taken an interest in a man,' Meg said.

'But that's another lie! I haven't taken an interest in a man.'

Charlie raised his eyebrows and looked at her stomach. Grace saw the look and blushed.

'Charlie, don't be coarse,' Meg scolded.

'I'm just saying, Gracie, you're not thinking about Johnny any more, are you?'

She shook her head, her eyes cast down.

'And you do think about Alex sometimes, don't you?'

'How can I help it, when his child is bumping around inside me?'

'All right,' Meg soothed. 'Let's just get the dray packed, and get those children over to their grandparents.'

Grace went about getting things ready. She was about to lift her packed suitcase when her brother came across and took it from her hands.

'Not in your condition, Grace,' he said.

'You see!' Grace turned to Meg. 'If he keeps that sort of molly-coddling up, everyone will know.'

'You and the baby are more important,' Charlie said, ignoring her protests. 'Just don't be picking up heavy things, and then I won't be taking them from you.'

***

The overnight train trip across the Wimmera and up through the Murray Mallee was long and arduous. By the time the train pulled into the Adelaide Railway Station, Grace was exhausted. She didn't even try to help Charlie and Meg with luggage, but instead allowed herself to be ushered into the ladies waiting room, where she was able to freshen herself up.

'You and I will go to the cafeteria and have morning tea while Charlie makes some enquiries,' Meg said.

Grace didn't argue. She knew Charlie had a plan, and while she was concerned she was doing the wrong thing, she didn't have the mental or emotional strength to fight him.

Meg ordered tea for the both of them, and they sat down to drink the fortifying brew.

'Ah, that's much better,' Meg said, as she replaced her plain china cup on its saucer. 'Nothing like a good cup of tea to help get one back on track for the day.'

Grace knew Meg was trying to be positive, but she couldn't even bring herself to smile.

'There's Charlie coming now. It looks like he's found the information we need.'

Grace watched her brother approach and saw that he was indeed looking satisfied with himself.

'I have Alex's address. We need to take another train out to Mitcham in about an hour,' he said.

'What else did you find out?' Meg asked.

'I found out about a home here, near the beachside.' He paused and searched Grace's face. She didn't respond. 'I'm hoping it won't be necessary, Grace. I'm hoping Alex will be able to find his way clear to help you.'

'He can't help me.' Grace managed to rouse enough energy to contradict him.

'You need to be more positive, Gracie. Alex is a good man, and I believe he will do what he can.'

'There's nothing he can do to get me out of this disaster.'

'Grace,' Meg placed her hand on Grace's arm. 'There is a possibility of marriage. You know that.'

Grace shook her head.

'Why are you being so difficult?' Charlie asked.

'I can't make this right by committing another wrong,' Grace said.

'If he is divorced, then he will be free to marry,' Charlie said.

'Free according to the laws of the land, but not in the eyes of God.'

'What are you talking about?' Charlie asked.

'The Scripture,' Grace said, a sudden burst of energy finding its way forward. 'You ask Meg what the Scripture says about marrying someone whose wife is still alive.'

Grace looked to Meg for her to speak. Charlie looked to her too.

'I know what Scripture you mean,' Meg said.

'It was Jesus who said it,' Grace said.

'Yes, but—'

'But what? If I find Alex has divorced his second wife, that he's wanting to marry me and take responsibility for this child, then I'll be effectively causing him to commit adultery.'

'He's already committed adultery, Grace,' Charlie said.

Grace dropped her face into her hands. 'I know, and it's my fault. I won't do it again. I can't. It's wrong.'

Charlie and Meg went quiet. Meg poured another cup of tea from the teapot for Charlie, and he drank in silence. Grace knew her brother well enough to know that he was digging-in to get his own way. She braced herself to resist him.

'We are going to see Alex,' Charlie said when he finished his tea. 'He needs to know about the baby, and it's only fair to talk to him about what's to be done.'

Grace wanted to argue, and she saw Meg look between them, anxious, as if she wanted to say something more, but she held her peace. Nothing more was said until the next train to Mitcham was announced to be ready for boarding. Grace followed along quietly, but she was in turmoil on the inside.

***

It hadn't been a long walk from the Mitcham Railway Station to the Torrens Arms Hotel. Charlie asked for two rooms and signed the register. Grace took the opportunity to lie down on the bed in her room the minute Meg left her alone. She needed to sleep, having hardly had any sleep at all on the journey across the state border, but her mind wouldn't stop buzzing.

Part of her longed to see Alex again; longed for him to take her in his arms and tell her it would be all right. Her conscience, however, would not let her alone. She felt shame, anger and grief over what she had done. If there had been no child, she would have hidden these feelings and continued with her life as if she had never met Alex Moreland and his children. It was *his* child, however, that would not allow her to forget him.

111

She wanted to pray, but every time she began to form a thought from her heart, she was met with another wave of guilt. God would not be interested in hearing from her. She was on her own. As far as she understood, God didn't have anything to do with fixing up people's sins.

She managed a few minutes of foggy sleep before Meg knocked on her door again.

'Grace.' Her voice came through the wood. 'Can I come in?'

Grace was tempted to roll over and pretend she hadn't heard, but she knew her sister-in-law and brother were doing the best they could to help her through this mess.

'Come in.'

The door opened and Meg entered. 'Are you ready?' she asked.

Grace pulled herself up from the bed. She wasn't ready—not physically, mentally or emotionally. There was little hope of her ever being ready. She still couldn't accept that meeting Alex was the best course of action.

'Come along,' Meg said as she picked up Grace's hat from the chair. 'Let's get you straightened up and presentable.'

'I don't want to be presentable, Meg. I'm not trying to lure him away from his wife. I wish you'd stop trying to make me do it.'

'If Alex Moreland has reconciled with Norma, then we will retreat quickly and quietly without saying anything, Grace.'

'Promise?'

'I promise.'

'What about Charlie? I'm afraid he'll just blab out that I'm pregnant, and not think of Alex's marriage.'

'Charlie is very mindful of how difficult this is,' Meg said. 'He's not trying to be insensitive, or to act thoughtlessly. It's a very complex situation.'

'Complex? Try impossible. I can't see there is any way other than going to the baby home and adopting the child out.'

'Is that what you really want?'

Grace didn't answer. To say she wished she'd never become pregnant was only half true. The connection she felt with the child was already too deep. She had not known what her sister and sister-in-law had, having borne children. She had kidded herself that being the maiden aunt was equally satisfying. Now she knew bearing a child was something different, something far more satisfying. Only she couldn't keep her baby, not without his father. She didn't want to give the baby up at all, but there was no choice. Charlie's scheme to get Alex to take responsibility was grasping at straws.

Meg fussed around Grace as if she were her mother, helping to straighten her hair and fix her hat. 'Let's just hope for the best,' she said. 'God will make a way.'

Grace hated to contradict her, but she was quite sure God had abandoned the project right back at the point of conception.

***

It was a good mile and a half from the hotel to the address that Charlie had as Alex's place of residence. He'd looked it up from the telephone book. The three of them had walked, and now stood at the bottom of the road. Grace was dismayed to see they had a steep road to climb before coming to the house about two hundred yards further along.

'How are you travelling?' Charlie asked.

'I'd prefer to sit here and wait for you,' Grace replied.

Charlie didn't reply, and Grace saw him raise his eyebrows at Meg. She knew what he was thinking. *Grace is being difficult. Help me out.*

As if on cue, Meg stepped in. 'Come on,' she said, taking Grace's arm. 'We'll scale this mountain together.'

One foot in front of another brought them closer and closer. As they approached the house, Grace saw a well-kept garden and small orchard. She refused to indulge any ideas about this property, chasing away the stab of hope. Hope was useless. Once they'd opened the garden gate and walked up the path, Grace felt as if she would be sick. She wanted more than anything else to run away from this meeting; yet she yearned for it at the same time.

A tall spindly woman answered Charlie's knock on the door.

'Yes?' Her tone was aloof and unfriendly, but then they were a group of strangers on her front porch.

'I wonder if Mr Moreland is in?' Charlie asked.

'Not home at the moment.'

'We've just dropped by to say hello,' Charlie continued. 'He worked for me for a few months, recently.'

'Oh.'

Grace watched the woman closely.

'Thank you so much for looking after him and the children. It has been so difficult getting work. I despaired that he'd never find anything. That's why he had to go all that way.'

Charlie nodded.

'You don't know how relieved I am that he's come back. It was a hard time, having my man away from me.'

Grace felt dizzy. *I'm going to faint.* Thankfully Meg had her by the arm and supported her. Mentally Grace thanked her for seeing and understanding.

'Are the children at home?' Charlie pushed on.

'No, they're at school. Listen, I'd love to have you in for a cup of tea, but I was just about to go and fetch the children myself. But I'll tell Alex you dropped by. He'll be sorry to have missed you.'

Charlie tipped his hat. 'We're staying at the Torrens Arms for the night if he wishes to call in.'

The woman nodded, stepped back and closed the door on them.

The walk back down the hill passed in a haze of clouded thought. Grace felt as if that was the final decision. As much as she had protested about seeing Alex, she now knew without a doubt. There was a wife, a home, a family. It was hopeless. She wanted to cry for her baby. She didn't want to give him up, but there was no other way.

Chapter Twelve

The three travellers took a tram car back into the city, and caught another to the beachside suburb of Brighton. Grace was in a daze. They were doing what had to be done, but she realised she must have been holding on to a thin thread of hope, because she felt bereft now it was gone. She hardly noticed what Charlie and Meg did. They hadn't pressed her with conversation. After all, they had all agreed that if the Alex solution was closed, they would help her go to a baby home.

Once they arrived at the baby home, Charlie did all the talking. Grace couldn't rouse herself from her state of depressed spirits. She was aware that Meg never left her side, and continued to hold her hand while paperwork was filled in.

'Do you wish to name the father?' the matron of the home asked.

Grace heard the question and suddenly snapped to attention. She cast worried eyes toward Charlie.

'Is it necessary?' Charlie asked.

'These details will not be available to the child after adoption. It is only for records. I take it the father doesn't know about the pregnancy.'

'We can add it later if we need to,' Charlie said. 'Leave it blank for now.'

The whole process seemed to be even more intrusion into a situation that Grace wished she could keep secret. Meg stayed with her while she was submitted to a medical examination. Grace felt warm tears flow down her face as the midwife spoke about probable delivery date and other factors regarding her child.

'We believe it is best if you do not see the baby when it is born,' she said. 'We will take it away immediately.'

'Where will you take him?' Grace asked.

'You don't need to worry,' the midwife said. 'The baby will be placed in a good home.'

'Straight away, or will they take him to an orphanage?'

'Miss Shore, you need to let the baby go and not worry about what happens afterwards. You will need a week or so to recover, and then you can go back home and forget this ever happened.'

Grace didn't say anything else. *As if I could ever forget this has happened.*

***

Meg was upset leaving Grace behind at the home. They had clung to each other, Grace crying, Meg crying. It felt so wrong to leave her there, and yet she knew there was no other option, unless they were prepared to take Grace home—pregnancy and all—and have the whole valley know that she had an illegitimate child.

'Why should it matter so much?' Meg asked her husband. 'It's not the baby's fault. Why should we abandon it like that?'

Charlie didn't answer straight away.

'Aimee was illegitimate, and we took her in without a second thought.'

'I know,' Charlie said. 'I wish I could tell Mum and Dad and ask them to support her.'

'Why can't you?'

'Grace won't let me. It's her secret, Meg. She has to make the decision.'

'But she doesn't want to give the baby away.'

Charlie was quiet again for a few minutes, before he spoke again.

'She was lying, you know?'

'Who, Grace?'

'No, that woman. Norma. Alex hasn't come back to her. I'd stake my life on it.'

'But she said she was glad to have him and the children back.'

'If that's true, it would mean Alex is a liar. He told me he would never take his children back to her. He told me she had abused them.'

'Do you think Alex lied to us?'

'No.'

'But what if he did?'

'Then I'll knock his block off for what he's put Grace through.'

'It's a good job that we are going back home then, if you're going to get violent.'

'I'm going back to see him.' Charlie sounded firm.

'We've just bought tickets home.'

'We can use them tomorrow. Today we are going to go back to Mitcham, and this time I'm not going to leave until I've had a man–to-man chat with Mr Alex Moreland.'

Meg knew when her husband had his mind made up. She wasn't going to tell Charlie, but she was pleased. The situation was unresolved on Alex's side. He needed to explain himself, and if necessary, Charlie could knock his block off. Perhaps he deserved it.

***

'Do you remember the name of the general store?' Charlie asked Meg as they walked through the main street of Mitcham.

'Which general store?'

'The one owned by Alex's father-in-law.'

'I don't know as I ever heard about it,' Meg answered. 'You were the one he talked to about his private life, not me.'

'I don't think he said, but that store over there is just as likely to be the one as any other.'

'If it's not, then perhaps they will know where he is.'

Charlie nodded. They crossed the street and walked in the front doors of Johnson and Sons general store. The moment they were inside they knew they had the right place.

'Mr Shore!' It was Jimmy. He was smiling as he came up to them.

'How are you, Jimmy?' Charlie said as he shook the boy's hand.

'I'm working as storeman after school, helping my grandfather.'

'I'm sure he is pleased to have you.'

At that moment an older man came up to them.

'Samuel Johnson.' He introduced himself. 'I see our Jimmy knows you.'

'Mr and Mrs Shore were Dad's employers in Victoria,' Jimmy said, sounding pleased to introduce them. 'They were very kind to us when we were there.'

'How do you do.' Samuel held out his hand. 'Pleased to meet you.'

'Likewise,' Charlie replied. 'My wife, Meg.'

Meg nodded her head and smiled.

'Have you come to visit someone?' Jimmy asked.

'Yes. Your dad, if he's around.'

'He's got some work fruit picking up in the hills,' Samuel said. 'He doesn't usually get back until the late train in the evenings. Work's been hard to find.'

Charlie nodded. 'It's been tough all over the place.'

'Can I invite you folks to tea?' Samuel asked. 'I think Alex would be pleased to see you, and the girls too, of course.'

'They're living with you?' Charlie asked.

'We can't live in our old house,' Jimmy volunteered.

'That'll do, Jimmy.' Samuel interrupted him. 'Off you go, back to the storeroom. I'm sure Mr and Mrs Shore will join us for tea. You can talk to them more then.'

Jimmy withdrew, respectfully.

'Alex told us about his unfortunate family situation,' Charlie said. 'We had already been to his house and the woman ...'

'Norma.'

'Norma told us they were all living there happily reunited.'

Samuel gave a derisive sniff. 'She's a piece of work, that woman. I beg your pardon, Mrs Shore.' He seemed to remember himself just in time.

'I suspected she might not have been telling us the truth.'

'I'm beginning to think she couldn't lie straight in bed. Alex has made a proper mess marrying her.'

You don't know the half of it. Meg didn't speak these thoughts out loud. There would be more time later to investigate the particulars of the case.

'We would be grateful for the opportunity to catch up with Alex,' Charlie said. 'What time would you like us to come?'

'If you come by around six o'clock, you can catch up with the children, if you like,' Samuel said. 'Alex doesn't get home until nearly half-past seven, and the children are heading off to bed shortly after.'

'That would be lovely. Thank you so much for the invitation.' Meg gave her warmest smile, though she felt like a fraud. They were going to come into this home with earth-shattering news. Alex and the children already had enough problems, without them bringing news of more.

***

The moment Meg saw Jean Moreland, she feared the child would burst with enthusiasm. She chattered on, as she had done when she'd stayed with them in Green Valley.

But Irene appeared to have changed. She was emerging as a proper young lady, even though she wasn't yet twelve years old. She had obviously taken on a lot of domestic responsibility, with her grandmother wheelchair-bound. Mrs Johnson gave clear instructions, but it was Irene who moved around the kitchen and brought everything together. Meg was glad to see how happy she looked. She was growing up and she needed a mother-figure in her life. This thought led to the problem that hung over them all. Irene needed a step-mother, but she had one already. Norma. However it would seem Norma was not just unsuitable, but dangerous.

And then there was Grace. Meg knew how good Grace was with children—and she didn't know how she would cope without her the next five months. Could Grace ever be Irene's step-mother? It would be a perfect fit, but even if Alex was clear to propose marriage, which from Mr Johnson's account he wasn't, Grace still struggled with the idea of marrying a divorcee.

Meg shook her head. *This whole situation is ugly. Ugly and stupid.* They all wanted to do the right thing, but now that so many mistakes had been made, what was the right thing to do?

'Thank you so much for tea,' Meg said to her hostess. 'And thank you, Irene, for serving it so well. You have done a wonderful job.'

Meg saw Irene flush with pleasure.

'She has grown up so quickly,' Doris said. 'She reminds me of my Nancy, to look at.'

'Jean favours her father though, I suspect,' Meg said.

'Yes, she looks a lot like Alex's side of the family, though her incorrigible personality is Nancy all over. Nancy was the one who nearly chattered me to death when she was a girl.'

Meg smiled. She felt Doris enjoyed talking about her deceased daughter, and it was good for the girls to hear their mother spoken of so fondly.

'I have two sons and a daughter,' Meg said. 'My Evie loved your girls. They got on very well together.'

'Yes, they've told me all about your children,' Doris answered. 'It seemed as if they were happy there. I'm not altogether sure why Alex came back.'

'Norma, I suspect.'

'He doesn't have any intention of reconciliation. He would have been better to just stay where he was, employed, the children happy with such good family connections. Now he's back here, and everyone is talking about why they are staying here and not in his own house.'

'Is he intending to stay, do you know?' Meg asked.

'He and Samuel talk about all sorts of things, but they don't always let me in on the secrets. Though I do happen to know that—' She broke off, as if reconsidering the wisdom of speaking out loud.

Meg didn't prompt her. She suspected that Doris knew about Grace, but she didn't know Grace was pregnant. Meg didn't want to be the one to divulge that secret. She continued to drink her tea and pretended not to be interested in what Doris knew.

Alex groaned when he walked up onto the veranda of the Johnson's home. He could tell they had guests, but he was bone tired. To get to this fruit picking job he had to catch the seven o'clock train in the morning, and didn't get back home until well after seven at night. He just wanted to come in, eat his tea and go to bed. The dejection he felt at being trapped by Norma didn't help. He wished he could still be in Green Valley. He had enjoyed the work and the family there. He didn't have to think of Norma, and he didn't have to know that the neighbours were gossiping about him.

'Daddy!' Jean raced up to the front door when he opened it. 'Guess who has come to visit.'

'Who, darlin'?' He tried to sound enthusiastic for her sake.

'Mr and Mrs Shore, from Green Valley.'

A jolt of something coursed through his body. He had just been thinking about them, and here they were.

'Come on.' Jean dragged him through the hall into the dining room.

'Alex. Good to see you, mate.' Charlie stood up from the table and held his hand out.

'Hello, Alex,' Meg said, smiling at him. 'How are you?'

Alex was momentarily shocked, and took a few moments to gather his wits.

'This is a surprise,' he said. 'What brings you all the way over here?'

'We had some business to attend to,' Charlie said. 'Thought we'd take the opportunity to drop in and see you before we went back home.'

'I'm glad you did,' Alex said. 'It's been a few months since I was there. How did you recover from that flood?'

'Slowly but surely,' Meg replied. 'The house still smells a bit musty at times, but we keep at it with open windows.'

Alex sat down at the table and Irene brought his tea to him from the warming oven.

'Thanks, sweet-pea,' he said.

'I hope you don't mind us disturbing your tea time,' Charlie said. 'Your father-in-law was kind enough to invite us to eat with the family.'

'Not at all,' Alex said. 'I'm sorry I wasn't here on time to eat with the rest of the family. My work is out a way, and it takes forever to get home.'

Talk around the table continued on, mainly about the children, and what they were currently doing with school and helping with their grandparents. Alex ate his tea as fast as he could. He desperately wanted to ask after Grace, but felt it wasn't appropriate. He hoped that they might offer the information, but they didn't.

'Perhaps Grandpa can read with you tonight,' Doris said to Jean, once the table was cleared. 'I think your father might like to catch up with his visitors.'

'Could Mrs Shore read with me?' Jean asked.

'I'm sure she would be happy to,' Charlie said. Alex saw Meg give a look to her husband. Something was amiss; he could tell.

'Could I have a few minutes to talk business?' Charlie asked Alex.

There it was. Alex knew they hadn't just dropped by. Something was wrong. He pushed back from the table.

'You kids go and get ready for bed.' Alex gave the order. 'If Mrs Shore doesn't mind, she can read with you for a while.'

'I don't mind,' Meg said, though Alex suspected she would have preferred to be in the discussion.

'Why don't you fellas go out and get some fresh air for a bit?' Samuel suggested.

Now Alex was sure something was wrong, and Samuel seemed to know it too.

Once they were outside Alex turned to his friend. 'Why did you really drop by?' he asked.

Charlie took a huge breath. 'It's Grace,' he said.

'Is she all right?' Alex felt a jolt of panic.

'She's pregnant, Alex, with your child.'

Alex felt the air leave his lungs and didn't know if he would be able to breathe in again.

'Are you sure?' His mouth had suddenly gone dry.

'Come on, Alex. You've had kids before. You know that after nearly five months we would be sure.'

Alex walked away from Charlie, lifted his head heavenward and closed his eyes. 'What am I going to do now?'

'I saw Norma yesterday.'

'Where?'

'At your house. We went there to find you.'

'I don't live there.'

'She told us you and the children were there, and she was thrilled to have you all back.'

Alex wanted to swear, but didn't.

'Grace was with us.'

'And she heard that?'

'Yes.'

This time he did swear. 'That woman is determined to destroy me.'

'Which one? Norma or Grace?'

Alex glared at Charlie in the dim light. 'What am I going to do, Charlie?'

'About?'

'About Grace. You don't suppose I'm going to leave her to deal with this on her own, do you?'

'What do you propose to do, as a married man?'

'I've asked for a divorce.'

'From what I heard yesterday, it doesn't appear as if Norma is willing to part from you.'

'We parted years ago. About a month after we married, to be exact.'

'Legally?'

'She doesn't really care about me. It's the property.'

'You have a nice piece of property there, but it can't be worth that much.'

'She wants the Johnson's store.'

'How? She's not a blood relative.'

'She means to take control through me and the children.'

'You're an heir, then?'

'No, only the executor and trustee. At the moment, anyway. Samuel is trying to change his will and leave me out of it.'

'Do you think Norma is only interested in the property? You don't think she has any feelings for you?'

'I don't care if she does. I still haven't forgiven her for the way she treated the children.'

'You're going to have to sooner or later, you know.'

'What?' Alex turned around to face Charlie again.

'Forgive her.'

Alex broke a stick from a bush and threw it. 'Not likely. I wouldn't trust her within ten yards of them.'

'I didn't say trust; I said forgive. There is a difference.'

'You think so?' This time Alex kicked at some loose stones on the path.

'I do.' Charlie's tone was matter-of-fact.

'Anyway, I'm not concerned about Norma at this point. What about Grace? You said she was here yesterday. Where is she now?'

'The Methodist Babies Home at Brighton.'

Alex put his head in his hands.

'Do you know the place?' Charlie asked.

Alex nodded. 'I've heard of it. It's not the sort of place that is brought up in polite conversation though.'

'No, I gathered that much.'

'I can't leave her there.'

'We have to, Alex. There isn't an option.'

'That's a place where you go in pregnant and come out with no sign of a baby. They get rid of them.'

'They adopt them out,' Charlie corrected.

'I'm not happy with that, either.'

'Do you have any choice?'

'Did you have a choice when Aimee was in need of a home?'
Charlie nodded.

'You wouldn't have left her, would you?' Alex asked.

'Grace is afraid of the family reputation being ruined.'

'But how can she just leave a baby like that?'

'She doesn't want to. She is beside herself, Alex. Ripped in two by it all.'

Alex groaned. 'It's all my fault.'

'Yep. It is.'

'Wouldn't your parents take them in?' Alex asked. 'They managed with your situation.'

'Truthfully, I think they probably would. The thing is, Grace doesn't think she can face the disgrace. The community would be alive with gossip for years.'

'How long do I have?' Alex asked.

'How long for what?'

'Before the baby is due?'

'When was the flood?'

'June, wasn't it?'

'It's nearly November now. I reckon you have until March.'

Alex paced back and forth, agitated.

'What if you can't get a divorce?' Charlie asked.

'Then I'll take the baby. If she can't, I will. My reputation is already completely ruined as it is. What's one more misdemeanour?'

'What about the Johnsons? How will they feel about it? They don't have any blood relationship to Grace's baby, and their reputation and business will be affected too.'

Alex hadn't thought about that. At the moment, he was heavily reliant on the Johnson's generosity and support. He knew they were happy because they saw the children, and even had the help of the children in a time when they couldn't afford to pay extra staff. But to ask them to sacrifice their good name was a big ask. They already had to deflect questions about why he hadn't moved back to his own home. To bring his illegitimate child into the mix would be a huge imposition.

'I have four months or so. I'll talk to Samuel and Doris. I have to work something out, Charlie. I can't let Grace give our baby away.'

Chapter Thirteen

Grace had adapted to the routine expected of the girls in the home. They were allotted chores in the laundry and cleaning around the dormitories. She was older than most of the others. They chatted amongst themselves and talked about how they'd gotten into trouble. In times past, Grace would have disapproved of their silly flirting and the dangerous games they played behind their parents' backs. However, being as she was in the same position, and there was a face and a name to the man she had fallen with, she was less inclined to be judgemental. It was easy to get into this sort of trouble. It only took one mistake.

Grace wasn't open to making friends. Her spirits were still very low, and though she wished she could pretend, each week's passing meant she was closer to having the baby ripped away from her.

'Grace Shore.' One of the nursing staff called her as she was folding nappies in the laundry.

'Yes.'

'There is someone here to see you.'

Grace fully expected it to be Charlie or Meg. She was preparing to scold them for making such a long journey back to see her. It was too far. But when she entered the common room lounge, it was Alex who stood up to face her. The moment she saw him she burst into tears.

'Grace, don't cry,' he said. 'I'm sorry. I'm so sorry.'

She knew he had stepped to within a couple of feet from her. She longed for him to take her in his arms, but that was how they'd gotten into this mess in the first place. She didn't move.

127

'What can I do to help you?' Alex asked.

Grace lifted her teary eyes to meet his gaze. 'There isn't anything you can do, Alex, is there?'

'When I can, I will get a divorce, and then I will marry you.'

Grace shook her head in denial. 'I can't.'

'Why not?' Alex sounded hurt.

'That would be wrong, Alex. The Bible doesn't allow remarriage after divorce.'

'At this point, I'm not really concerned about what the Bible says,' Alex said. 'I'm concerned for my child, and his mother. I don't want you to give him away, Grace.'

'I can't keep him. How could I keep him? It would destroy my parents.'

'Would it, Grace. Would it really? Have you talked to them about it?'

'I don't want them to know. I've never done anything like this before. It would be such a disappointment to them.'

'Haven't they faced disappointment before?'

'Not from me,' Grace said. 'I've never done anything wrong before.'

'Really? Are you that good?'

Grace hung her head.

'Look, Grace. This is my child too. If you won't keep him, then I'll take him.'

Grace's gaze snapped back up.

'How?' she asked.

'I don't know how; not just yet. All I know is that I don't care what the neighbours will say. They've already got me pegged as a disgrace for living separately from Norma.'

'You don't live with her?'

'No. I haven't lived with her for over four years. I know she told you we'd moved back into the house, but it was a lie.'

'How do you know I was there? How did you know I was here?'

'Charlie and Meg came to see me several weeks ago, before they returned to Green Valley. I've been wracking my brains trying to find a solution to our dilemma.'

'But you haven't, have you?'

'I mean to have my name filled in the paperwork as the father of this child. And I plan to make it plain that the child is not available for adoption.'

Grace started to cry again. She wasn't normally an emotional sort of person, but she was so lost and hurting, she just couldn't help it. She felt Alex's arms go around her, and for a short moment she allowed herself to be comforted in his embrace. But all too quickly, she remembered their situation.

'I can't, Alex.' She pulled back from him.

'I know, but I'm still going to fill in the paperwork.'

***

Grace went with Alex into the matron's office.

'I am the father of Grace's baby,' Alex said without preamble.

'I see.' Grace couldn't tell if the tone in the matron's voice was one of disapproval or not.

'I wish to be named as the father, and also wish to make it clear that this baby is not available for adoption.'

'Well, Mr Moreland, the best thing for you in this situation would be to do the honourable thing and marry your baby's mother.'

'Unfortunately, I can't at this point.'

'You're already married, then?' Now Grace knew she heard disapproval.

'Legally, yes. I have been estranged from my wife for nearly four years.'

'I'm not here to deliver any lectures, Mr Moreland, but I'm sure you know that doesn't make your relationship with Miss Shore legitimate.'

'I am aware of that. I would also like to make it very clear that Miss Shore is not a woman of loose morals. Our situation was under extenuating circumstances, a one-off occasion, and not something that she would normally have engaged in.'

'I'm sure that is none of my business,' the matron said.

'I'm sure it's not, but I don't like your judgemental tone.'

'You have committed, adultery, sir, and got a young woman pregnant. You do understand that is not acceptable.'

'I know, only too well. I'm just—'

'Please leave it, Alex.' Grace placed her hand on his arm. 'It is what it is. We can't change it.'

***

Alex hated leaving Grace. She wasn't the capable, friendly woman he'd known prior to the flood. The word he would use was "fragile". She was in a place where she had no control over what was happening to her, and Alex knew that it was his fault. It was ironic; the way he'd treated her so aggressively to start, trying to make sure she kept her distance, yet that distance was swallowed up by floodwaters. He knew he should feel utter contempt for his actions, but he couldn't be completely sorry. She was a beautiful person, and now she carried his child, and he loved her—not like he had loved Nancy, but still he loved her. He wanted to be with her, to give her his name and take responsibility for his child. But sleeping with Grace had been his second mistake. If it had been his first mistake, he could have married her and corrected all this. But unfortunately his first mistake had been marriage to Norma.

Alex didn't have any answers to his problems. He hadn't talked to Samuel and Doris about the baby yet. He knew it was going to be a terrible burden for them. But he needed to talk to someone.

'Alex Moreland!' The Reverend Matthew Decker reached out and grabbed Alex in a strong embrace, thumping him firmly on the back. 'It's been too long since I've seen you, mate.'

'I've been working over in Victoria for a couple of years.'

'I'd heard you were back the last couple of months.'

'I needed to sort some family stuff out.'

Matthew stared at him for a couple of seconds, then thumped him on the arm again. 'Come inside for a cuppa, mate. Let's talk about old times.'

Alex followed his friend inside. Old times. Matthew meant those years they'd served together in the AIF in Europe. He also knew that a bit of war talk would only be the lead-in to what was the real issue. Matthew Decker had served as padre in their unit. He was a man of prayer as well as action, and Alex knew he was also a man who'd share any burden.

'So what are you going to do about Norma?' Matthew eventually got around to the topic.

'You know why I left, don't you?'

'I heard from the Johnsons. I didn't know how much they might have exaggerated the abuse.'

'Whip marks, signs of malnutrition, no clothes that actually fit, and that's what I saw with my own eyes. Irene tells me he slept in the chook shed because she wouldn't allow him indoors.'

'I have a feeling that could be reported to the police.'

Alex shrugged his shoulders. 'Too late now. I just ran and left her with the property. I didn't intend to come back.'

'So why did you?'

'I got involved with another woman.'

Matthew didn't say anything, but Alex could tell by the look on his face that he was struggling to think of what to say.

'I didn't intend to,' Alex said. 'I had avoided her like the plague until we got thrown together during a flood. I saved her from drowning, then we had to take refuge in the ceiling space of the farm house to escape the floodwaters. We were stuck for a couple of days.'

'And?'

'And now she's pregnant.'

'Oh dear.'

'But I can't marry her because Norma refuses to divorce me.'

'Oh dear,' Matthew repeated.

'It's wrong on so many different levels. I don't know which option to take that makes me least despicable.'

'Oh, Alex, you are in a pack of trouble.'

'Thanks for that, Matt. I hadn't realised that before now.'

Matthew actually laughed. Perhaps it wasn't quite appropriate, but then Alex decided to laugh as well. Matthew had always been a cheerful bloke: one who could see the funny side of just about anything, even in the trenches. At this point, Alex figured his situation wasn't quite as bad as the trenches. Not far off, but not quite.

Matthew brewed a second pot of tea while they sat and talked in more depth about the situation.

'I'm going to need to think about this, Alex,' he said after a long discussion. 'I will pray for you too, of course, but I don't want to dish out advice right now without seeking a little bit of wisdom from above.'

'Do you really think God is interested in my sordid affairs?'

'Well if he doesn't care about you, mate, I know he cares about your baby, don't you think?'

Alex thought about that for a bit. Generally society frowned on bastards—thought they were of questionable breeding, and likely to be trouble. Did God really care about them?

'The baby is innocent, Alex.' It was as if Matthew read his thoughts. 'And the poor little soul needs his mother and father.'

'I agree,' Alex said. 'But what about Norma?'

'Too hard a question for me to answer today. I need to think and pray on this one. Come by next week, and let's talk again.'

***

Alex was glad of the work he'd managed to get, picking fruit up in the Adelaide Hills. It was the stone fruit season, and while it was busy right at the moment, he knew the work wouldn't last. As he worked in the cherry orchards, he had plenty of time to think about his family situation. He'd been glad of the open discussion he'd had with his friend, the minister. Matthew had a way of making even the worst of situations seem as if there might be some hope somewhere. Alex wiped the sweat from his forehead. Even with Matthew's optimism, Alex still couldn't see how he was going to work it all out, but he knew he should at least tell Samuel and Doris about the new development. It was only right, considering he was already imposing on their good grace.

Though he was always weary by the time he got home on the train,

Alex had made up his mind that this was a discussion that could not be delayed any longer.

'Can I talk to you after tea?' He addressed both his parents-in-law.

'Yes, after the children are in bed,' Samuel said. 'Actually, I have some news I want to share with you as well.'

Alex was anxious to get this discussion over, but he took the time to spend reading with the children. Irene was the best reader out of the three, and she often took charge of reading out loud to the rest of them. They were reading one of Nancy's childhood books, *Pollyanna*. Alex was only half listening, but when Irene read about the *Glad Game*, Alex wondered if such a childish notion could possibly work in the real adult world—especially one that was as complicated as his.

'All right, now. That's enough for one night,' Alex announced when Irene reached the end of the chapter.

'Oh, Daddy, can't she read us another chapter?' Jean asked.

'Not tonight, Jeanie. I need to spend some time with Grandpa and Grandma.'

'Why?' Jimmy asked.

Alex knew his son was growing up, and was more aware of adult troubles than Jean was, but he didn't want to discuss this with him.

'It's not for you kids to know about,' he said. 'Grown-up stuff.'

Alex saw a look on Jimmy's face. He had just turned fourteen, was working as a storeman, and Alex thought he was probably annoyed that he was being fobbed off as a child. No matter. He still wasn't going to indulge him.

'We will chat about it later,' Alex said to Jimmy. 'Now off to bed, please.'

Alex waited until they were all in their beds. He didn't want to open up this topic and risk having the children overhear the disagreement— and he was sure there would be a disagreement.

'Do you want another cup of tea?' Samuel asked as Alex came into their lounge room. Alex shook his head. His stomach was churning and his recent meal was already threatening to cause trouble.

'Do you want to go first, or shall I?' Samuel asked as Alex sat down.

'You can,' Alex replied, glad to have a few minutes reprieve.

'I've heard back from my lawyer today. We have changed my will, leaving my nephew, William, as executor, trustee and power of attorney instead of you.'

Alex nodded. 'Was it costly?'

'Affordable. I feel better knowing that the children's interests will have an outside arbitrator and that it won't come down to a domestic dispute between you and your wife.'

Alex's shoulders slumped. They were determined to see the marriage as unbreakable.

'Are you all right with that?' Samuel asked. 'I just need you to make sure William knows your current address at all times, in case he needs to get in contact with you or the children.'

'Of course.'

'Which brings me to the next subject.'

Here it comes, Alex thought.

'How long do you plan to stay here with us?' Doris asked the question, as much a part of the conversation.

'Until I've sorted out my domestic issues, if I may impose that long?'

'It wouldn't be too hard for you to just move back to your own home,' Doris said.

'It is impossible, Doris. I'm sorry. And I'm afraid the situation is now more serious than it was before.'

'Why? What's happened?' Samuel asked.

Alex sighed deeply and studied his hands that were clasped together between his knees, desperately searching for the strength to see this through.

'Is something wrong?' Samuel asked.

Alex nodded. 'I'm afraid so.'

'What?' Doris asked.

'There's a baby.'

There was a stunned silence for a long moment. Alex sensed both of them looking at him, but he didn't have the courage to return their gaze.

'Do you mean to tell us that your affair has left the woman pregnant?' Doris sounded disapproving.

'Grace is pregnant, yes. She is due in March next year.'

Another long pause.

'She will get rid of it, of course.' Doris broke the silence.

Alex took another deep breath.

'I'm not going to let her,' he said. 'I'm going to take the child, if she can't.'

'Alex, you cannot be serious,' Doris said. 'How on earth are you going to take care of an illegitimate child?'

'Illegitimacy has nothing to do with it,' Alex said. 'The child is mine, as much as Jimmy, Irene or Jean.'

'Don't you be lumping a little bastard with my grandchildren,' Samuel growled. 'Nancy was a decent young woman, and I don't want the issue of some tramp being together with them.'

Alex was stunned. He had great respect for his parents-in-law, and to hear them take such a harsh stand against an innocent little child was like a punch to his gut. He literally felt winded by it.

'Let her adopt it out,' Doris said. 'We have enough disgrace as it is. You can't bring it here, and I don't want our grandchildren to mix with it.'

'I'm sorry you feel like this,' Alex said, trying to keep his tone even, despite the growing fury he felt. 'However, this child is my flesh and blood, and will be the brother or sister of Jimmy, Irene and Jean.'

'You can't do that, Alex,' Samuel objected. 'It's not fair to the children.'

'How is it not fair? If my marriage to Norma had worked out, we would've had children. They would have been half-brothers or sisters. The only difference here is that the mother involved is a decent, kind and caring woman.'

'She is obviously not a decent woman, or she wouldn't be in this situation.'

'Well, I'm sorry you feel this way, but I am immovable on this.'

Samuel stood up and walked over to the window. Alex didn't look directly at her, but he could feel the animosity coming from Doris's direction.

'You will not bring a bastard child into this home,' Samuel eventually said. 'You'll have to make other arrangements.

Alex nodded. He hadn't expected them to be happy about the announcement, but he hadn't quite expected this level of hostility either. He left the room knowing he couldn't really blame them. He had brought one disgrace after another into their home and this was the straw that had broken the camel's back.

Chapter Fourteen

Alex went to church on Sunday morning, something he hadn't done since he'd been back from interstate. He accompanied Doris and Samuel with the children, but despite the friendly cheerful front the Johnsons put on, Alex knew they were upset with him. After the service they gathered out the front of the church and chatted with the other church members.

'How is Norma?' One of Doris's CWA friends spoke to Alex. 'You were away a long time.'

Alex didn't want to answer, but the woman was persistent just in the way she held him in her gaze.

'We're separated,' Alex said bluntly.

'Oh, dear. I'm sorry to hear that,' the woman said. Predictably, she then turned aside and looked for someone less troublesome to talk to.

'Do you have to announce it to everyone?' Doris said in a low tone near his ear. 'I don't want the whole community to know.'

Alex didn't have the heart to make excuses. He walked away from his family and sought out his friend, Matthew.

'A bit brave of you to face the religious crowd on a Sunday morning,' Matthew said.

'A bit stupid of me, I'm thinking.'

'Come around after lunch. I've been praying about your crisis, and have a bit of a plan.'

Matthew then turned from Alex to greet another parishioner. Though Alex knew most of the folks standing about, he also knew they would either be curious about Norma, or they would already know and were gossiping about it. In any case, he didn't want to engage.

'Come on, kids. We're going home.' He tried to round up his children.

'Oh, Daddy. I'm playing with Heather. Can't I come home later with Grandpa?'

Alex glared at Jean. Typically the social butterfly, she was with another little girl her age. Alex didn't feel like making a scene so he nodded his head.

'Make sure you keep an eye out for when they're ready to leave,' he said.

Irene and Jimmy weren't so keen to stay and started to walk back with him.

'Grandpa and Grandma seem like they're angry with you,' Jimmy said. 'What have you said to them?'

'They are upset with me,' Alex admitted. 'I can't really talk to you about it at the moment. Grandpa and Grandma are doing what they think is best.'

'Are you doing something wrong, Dad?' Irene asked.

'I have made some mistakes,' he replied. 'I should never have married Norma. She treated you children badly, but marriage is a very important commitment. Everybody thinks we should move back into our house with her.'

'No, Dad. No!' Jimmy's face paled, and Alex's gut tightened when he saw it. 'I won't live there again, ever.'

'Settle down, son,' Alex said. 'I'm not going to move back. It's just that everybody else thinks I should.'

'How is this everyone else's concern? They don't know what she did to me.'

'I know. I'm not moving back.'

'I'll tell Grandpa myself. He can't make you.'

'There's more to it than that,' Alex said. 'I don't want you to say anything to Grandpa and Grandma. I'm trying to sort it out. One day soon, I hope we might go back to Green Valley.'

He watched his two older children to see how they would respond to that. 'Would you mind it if we left Mitcham?'

They were both quiet for a moment.

'I liked it in Green Valley,' Irene said. 'The Shores are really nice people.'

'But I'd miss Grandpa and Grandma,' Jimmy said. 'I like working in the store.'

Alex nodded. More complications for him to try to work out.

***

'Tea?' Matthew ushered Alex into his church office.

'If you think it will help,' Alex replied.

'Life always seems much easier to handle if one has a good cup of tea.' Matthew moved across to the door and called out to his wife. 'Could you make us a pot of tea, love?'

'I've a feeling alcohol might work better at this point,' Alex said, allowing his low spirits to show.

'You want me to add drunkenness to the list of misdemeanours?' Matthew had a pencil in hand and was grinning at him.

'Have you been listing my misdemeanours?' Alex asked.

'Not yet, but I think it might help if we saw it all on paper.'

'Spare me,' Alex said. 'I feel rotten enough without seeing it all listed down.'

Just then the office door opened and Mrs Decker brought a tea tray in and put it down on the desk between them. 'How are you Alex?' she asked.

'Good, thank you,' he replied.

'Which is a complete lie,' Matthew said. 'Still, he is fit and healthy, so we can be thankful for that.

Rosie Decker laughed along with her husband. 'I'm sure things will come good soon,' she said as she left the office.

'Does she know?' Alex asked after she'd left the room.

'Everyone knows about Norma. Did you think it was a secret?'

'I had hoped it might have gone unnoticed.'

'You've been away four years.'

'I was away working.'

139

'With the children?'

'So I ran out on her. And I don't mean to go back.'

'Good. That will go on the top of the list.'

Alex rolled his eyes. Matthew was in fine spirits, ready to make a joke out of everything. He wasn't sure how he felt about that. Still it was better than the hostility he'd faced at the Johnsons. Perhaps he preferred Matthew's approach.

'So I was thinking, old friend, it might be good to write down the names of those people who are affected by this situation.'

'How will that help?'

'I just think it will help us to look at the situation from a practical point of view, and help us decide what's best.'

Alex shrugged his shoulders. He didn't have a better idea.

'OK. First, Norma,' Matthew said.

'I'd put her last.'

'Why?'

'Because she doesn't deserve any consideration.'

'Harsh words, mate, from a man who's abandoned his wife, committed adultery, and got another woman pregnant.'

'Are you saying you think my sins are worse than hers?'

'If you want to start scoring on whose sins are the worst, you're not gonna come out on top. I think we should just leave sin alone for a bit and concentrate on the practical aspects of the situation.'

'How can I leave sin out of it? That's what God is all about, isn't it—Judgement for our sins?'

'You haven't been listening to my sermons, have you? No, you've been away.'

Alex raised his eyebrows.

'Sin doesn't really have anything to do with it,' Matthew said.

'That sounds like heresy, even to me.'

'Did you ever hear that God sent a Saviour? That Jesus Christ, the son of God, shed his blood for our sins? Made a way for us to come before God, clean?'

Alex took a breath and considered the words.

'You have heard of it, I assume?' Matthew pressed.

'Of course, but …'

'So what is the point of a Saviour if we are never saved? The sin factor has been taken care of.'

'That makes it all a bit easy, doesn't it? If it were that easy, everybody would just sin and play the "Saviour" trump card.'

'That's right. That's exactly what everybody does.'

'Well, that's not right, is it?'

'No, not right, but that's what happens. We all struggle to live a righteous life. Even me.'

'What trouble have you got into?' Alex asked.

'A touch of covetousness here and there, an odd stab of lust …'

'Come on, Matt! We all know you're a saint.'

'I'm the same as you, Alex. A sinner saved by grace.'

'Yes, but you don't have all the problems I do.'

'Ah, yes, that's true. Perhaps my sin doesn't quite have the same catastrophic consequences. Yours might take a little more working through, practically.'

'That is an understatement, if ever I heard one.'

'Right, so back to the list: Who is going to be affected by the decisions that might be made here?'

Matthew prodded Alex for some time until he had just about everybody listed: his children, his in-laws, Norma, Grace, Grace's family, the new baby and himself.

'I guess I don't really matter, do I?' Alex said, allowing his head to hang down.

'You are the key player,' Matthew replied. 'The decisions you make will affect everybody. That is why we have to think it through carefully.'

'If it were up to how I feel, I'd marry Grace and not bother about what everyone else thought.'

'But it's not up to how you feel. It was how you felt that got you into this mess. You felt desperate for help with the children after Nancy died;

you felt so full of grief you didn't stop to think what marrying Norma would actually mean; you felt overpowered by physical attraction to Grace. Stop feeling for a moment, and let's just think.'

Matthew was being provoking. Alex wanted to defend himself, but reason told him arguing with Matthew wasn't going to help. He needed to walk this road, no matter how tough it was.

***

It was nearly dark, and Alex had been working through his family issues with Matthew for the entire afternoon.

'Are you staying for tea, Alex?' Rosie had popped her head in the study door again. It was the third time—she'd already refreshed the teapot twice.

'I need to be going,' Alex said. 'Thank you. I'm sorry for taking up Matthew's time all day.'

'Have you got it all sorted out?'

Alex looked to Matthew to gauge what sort of response he should give.

'Do you mind if we ask her opinion?' Matthew said.

Alex shrugged his shoulders. 'I guess not. She already knows about Norma.'

Rosie swept into the room and took the other office chair.

'I'm really sorry things have gone bad for you, Alex,' she said.

'Listen, Rosie. I'm trusting you'll keep this information to yourself,' Matthew said.

'Matthew Decker! What a thing to say! As if I would share sensitive information around.'

'Just wanted to make sure.'

Alex was amused at the couples' way of relating. She was a feisty soul, and he imagined that Matthew had some lively discussions with her at times.

'We've narrowed down the two people who are most affected by whatever decision Alex makes. Norma and the new baby.'

Alex waited for her to ask, "what baby" but she didn't. She obviously already knew. Matthew must have talked to her about it already.

'If Alex goes back to Norma, then his children, particularly Jimmy, will be unhappy, and perhaps in danger of further abuse. His new baby will be given up for adoption, and be brought up with the stamp of illegitimacy and no real family connection. If Alex pushes for a divorce, then Norma will wear the stamp of disgrace as a divorcee, abandoned and betrayed by her husband.'

'Both will be provided for?' Rosie asked.

'Alex will settle property on Norma, if they divorce, yes. The baby might be placed in a family, or it might be brought up in an orphanage. Either way, there is no guarantee that it will be loved or wanted.'

'I can't bear to think of the poor little child growing up alone, knowing that he doesn't have anyone who really cares for him, and thinking his real parents didn't want him.'

'I do want him,' Alex said. 'With all my heart. So does his mother.'

'Will Norma accept property for a divorce?'

'Last time we spoke, she was fairly determined to hold on to the marriage.'

'Even though she knows that you have betrayed her.'

Alex felt a stab of guilt. That's what it amounted to, wasn't it? Betrayal.

'She's willing to forgive me.'

'By the tone of your voice, I'm guessing the forgiveness isn't really a passionate lover's forgiveness.'

'We were never passionate lovers. I married her because it was convenient to have someone look after my children.'

'That sounds like you were very selfish, Alex,' Rosie said.

Alex hadn't heard it put quite like that before, and was a little stunned. He wanted to make excuses, but when he recalled the word he had used—convenient—he realised it was a selfish decision. It was one he'd made while focussed only on himself. He had considered the children, of course, but he hadn't given any thought to what it meant for Norma. He felt a stab of guilt.

'And you believe she abused your children?' Rosie continued, apparently not concerned with pursuing this extra fault of his.

'I saw it with my own eyes. It's not just a suspicion.'

Rosie Decker took a deep breath. 'You understand she tells a different story?'

'What is her story?' Alex asked.

'That you were forced to leave home to find work; that your children were so difficult they refused to stay with her, but that she is glad you've all returned home.'

'We aren't back home.'

'I think everybody knows that, but she is sticking to her story.'

'Back to the problem at hand, Rosie,' Matthew said. 'Should Alex do what's best for the child, or for Norma? Who will be the most affected?'

Rosie took a moment to consider. 'From my point of view, I feel the child is still innocent, is still secure with his mother and has no idea that he is at risk of being torn away and branded. Norma already knows, and so does everybody else. To divorce is just an official acknowledgement of the separation and betrayal that happened years ago. If it comes down to a choice between the two, I would protect the child.'

Alex released a sigh of relief.

'Neither option is great, Alex,' she said.

'I know.'

'He wouldn't take his children back to Norma, even if he didn't push for a divorce,' Matthew said. 'Jimmy particularly is anxious that he might. The best Norma will ever get is an estranged husband and family. Unfortunately, she has behaved in a manner that has caused hurt and distrust.'

'You have to protect the new baby, Alex, and ask God to forgive you for what it means to Norma.'

'I'm not sure God will be interested in my pleas for forgiveness.'

'He'll be interested, mate. He's already bought and paid for it with his blood. Don't be underestimating the power of forgiveness.'

Chapter Fifteen

The tension that existed between Samuel, Doris and Alex was almost unbearable. Alex tried to pretend everything was normal, but the atmosphere bristled with unspoken disapproval. Eventually Samuel called him in for a private conversation.

'Have you made your decision yet?' Samuel asked.

Alex nodded.

'And?'

'I mean to protect my children, *all* of them.'

'By that, you mean to include the bastard child.'

'If I can make it happen, the child will be born to my wife.'

'You can't marry her while you're still married to Norma.'

'I mean to press for a divorce again. I'm hoping you will allow me to show her your new will.'

Samuel was quiet for a time.

'I'm not happy with your decision, Alex. I don't like what it means for the children.'

'I'm sorry, Samuel, but what you are thinking about is yourself and your own reputation. I know my decision will affect your reputation, and I'm sorry about that. I know it is my fault, and I know it hurts you.'

Samuel opened his mouth to speak, but Alex cut him off.

'At this point, I'm thinking about an innocent child who stands to be rejected, neglected, branded and bullied because I have to choose between him and my reputation. I can only apologise to you, and once all is secure, I will leave this state with my family. You won't need to be reminded of the disgrace.'

Samuel's face was like granite.

'I will not keep your grandchildren from you, Samuel. When things are less tight financially, I will arrange for them to visit you. I don't mean to hurt you, but I will not punish my fifth child when it is my fault.'

'Fifth child?'

'My fourth child is in the grave with Nancy, remember.'

Samuel ducked his head and Alex thought he saw moisture.

'I'm sorry, Samuel. I really am. I wish I could do what was best for everybody concerned, but to brush Grace's baby aside is just pretending for everyone else's sake. The baby is the one who will suffer a lifetime of rejection. I can't do it.'

Alex waited for several long moments while Samuel appeared to pull himself together.

'I'll get the new paperwork for you,' he said, and walked out of the lounge room.

***

Norma sat at their kitchen table, stony-faced.

'Why are you showing me this?' she asked Alex.

'I want you to understand that in refusing to let us go, you will gain nothing in the long run.'

'What about my house, garden, orchard, animals?'

'I'm not going to take your home away from you,' Alex said. 'Listen Norma, I realise that I have done the wrong thing by you—'

'And I said I would forgive you.'

'But I'm not sure I can forgive you,' he said.

'For Pete's sake, Alex! I don't know why you put so much stock in the things those children say.'

'Stop it, please,' Alex said. 'I don't trust you. I don't love you like I should, and I'm not prepared to resume domestic relations. If you do not press for a divorce, you will have nothing more than the disgrace of being deserted. I'm not coming back.'

Norma looked angry. 'I suppose you put the Johnsons up to cutting me out of the will.'

'You were never in the will.'

'Yes, but you knew I wanted that store, and as your wife I had some chance.'

'What you wanted had no bearing on the case. It was never intended for you, and now they've made sure you can't manipulate my children to get control.'

'You did that deliberately to hurt me.'

'I did it to protect my children, Norma.'

She sat with a sullen pout on her face. Alex didn't quite know what to do next.

'If you will let me go, I am prepared to let you have half of this property.'

'Half?' she said. 'I want it all, Alex. You haven't left me with anything else.'

'What about my children? What do they get?' Alex asked.

'They get the store.'

Alex was quiet. The only person who was left was him, and at this point he didn't feel as if he deserved anything at all. But then he remembered Grace and his new child.

'No. I am only allowing you half. Once it's sold, you'll get half the value.'

'You can't sell it in this economy. We won't get anything for it.'

Alex knew she was right.

'I won't sell until the economy recovers, then you can either pay me for my half, or take half the proceeds once I sell to someone else.'

'How am I supposed to earn money to pay for half?'

Alex shrugged.

'Don't you care at all?'

He didn't really care about her—he could admit that to himself—but he did care about his own sense of self-respect. 'I won't sell the property until you are in a good position.'

Silence descended again.

'I'll think about it,' she said after a long pause. 'You haven't really given me much choice, have you?'

'I'm sorry,' Alex said.

'Are you?'

Alex didn't want to answer. He knew he still hadn't forgiven her. He had Matthew's voice echoing in his thoughts about how he needed to forgive her, but he was resisting.

'You have the information, Norma. Please let me know if you are willing to proceed.'

He got up from the kitchen table and left the house. His house. The place he'd brought his childhood sweetheart as a new bride; the place his three children had been born; and the place Nancy had given her last breath. The price for his bad decisions was high, and it hurt.

***

After nearly three months, Grace was resigned to the loneliness and homesickness. Sometimes, when her baby was particularly active, she was tempted to talk to him, but she was reluctant to get attached if she was going to have to give him away.

What a ridiculous thought. You are my own flesh and blood. Even if they take you away, and I never see you again, I am attached and will be for life.

Such thoughts brought on bouts of melancholy, sometimes with tears, sometimes with just a numbness of soul. She wasn't really aware of what others in the home thought about the way she was, nor did she really care.

'Grace, why don't you come down to chapel?' One of the nurses in the home sat down next to her to try yet again to rouse her from her depression. 'It's Christmas Eve. Come and sing some carols with us.'

Grace had been aware that Christmas was approaching. The home had given the girls decorations to hang up, and had put up a tree. She had gone through the motions, but refused to engage.

'Come on,' the nurse persisted. 'It might cheer you up.'

Grace got up from her chair and followed the friendly nurse. Ivy, that was her name. Grace doubted chapel would cheer her up, but she went anyway.

Several times during the service Grace wished she could just run out of the room and hide in her bed. The dear carols—so much a part of happy childhood memories—stung her. Then the minister talked about the Christ child, born as a tiny baby in the stable. As he spoke, Grace's baby decided to move around. She placed her hand over her abdomen, and allowed tears to flow. The Christ child came to bring peace on earth and hope to all mankind, but she felt no peace in her place of hopelessness.

'Miss Shore?' The minister approached her as soon as the service was finished. She looked up to acknowledge him. 'My name is Matthew Decker.' He grasped her hand in a warm handshake. 'Alex Moreland is a good friend of mine.'

At the mention of Alex's name, Grace gasped and then frowned, carefully drawing her hand back.

'I know the little one you carry is his child,' Matthew said. 'He and I have been talking about how we can make a safe and secure home for him with his parents.'

'What do you mean?' Grace asked.

'I mean Alex has decided the needs of your child are more important than any of the other demands being placed on him at the moment.'

'But I haven't seen Alex in nearly six weeks.'

'He doesn't feel free to come until he's sorted out the business with Norma.'

'How is he going to sort it out?'

'He is still hoping for a divorce.'

Grace didn't say anything. She still struggled with the idea.

'It's the only thing he can do if he's to do anything for you and your baby.'

Grace nodded, hoping her doubts didn't show too much.

'Nothing has come of it as yet,' Matthew went on, 'but Alex is determined he will make a home for the baby.'

'I don't know how he will do that if he doesn't have support.'

'We're praying something will work out soon.'

'Alex is praying?'

'Well, I'm praying, and he is worrying.'

'Do you think God really cares about this situation, Reverend?'

'As I said to Alex, I am certain He cares about your child, even if you can't accept He might care about you.'

'Oh, I wish that were true,' Grace said, before she could think about what she had said.

'You doubt that God cares about the baby?'

'Every good Christian person I know wouldn't approve of this baby at all. They would sooner he be adopted out and away from sight. I'm sure you know that.'

'Perhaps you might need to amend the titles. People are quick to classify themselves as *good* Christian people, but not so quick to examine what their attitudes really mean. I'm sure they are upstanding in the community, but sometimes some really ugly attitudes can breed when people indulge in self-righteousness.'

Grace felt chastened by his words. She knew she had indulged in self-righteousness. She still thought she wasn't quite as bad as some of the other girls in the home. It was an alarming revelation.

'Anyway, I just wanted to wish you a Merry Christmas, and encourage you to put hope in the Lord. He loves your little one, and He loves you.'

Grace didn't quite know how to feel after the minister left. She wanted to reach out and take hope with both hands, but still doubted that God would interest Himself with such a creature of sin.

***

The modest Christmas celebrations at the babies' home were just enough to Grace's way of thinking. Not loud and indulgent, but at least an acknowledgement of what the day meant. After having spoken with the Reverend the night before, Grace felt her spirits were a little lighter than they had been. She was tempted to hope, at least on Christmas Day. All the girls seemed ready to enjoy the day of rest, and several games were organised for them to play. Grace didn't feel quite that hopeful, so she just sat to one side and watched. Once or twice the proposed game was a little too boisterous, and one of the nurses who was included in the party advised that so many pregnant women could easily injure themselves. Grace smiled. It did look rather funny.

'Are you feeling better today?' Ivy, the young nurse who'd urged her to chapel the evening before was back on duty and sat down next to her.

'I am, a little. Thank you.'

'I saw you chatting with the reverend last night.'

'He is a friend of Alex's.'

'Your baby's father?'

Grace nodded.

'Do you think he will try to help you?'

'Reverend Decker?'

Ivy smiled. 'No, the baby's father.'

'Reverend Decker said he was desperately trying.'

'What will you do?'

'Wait and see. I'm a little afraid to raise my hopes for fear it will end in disappointment.'

Ivy smiled at her and squeezed her hand. 'I'm praying it will work out for you and your baby.

'Thank you.' Grace responded well to this particular nurse. She always seemed so caring and kind. The other nurses cared too, she supposed, but not with the same attitude. They were generally more stern, and every now and again, a hint of judgement would show in the things they said. Grace had hardened herself to these comments. After all, she knew they were probably right.

'Oh, look! He's here.'

Grace looked up to see where Ivy was pointing, and saw Alex standing in the foyer outside the common room.

'Quickly, Grace. Go to him, before he gets swamped by the other girls.'

At nearly seven months pregnant, nothing happened quickly. Grace put her hand on the back of her chair and pulled herself up. She didn't know if she was glad or anxious to see Alex. She felt something, and it made her stomach churn and her heart hammer.

'Hello, Grace.' Alex stepped towards her the moment he saw her coming. 'Merry Christmas.' He leaned in and gave her a quick kiss on the cheek.

'Thank you, Alex. Merry Christmas to you too.'

They stood awkwardly for a few moments before Ivy came over to them. 'Why don't you go into the sitting room and have a cup of tea.'

Grace turned and led the way further down the hall to another room on the right. She found that there was a tea tray already there, with a teapot covered in a cosy.

'Would you like tea?' she asked Alex.

'Yes, please.'

Grace noticed that he seemed ill at ease. She felt ill at ease too. Their past together had been so short and so chequered that it was hard to figure out how they should relate to one another. She poured the tea and brought the cup and saucer over to him.

'Milk and sugar?' she asked as she handed it to him.

Alex nodded, and she brought the sugar bowl and milk jug to him.

They sat down with their cups and after another couple of awkward minutes, Alex spoke.

'She has finally agreed.'

'Who?' Grace asked, though she thought she probably already knew.

'Norma. She's going to let us go.'

'You make it sound like she's held you prisoner.'

'She has ... held us prisoner, I mean. If not physically, at least on so many other levels.'

'Poor Norma.'

'Do you feel sorry for her?'

'I can't help it, Alex. Look what we've done to her.'

Alex turned his attention to his cup and took several sips.

'I didn't come here to talk about Norma,' he said.

Grace took a breath and managed to hold his gaze without turning away, though she found it difficult.

'We have to wait until all the paperwork has been brought before a court, and then the divorce will be filed. Then I plan to come back and ask you to marry me.'

Grace wanted to feel overwhelmed with happiness, but her guilt was so strong it seemed to dampen those feelings.

'Will you say yes?'

Grace thought she heard uncertainty in his voice. 'I don't know.'

Alex's face paled, and a frown furrowed his brow.

'You can't look after the baby on your own,' he said. 'I want to take my place as his father. I want us to be together, at least for his sake.'

Grace nodded.

'I know how I treated you in the beginning was horrible, but you know why I did it.'

'Yes, I know. I understand, Alex. Perhaps if you had kept your awful personality up, we might not be in this fix, but you let your guard down, and now I've seen someone entirely different.'

'Do you think you could grow to love me?'

'I think I love you now,' Grace said. 'It's just that I can't seem to shake this awful guilt for what we've done, and I'm worried that by marrying we are going against God again.'

Alex put his cup and saucer on the nearby table and turned back to her. 'What about our baby?' he asked. 'I can't—I won't—throw him out to fend for himself when we can come together and love him as a family.'

The baby chose that moment to make what felt like some monstrous movements, and Grace laid her hand over the protruding bump he'd caused. She was surprised when Alex placed his large, work-worn hand over the top of hers, and the baby moved again. Was it a response?

'He knows I'm here,' Alex said. 'Don't you, little mate?'

'You keep talking about him as if you know it's a he.'

'I guess I'm imagining him as a he. A brother for Jimmy.'

'What sex was your little one who died?'

Alex took a deep breath. Grace saw pain in his eyes.

'It was another little girl. I named her after Nancy's mother, though she was stillborn. She's buried with her mother.'

'I'm sorry, Alex. That must still be painful for you.'

'It's been seven years since they both passed. I guess the pain isn't as hard to bear as it used to be.'

The baby moved again, so vigorously that both Grace and Alex laughed.

'This is about him,' Alex said. 'He doesn't want us to get distracted.'

'I'm sorry Alex, but just having you this close and touching me is quite distracting, and we aren't married.'

Alex removed his hand.

'Then you do feel something for me?'

'I would have thought that night of refuge in the roof might have given you a clue.'

'Yes, but that was the heat of the moment. Are you willing to forgive me for crossing the boundaries?'

'We have to forgive each other, I think.'

'Can you do it?'

'I'm trying. I find forgiving you is easier than forgiving myself.'

'Because you're still worried about Norma?'

'I've already fallen once, and now you're about to ask me to commit myself to you—a divorcee, when your wife is still alive.'

Alex pursed his lips and didn't say anything else on that subject.

'I'll leave you to think about it, Grace, but I will return, just as soon as I have the official and legal right to do so. I hope we can find a happy solution.'

She nodded.

'Is that all right?' he said. 'How do you feel about it?'

'Don't ask me how I feel about it. If I went with how I felt, we'd really be in trouble.'

Alex held her gaze.

'You mean ...'

'Don't ask me.' Grace cut him off. 'Leave me to think about it, Alex.'

Alex stood up, and held out his hand to help her up. Without saying anything else, he kissed two of his fingers and pressed them against her abdomen, and then again, and pressed them against her cheek. Then he walked out of the sitting room.

Don't ask me how I feel, Alex. I want you, but I'm not sure I can have you.

Chapter Sixteen

Meg noticed Charlie was short tempered during the evening meal. They were sitting at the dining table at Wallace Hill, sharing family time with his parents. Charlie had scolded the children several times for nonsense issues, and she wanted to scold him. She knew why he was tense, but that didn't give him the right to take out his worry on the rest of the family.

Thankfully, they managed to finish their dessert without him going too far, and she was grateful when he hurried the children into the next room to play.

'What's the matter, Charlie?' Emily Shore asked. Meg might have known his mother would pick up on his agitation.

'We need to talk to you about something serious,' he said. 'Could we go to the study, to make sure the children don't overhear?'

'Are you intending to start an argument with your father?' she asked.

Charlie didn't answer his mother, but got up from the table and moved out into the hallway. Meg got up as well and followed. She took a deep breath for courage. She knew exactly what the subject was, and she had a fair idea how Charlie's parents would respond.

'What's eating you, Charlie?' Colin Shore asked straight out.

'I've a letter here from Alex Moreland.'

'Oh, how is he?' Emily Shore sounded genuinely interested.

'I think you should both read it.'

Meg sensed the anxious tension rise.

'Why don't you just tell them instead of drawing it out like this?'

'Tell us what?' Colin asked.

Charlie looked at Meg and raised his eyebrows as he nodded his head—his signal for her to speak.

'When we took Grace with us on our trip to South Australia, the business we needed to attend to was about Grace.'

'What do you mean?' Emily asked.

'Grace was four months pregnant, and we needed to help her sort the problem out without the whole of Green Valley knowing about it.'

'What in heaven's name are you talking about?' Predictably, Colin exploded. 'How could she be pregnant?'

'Alex Moreland?' Emily asked, her face going pale. 'I thought there was some emotional connection between them, and hoped that Grace had finally found someone, but I didn't think they would ever …'

'Well, if he's gone and violated her, why hasn't he had the decency to ask my permission to marry her?' Colin's temper was aroused.

'He was already married, Dad,' Charlie said, 'and it's no use you huffing and puffing about it now. The damage has already been done.'

'Married!' Emily said. 'He told us his wife had died.'

'The children's mother died, yes. This was his second wife.'

'God forbid.'

'Dad!' Charlie frowned at his father.

'So when you told us she was staying with some people in Adelaide …?'

'She is in the Methodist Babies Home there.'

'Thunder and turf!'

'Dad!' Charlie complained again. 'Is this really helping?'

'Didn't I have enough trouble with you and your floozie wife?'

'Col!' Emily tried to intervene.

'There's no need to be dredging up the past,' Charlie said. 'I thought we'd moved beyond all that.'

'And here you are, telling me my daughter is pregnant to a married man, and that you kept that information from me.'

'Why did you need to know? What could you have done?'

'I could have shot that Moreland fellow, for a start.'

'Col!'

Meg took a deep breath. Charlie and his father were a pair of hot-headed fellows.

'That's enough.' She raised her voice with authority and stood between them, giving one, then the other, her best mother's stare. 'Your wounded pride is not going to help the situation. You need to calm down and listen for a while.'

Charlie was used to her standing up to *him* and making him see sense. His father … not as much.

'Mr Moreland has …'

'Mr Moreland has a nerve doing anything at all,' Col cut her off.

'Dad, just be quiet, will you, and listen.'

Meg took another breath.

'Mr Moreland proposes to marry Grace before the baby is born, and then he is asking if he may bring her back here, with the whole family, as his people in South Australia aren't happy with the situation as it stands.'

'And he thinks we will be?'

'Col!' Emily kept up her efforts trying to keep her husband in check.

'Well, what does he think? Our friends and neighbours can count, Emily. It won't be hard for them to figure out they're bringing back an illegitimate child. And besides, what does he propose to do with his current wife?'

'They have filed for divorce.'

'Oh, dear.' This time it was Emily who seemed dismayed. 'What a disgrace.'

'Mum, for pity's sake, if you hadn't worked through this sort of thing before with me and Janielle, and hadn't accepted Aimee, I would be tempted to think this is a lost cause.'

'But divorce, Charlie.'

'Adultery, divorce, gossip, pride …'

'Don't be bringing this back to our doorstep,' Col said.

'If the cap fits…'

'I've a right to my self-respect and pride, and I have a reputation.'

'And all of that is more important than your grandchild?' Meg asked.

'Moreland's by-blow is no grandchild of mine.'

'But he is, Dad, don't you see?' Meg stepped up again. 'This poor little soul has done nothing wrong, and you have already rejected it as if it is something distasteful.'

'Because it is a bastard.'

'Col!'

'Dad!'

'What about Grace? What about how she's feeling at the moment.' Meg pressed on.

'Well, how could she have let Moreland get to her? I thought he was all against women.'

'Did he force her?' Emily sounded horrified that this might be the case.

'No, it was a mutual thing. Grace was adamant about that.'

'When did this happen?' Emily asked.

'During the flood, while they were trapped in the roof of the house together for a few days.'

Colin had gone quiet. Meg supposed he was imagining how such a situation could foster such an outcome. She certainly could.

'Anyway, I'm going to leave the letter with you to read, once you've had a chance to think about it, and then you will understand all the circumstances surrounding the situation.'

Meg placed a thick envelope on the desk. In fact, Alex had written eight double-sided pages, and in it he had begged for forgiveness and hoped for understanding. Meg also hoped that her parents-in-law would help their daughter and grandchild, and not reject them out of misplaced anger.

***

Grace was feeling uncomfortable. She wasn't sleeping well—mostly because she couldn't find a comfortable position to lie in—but then her mind would go over and over the particulars of her situation, and anxiety would make sure that sleep eluded her.

'Grace, you are looking really tired.'

Grace felt she had become quite close to Ivy, and she appreciated her concern.

'I'm not sleeping well.'

'It is more difficult as the baby takes up more room,' Ivy said.

'I worry all night. I'd say I tossed and turned, but the effort to turn is too hard, so I just lie in one position and worry.'

'Have you heard more from Alex?'

Grace shook her head. 'He said he won't come back until it is all officially done. It looks bad.'

Ivy gave a wry smile.

'That's a ridiculous thing to say, isn't it? It is bad. How can his coming here ever look good?'

'Perhaps it will all end well.' Ivy tried to encourage her.

'I'm still not sure.'

'Are you afraid that Alex will back out and abandon you?'

Grace frowned. 'No. He's the one who is sure. It's me. I'm not sure.'

'About what?'

'About what the best thing to do is.'

'I don't understand.'

'Even if I agree to marry Alex, his family and community will know, and my family and community will know.'

'Know what?'

'That we had an affair, and this baby was conceived out of wedlock.'

'And?'

'I'm not sure it would be better for all involved if that was kept secret.'

'The only way to keep it secret is to give the baby up for adoption.'

'I know.'

'Grace, do you understand what you're saying?'

'Ivy, I don't think you understand. My parents have a reputation to protect.'

Ivy didn't respond but held her gaze, a look of consternation fixed firmly on her brow.

'Not only will they have to bear the disgrace of having an illegitimate grandchild, then I'm proposing to bring a divorcee into the family.'

Ivy still didn't say anything.

'Can't you see how dreadful that will be for my family?'

Grace could feel herself getting worked up, and now she'd vented the depths of her worry, she wanted Ivy to respond—to tell her she understood. She waited, but Ivy didn't say anything, and eventually left her room. Grace was agitated, even a little angry. It had taken her a long time to work up enough courage to share her worries, and now Ivy had just walked away.

It was another whole day before she saw Ivy again, and by this time Grace was struggling with resentment at having been left mid-conversation. She was determined she wouldn't bring the subject up again.

'I need to apologise for walking out on you yesterday,' Ivy said, after she'd finished examining Grace. 'I needed to think carefully about how I should respond.'

Grace nodded, still guarded and not sure she would open up again.

'I don't have a lot of time now, but I need to tell you some things about my background that may help you put things into perspective. Can I meet you for afternoon tea after my shift finishes?'

Grace was not a vindictive soul, despite the fact that she felt vulnerable and exposed. 'Yes, all right.'

Ivy gave her a warm smile and left her to the hand-sewing piled next to her.

***

'I came to work here because this is where I came from.' This was Ivy's opening statement when she and Grace sat down together with tea.

'You were born here?' Grace asked.

'No. This place didn't exist then, but the situation did. I was left at an orphanage when I was a tiny baby.'

Grace felt a stab of guilt.

'I don't know who my mother was, or why she felt she had to abandon me. Sometimes I watch the different girls who come through here and try to imagine if that was who my mother was.'

'I'm sorry, Ivy,' Grace said.

'I was bought up in the orphanage until I was eleven. Then a family adopted me.'

'Were you happy? Was it a good family?'

Ivy gave a sharp laugh and shook her head.

'They didn't want me for a child—they already had six small children. They wanted a handmaid they didn't have to pay.'

Grace felt a lump of emotional tension form in the pit of her stomach.

'They barely tolerated me. They snapped orders at me often enough, and if something went wrong with one of their children, they would often blame me. I took a number of beatings because of something one of their children had done.'

'I'm sorry,' Grace said.

'And they made sure I knew I was a bastard child. I never got anything new. I never got a birthday or Christmas gift, and was never invited to any parties their children attended. When I was fourteen I left and got a job in a shoemaking factory.'

'Fourteen! Who looked after you?'

'I looked after myself. And I educated myself. When I was confident enough, I came to this place and began to volunteer. Eventually one of the older matrons offered to apprentice me as a nurse. I've been here ever since.'

Grace felt tears running down her face. Her heart ached for Ivy, and she knew that Ivy's story could likely become her child's story too. There was no guarantee that a good and loving family would take the baby. Once she let him go, it would be left to chance.

'I'm sorry to be so judgemental towards you,' Ivy said, 'but when you talk about your family's reputation as a reason to abandon your baby, I just can't understand how that could be more important. I would have given anything for just one parent to love me.'

Now Ivy had tears running down her face too, and Grace felt awful. She leaned toward her and took her hand.

'I feel so ashamed, Ivy. I'm so sorry to have shown you my selfishness, when you've always shown me nothing but kindness and concern.'

Ivy squeezed her hand back, and then took a handkerchief to her nose. 'I don't think I've ever told anyone that story, Grace. It's just that I couldn't bear to see you turn your back on the opportunity Alex is offering you, not for your sake, but for your baby's. All I could think was: what if that had been my mother's situation. If only someone had done the same for her. For me.'

Chapter Seventeen

'It's official,' Alex said to Matthew outside the church, following the morning service.

'Do you want to talk about it?' Matthew asked.

'When you have time, yes, if you don't mind.'

'This afternoon.'

Alex only had Sunday afternoon free, so was glad that Matthew had time for him then. Every other day he worked at one job or another. He was not only trying to provide for his children, but trying to save up enough money to get them all back to Green Valley, including Grace and the new baby. He hadn't heard back from Grace's parents, but Charlie had dropped him a line and let him know they knew. That hadn't sounded terribly promising, but Alex was willing to gamble that his chances of acceptance were better there than they were in his current position. Doris Johnson had become cold and distant towards him. Samuel's anger was obvious, and only worsened the more people gossiped. Norma had allowed people to know that she was divorcing him for his unfaithfulness. Alex wanted to get away from the small community as soon as possible.

'So, what now?' Matthew asked the moment they sat down in his study.

'Can you organise the notice of intention to marry?' Alex asked.

Matthew nodded. 'The sooner the better, I'm assuming. When is the baby due?'

'According to my calculations, in about three weeks.'

'I'll take the tram into the city tomorrow and see if the office of Births, Deaths and Marriages can hurry the paperwork along.'

'Thanks, mate.'

'How are you coping, Alex?'

'I just do what I have to do. I know everyone is talking about me, and I know there is speculation as to my having a mistress. Doris and Samuel are taking it hard.'

'I'm sorry, mate. It's the price you pay.'

'Yeah. I'm worried about the kids too. I'm worried about what they will hear, and how people will treat them.'

'We talked about all this before. It's a storm you're going to have to weather. In the long run, the other option just wasn't tenable for any of your children, especially not Grace's baby.'

'I think the thing I struggle with the most is that the children are the ones who suffer for something I did. God forgives me—so you tell me—but people don't, and they seem to feel it's their right to make my children pay for my sin as well. I sometimes wonder if Christianity is just about judgement and making people pay, is it really worth the effort to believe at all?'

'God's work through Jesus Christ was about forgiveness of sin, and restoration of sinners back to fellowship with Him. You can accept that for yourself because you know you've sinned. You're willing to admit you've done wrong, and laid it before Him. Where the rest of the Christian community often falls foul is they don't see they have ever done anything wrong. They sit in their decent homes, with their respectable families and preen their feathers about how good they are. They don't even realise they have also been saved from sin by the same grace of God. Self-righteousness, pride and gossip are the acceptable sins of the church.'

'You think it's acceptable to gossip?'

'No. What I mean is, Christians don't seem to rate gossip and pride as serious sins. They're kidding themselves.'

'Sit in my position, and I'll tell you how devastating gossip is. It's killing me.'

'I know, mate. We're just going to have to ride it.'

Alex didn't have the courage to hope for much at the moment, so he just nodded.

'Hopefully the paperwork can be released in a week. Then you can take care of your baby's legitimacy. That will be one worry off your mind.'

Alex nodded again. The list of worries on his mind was so long that even this one step didn't rate much.

Chapter Eighteen

Grace was restless and uncomfortable. She knew that she was not due to deliver for another ten days or so, but she wished that she could get on with it right now. Her ankles were swollen with the heat of late summer; her stomach distended to what she felt must be the absolute limit. She fought to find another position where she could sit and continue with the sewing she had by her side. Finally, she found a spot she felt was bearable. Still, she worried as she took up her needlework. Alex hadn't returned. Once or twice she was tempted to believe that he had given up on her, but then she remembered that Alex had insisted he would take responsibility. He had his name and address listed in the paperwork.

As if thinking about him had conjured him up, Alex appeared at the door of the common room. Grace smiled automatically. She couldn't help her response, despite the fact that she still told herself that she should act sombre and contrite. She knew she had come to love him, in spite of every objection. However, when she saw his downcast expression, a fear gripped her heart. She pulled herself forward with great effort and began to lever herself out of the chair.

'Don't get up, Grace,' Alex said, coming across the room.

Grace was already standing by the time he'd reached her. She wished she could hold out her hands to him, or lean into his embrace, or even just receive a kiss—but none of these things seemed appropriate. There was also the strange sadness that hung over him.

'Are you all right?' she asked. 'Has something gone wrong?'

Alex gave a smile that didn't reach his eyes. 'Everything has gone wrong,' he said. 'I'm still waiting for the day when something will go right.'

Grace wanted to ask about his freedom to marry, but she was afraid it was going to be bad news, and didn't have the courage.

'Can we go somewhere a little more private?' Alex asked.

'We can sit in the rose garden under the tree, if you'd like some fresh air.'

Alex nodded and held out his arm for her to take.

'How are you feeling?' he asked, as they walked outside.

'Ready to burst.'

'You look about ready,' Alex said.

Grace frowned at him.

'I'm sorry,' he said. 'That's not a nice thing to say to a lady, especially when I'm hoping she will accept a marriage proposal.'

'You're going to propose?' Grace asked, releasing a sigh of relief.

'I said I'd come back when I was free to do so. I'm here.'

'You don't look very happy.'

'I know. I'm sorry. It's not you.'

'What's the matter?' Grace slid her hand down his arm and covered his hand with hers.

'My in-laws, my children, the community gossip vine, my ex-wife, your parents. Everything is wrong. No matter which way I turn, it seems I'm the villain, and I have nothing to defend myself with.'

Grace took his hand and placed it on her swollen abdomen.

'Here,' she said. 'Turn your attention here. This little person is thrilled to know that his daddy loves him enough to sacrifice everything.'

'So you're going to accept,' Alex said, capturing her gaze.

'For the sake of this child, yes, I will accept.'

Alex looked down where his hand lay. Grace could tell he was still in low spirits.

'What about for your sake, or mine?' he asked quietly.

Grace was still for a few moments. This was the question she still couldn't answer.

'Grace, I need to know. I've gone into a marriage before without fully understanding what it means. I need to know exactly what I should expect from you.'

'I will look after you and all your children with all my heart and soul. I love you all …'

'But?'

'But I still struggle with it all. I'm worried I'm doing the wrong thing by you.'

'I don't mean to be contentious,' Alex said, 'but isn't it too late? Is this just to punish me some more?'

'Punish you? No! Why would I want to punish you?'

'Is it to punish you, then? Can't you accept forgiveness and move on?'

'Alex, I'm not sure I can explain it. I guess you're right. I do feel guilty, still.'

'Will you ever be able to let it go? For the baby's sake at least.'

'I hope so.'

'So do I. I know I don't deserve much, but I hope to build a home full of peace, if not full of love.'

Grace nodded at the statement, but was suddenly alarmed as she felt a gushing of water come away from between her legs.

'Oh no!'

'What is it?'

'Oh, dear. I think my waters have broken.'

Alex stood up and looked at her. Grace felt self-conscious under his gaze.

'Yes, that's what it looks like,' he said, matter-of-fact.

'I haven't done this before. I think it means the baby is coming early.'

'Yes. That's what it means. This is the point I usually exit and leave the doctoring to professionals.'

'I keep forgetting that you've done this before.'

'I'll get one of the nursing staff,' Alex said, 'and then I'll call Matthew Decker.'

'Why?' Grace asked.

'To marry us before the baby is born.'

Alex had waited out four births in his life so far. He had always felt a level of anxiety, but this time it was far worse. When his last daughter had been born, he had lost both his wife and the baby. He knew the doctor had been worried about complications in Nancy's last pregnancy—and he knew this time the nursing staff had reassured him that Grace and the baby were fine—but he couldn't help but feel anxious.

'You're doing a fine impersonation of a nervous father pacing the floor,' Matthew Decker said as he walked into the foyer of the babies' home.

'I'm worried on so many different levels, I can't even begin to explain it.'

'Yes, well, first things first. You need to be the waiting husband, and there are some formalities that need to be conducted before we can pronounce that title over you. Has she begun labour yet?'

'The waters broke about three hours ago. There was no pain at that stage. You sure took your time getting here.'

'I wasn't sitting by the phone waiting for your call, you know.'

'I'll speak to the matron and see if it is possible.'

Alex left his friend in the foyer and walked directly toward the delivery ward area. He was glad when he found Ivy. She had always been a friend to Grace.

'Is the minister here yet?' Ivy asked.

Alex nodded.

'Well, don't just stand around. We don't have forever.'

Alex returned to fetch his friend, and the pair of them were ushered into a delivery room.

'Have you ever been inside a delivery room before?' Matthew asked.

'Not likely. This will be a first and last time, I hope.'

'Grace, your groom has brought the minister,' Ivy said. 'Are you ready?'

Grace was propped up on a bed, dressed in a white hospital gown. She looked surprisingly well, and Alex couldn't help but feel that she was glowing. That was until he saw a shadow of pain cross her features. He could tell the labour had begun, even if she wasn't admitting it.

'Alex, you can stand next to your bride, and hold hands with her. We'll do the short version today, if that's all right with you.' Matthew gave the direction and opened his prayer book, ready to proceed.

Alex moved across to Grace's side and took her hand in his, lacing his fingers with hers. He had only just got into position when he felt his hand being squeezed, but by its intensity, he knew it was not as a communication of affection. He studied her face and saw that she was obviously in the grip of another contraction.

'You're in labour, aren't you?' Alex asked.

Grace didn't reply immediately, as she was holding her breath.

'You need to breathe through the pain,' Ivy said, coming around to her other side. 'If this is too much, we can send the men away, and do the wedding after.'

'No,' Grace forced out between clenched teeth. 'I want to be married when the baby appears.'

'All right then. Hurry it along, please, Reverend Decker,' Ivy said.

Alex hardly knew what was being said as Matthew began to read the wedding service. If he was reading the short version, it didn't seem to be very quick. He didn't count, but in the time it took him to reach the part where he was to respond with "I will" Grace had nearly wrenched his fingers from his hand several times.

'Grace Shore, will you take this man, Alexander Moreland, to be your husband? Will you love him, honour him, and keep faithful to him, for better or worse, through sickness and in health, for richer or poorer, until you are parted by death?'

The small group of witnesses waited while Grace held her breath through another contraction.

'Breathe, Grace,' Ivy whispered.

Finally, she let out a breath. 'I will,' she said with extreme force. 'Get me the paper to sign, will you. For mercy's sake.'

'Now that's what I call enthusiasm,' Matthew said, smiling as he fetched the official records book.

Alex glared at his friend. 'Who wants to sign first?' Matthew asked.

'I will,' Grace said. 'Quickly, before another pain comes.'

But he hadn't got the book in front of her before she contorted again, this time allowing a low moan to accompany the death-like grip.

Matthew waited with the pen in hand until the pain subsided. Grace all but snatched it from him.

'Where?'

Matthew pointed out the two places where she should put her signature. She managed to get it filled in, then she threw the pen at Alex.

'Hurry up and sign,' she said, and then another contraction had her.

'All right gentlemen, I think that's enough.' The matron who had been in the room stepped forward and ushered them out. 'We will call you later, once Mrs Moreland has delivered.'

'Mrs Moreland,' Alex said as he walked away from the room. 'At least the staff recognise that it is a legal marriage.'

'Actually, not quite. I'll need to get their signatures as witnesses, but other than that, I think it will pass.'

Alex went with Matthew outside to the rose garden. His head was spinning with the intensity of it all. Doris Johnson had never allowed him to stay that long into Nancy's deliveries. He'd been ushered away very quickly, and had only to reappear once the storm had passed. Nancy had told him that giving birth was an excruciating ordeal, but he hadn't realised just how much pain was involved. The realisation rocked him quite a bit.

'She sure was feisty,' Matthew said.

'She was in pain.'

'Mmm. Imagine what it would be like if they ever decided that fathers had to stay for the duration of the birth.'

Alex gave Matthew a direct look. 'I think the birth rate would go down. No one likes to see that much suffering, especially knowing they are the cause of it.'

'So no more children for you then?'

'I will have four. I think that might be enough.'

'What if Grace wants more than just the one?'

Alex gave a sad smile.

'I don't think we'll be having any more. She has married me for the sake of the baby. I don't think she has married me for me.'

Matthew raised his eyebrows.

'She still feels guilty about Norma,' Alex said. 'She can't seem to let go of the fact that she has stolen her husband.'

'Time will change that, I think.'

'You think?'

'I probably shouldn't say anything, but Norma has another fellow.'

'So soon?' Alex turned to look at his friend, eyes wide.

'She has been seeing him for quite a while, over a year.'

'How do you know?'

'I just do. It was told to me in confidence by the man's worried mother.'

'And you didn't tell me.'

'It was a confidence.'

'You just broke it now. Why couldn't you have done so before?'

'Alex, that's beside the point. I'm just telling you, Norma isn't pining for her lost marriage. She isn't the broken-hearted victim Grace thinks she is.'

'But that is the point. Grace thinks she is, and she also thinks that she is going against God by marrying me.'

'But she just married you.'

'The needs of the baby have taken a higher priority. She couldn't give him away.'

'I think you have needs too, as does she, and she will eventually see that.'

'I don't have your confidence.'

'Alex, you and she are obviously physically attracted to each other, or we wouldn't be sitting here having this conversation. As time goes on, and you settle in as a family, I believe she'll forget about the past and take hold of the future.'

'Right at this moment, I'll be glad if I can see the baby safely delivered, and the name properly registered.'

'And Grace?'

'And Grace come through hale and healthy. I need to get her back to her home and people.'

'You are her people now, Alex,' Matthew said, waving the marriage certificate in his hand. 'Don't forget that.'

***

Grace had accompanied her mother to attend Meg on two out of her three births. She knew giving birth was intense, but it was one thing to observe and another to go through it. Now she knew what every mother in her family had experienced. Pain, and lots of it. But the tightly-wrapped baby who was placed in her arms acted like an anaesthetic. Now the little girl was here, she couldn't imagine what terrible agony she would have had to endure if they'd taken her away without even being able to see her. She clung tightly to the baby, kissed her soft head and whispered to her.

'I'm sorry, my darling, sorry I ever considered giving you away.'

'Are you ready to see your husband now?' Ivy asked. 'He's been pacing around like a caged lion these last hours.'

'I expect you're used to that,' Grace said.

'No, not usually. Most girls who deliver do so without a father anywhere near.'

'I'm sorry,' Grace said. 'I keep forgetting where I am.'

'You don't know how pleased I am that he is here, and that he's desperate to see you both. It does my heart good.'

Grace smiled at the nurse. 'Thank you, Ivy. Thank you for being so understanding and supportive.'

Ivy just smiled. 'I'll get him then?'

Grace nodded. Her heart began to thump wildly. She had been very short and snappy when they'd conducted the wedding, but they had conducted it. Alex was now her husband, and she could hardly let

172

herself believe it. He was there to take care of them both, and for the first time in many months she allowed a small prayer of thanks to God.

'Grace?' Alex sounded tentative as he put his head around the door. 'Is it all right to come in?'

Grace smiled at him. 'Thank you for being here, Alex. Thank you for fighting for us.'

She felt tears overflow her eyes, and saw that he also was fighting emotion.

'It's a girl,' he eventually said.

'You sound surprised.'

'I was so sure that this time Jimmy would have his brother.'

'I hope you're not too disappointed.'

Alex moved close to the bed. 'May I?' He held out his arms.

Grace didn't have any qualms about passing the baby over to him. She knew he was confident with children. Seeing the love in his face as he studied his daughter's face made her feel warm with emotion.

'She's beautiful, Grace. What will you call her?'

'What will we call her?' Grace said. 'We are in this together, aren't we?'

Alex nodded. 'I just thought, that since I got to the party late …'

'You were there at the beginning. We will name her together.'

***

Alex was in love. For the time being at least, all he could think was how precious his newborn daughter was, and how beautiful her mother was. That there were so many other problems yet to deal with didn't have an audience in his mind today.

He was drawn back to the present when there was a knock on the door of the room. He stood up with the baby in his arms to open the door.

'Is it all right if I pop in and offer my congratulations?' Matthew Decker asked.

'Please come in,' Grace said. 'I want to apologise for my shortness during the wedding.'

'Yes, brides are usually less stressed when they take their vows.'

Alex felt himself smile with genuine amusement for the first time in a long time. He really appreciated his friend, the padre.

'Which brings me to a crucial point,' Matthew said.

'Did you get the nurses to sign as witnesses?' Alex asked.

'Yes. The paperwork is all legal and accounted for. It's just that I didn't get to pronounce you man and wife.'

Grace smiled. 'I don't really think I was in the mood for it at the time,' she said.

'How about now?' Matthew indicated that Alex should take his place next to Grace. 'Let me hold the baby while we finish the formalities.'

Alex grinned as he passed his daughter to his friend.

'I now pronounce you man and wife.' Matthew looked very pleased with himself. Alex took Grace's hand in his again, and this time when she squeezed it, he knew she meant it to be affectionate.

'You must now kiss the bride.'

'Must?' Alex said.

'It's part of the ceremony. Not negotiable.'

'You think so?'

'I know so.' Matthew nodded with raised eyebrows as if he expected them to follow his directive. 'Don't be missing the opportunity while you have someone to hold the baby.'

Alex felt a wave of happiness smother all other worries and concerns. 'You heard the minister,' he said to Grace. 'It's a non-negotiable part of the ceremony.'

'You do a lot of talking and not much action.'

With that challenge he took her face in his hands and kissed her. It might only be temporary, but at that moment he was breathless and overcome with joy.

'There you are my little angel,' he heard Matthew say. 'Your mother and father are safely married, and I would hazard a guess they are well on their way to being truly in love. You will be in good hands.'

Alex took a few extra moments to search his new wife's face. She smiled warmly at him, and he couldn't resist stealing another quick kiss. 'I love you,' he whispered, for her ears only.

'Well then,' Matthew interrupted the exchange. 'My work here is done. All I need to know is what you have named this darling child.'

'Margaret Emily,' Grace said.

'Family name?' Matthew asked.

'My mother was Margaret,' Alex said, 'and also our sister-in-law who has been so supportive.'

'And my mother is Emily,' Grace said.

'Perfect. I will be on my way now, as I know Rosie will want to know all the details before she goes to bed.'

'Could you wait just a few minutes?' Alex asked. 'It would be great if I could hitch a ride back with you, but I'd like to say a proper goodbye.'

'I'll wait for you out the front.'

Matthew left them alone and Alex sat on the bed next to Grace. She had the baby back in her arms and she looked radiant.

'I wish you didn't have to leave,' she said.

'Me too, but I have to work tomorrow, and the whole week. I won't be able to come back until next Saturday.'

Grace looked forlorn.

'The matron told me they will probably discharge you after two weeks. I need to earn as much as I can for train fares back to Green Valley.'

'I know. Thank you, Alex. You're doing so much for me.'

'You're my wife, and I love you.'

Grace smiled. 'Do you think we can really make it work?'

'We can try. Will you try with me?'

Grace nodded.

'I shouldn't keep Matthew waiting. I had better go.'

'I'm missing you already.'

Alex leaned in and captured her lips in another full and passionate kiss. 'I *must* kiss the bride.'

'Be safe this week,' Grace said.

Chapter Nineteen

Alex had thrown himself into work. He was missing Grace, and that puzzled him, since they had never spent much time in each other's company before—other than the days they were stranded. He longed to tell his older children about their new sister, but he waited, knowing that it would create a storm in the Johnson's house. It was a conflict that was waiting to happen, and he didn't have any great hopes that it would turn out well. He needed to be ready to leave when he made the announcement.

On the Friday evening he asked Samuel and Doris if he might have a private word with them after he'd seen the children off to bed.

'Well?' Doris said, her lack of patience evident. 'What have you got to land on us now?'

'Tomorrow morning, I will be telling the children about their new sister and step-mother.'

Doris sat stony-faced. Samuel was more agitated.

'You know how we feel about this.'

'I do,' Alex replied.

'Then why can't you just leave it?'

'I have a wife and baby I need to bring home from the hospital.'

'You've married her, then?' Samuel said.

'I told you I was going to.'

'I don't want you bringing her here,' Doris said.

'Then I will need to pack the children up before I go to the hospital, and we will all be leaving.'

Doris gave a small cry of alarm.

177

'How can you be so cruel to them?' Samuel said.

'I'm not the one refusing them the right to see their sister and step-mother.'

'That is a patched-up affair, Alex. I wouldn't be surprised if you only managed to sign the marriage certificate just as the baby was being born.'

Alex didn't admit the truth of that statement.

'I told you before, and I'll say it again, I don't want my grandchildren being subjected to this kind of immorality.'

'They are my children, Samuel. You don't have a right to be making such demands.'

'It is our right to expect you to do what is best for them, for Nancy's sake,' Doris protested. 'She would be horrified to know what you are proposing.'

Alex felt the accusation hit home.

'Nancy would be horrified to know that you are putting your reputation above kindness for an innocent baby.'

'If you'd let the baby be adopted out, then there wouldn't be a problem, would there?'

'I'm not going to argue with you about this. I have made up my mind, and tomorrow I will be telling the children. Either you show a little charity, or I'll be taking all of them with me without further ado.'

'Why don't you just leave them with us?' Samuel said. 'Take your mistress and bastard child, and leave us alone.'

Alex felt fury rise in his chest. He wanted very much to vent his anger, but he knew that he was coming from a bad position.

'I will not leave them here,' he said in a low tone. 'You couldn't manage them four years ago, and you won't be able to manage them now.'

'Nonsense,' Doris said. 'Irene is quite capable of cooking and cleaning, and Jimmy pays his way in the store.'

'They are children,' Alex said. 'I'm not leaving them here to be your domestic servants. They will be going to school with other children their age, and receiving an education.'

'Pfft,' Doris said. 'Irene has all the book learning she needs. What she requires now is an education in the domestic arts.'

Alex let out a loud breath of frustration.

'Neither of you are listening to me. These are my children, my responsibility, and I will be making the decision. Tomorrow, they will learn about their sister and step-mother. If you wish for them to stay for a few more days, then that is up to you. However, if you are going to be difficult, I will take them tomorrow, and we will sleep in the park under the bridge until I have enough money to buy our fare back to Victoria. That is the end of this discussion.'

Alex left the room before he said something else that he knew he would regret.

***

'Dad, I can hardly believe that you married Miss Shore.' Irene made the statement to her father as they walked away from the tram stop. 'You were always so nasty to her.'

'Not always,' Alex said. 'Actually, I liked her a lot early on, but I couldn't let anyone know that because of Norma.'

'Grandma says what you have done is really bad.'

'How much has Grandma talked to you about the situation?'

'Not much. Just that divorce is a disgrace to the family, and that you should have gone back to Norma.'

'You know that I couldn't, don't you?'

'If you had gone back to her, Jimmy and I would have run away.'

'Is that what Jimmy told you?'

'He was terrified you would. So was I. I'm glad you haven't gone back.'

'Irene, divorce is an unhappy solution. I'm not proud of it, and wish above all else that I'd never married Norma in the first place. I was stupid to have done it, and I'm sorry for the pain it has caused you.'

Irene appeared to accept Alex's apology. They walked on in silence for a few more minutes.

'You might hear people say some other things about me and your new step-mother ...'

'Miss Shore?'

'Yes, but you can't call her that now. She is Mrs Moreland now, and that name doesn't seem right for you either.'

'What should we call her?'

'Perhaps you can discuss that with her later. Right now, I just want you to know there are other things that people might say about us, and if you hear anything, I want you to come and talk to us about it. Unfortunately, things started out on the wrong foot, and I haven't been able to make everything right.'

'But people will forgive you, won't they?'

Alex shrugged his shoulders.

'Is what you have done really *that* bad?'

'I would like to discuss it with you more, but not now, if you don't mind. We are here, and I want to introduce you to your new sister.'

Irene smiled. 'I can't believe we are going to have a new baby.'

'Are you happy about that?'

'Oh, yes. I hope Miss Shore will let me help her with everything.'

'I'm sure she will be more than happy to have your help. You might not remember from when Jeanie was a baby, but babies are a lot of work.'

'I can't wait. Thank you for letting me come with you to pick them up.'

Alex smiled. At least with Irene he had an ally.

***

'Are you packed and ready to go?' Ivy asked.

'I didn't bring much with me. I've been wearing the hospital maternity dresses,' Grace said.

'Reverend Decker dropped off a layette for the baby. It is a gift from the church ladies to you.'

Grace was stunned. She didn't doubt that Matthew and his wife would give such a gift, but from what Alex had told her, she doubted that any of the church ladies knew that their sewing and knitting was being put in a gift box for the likes of her.

'You will need every little thing in that box,' Ivy said. 'Don't be too proud to accept it.'

'Oh, I'm very grateful,' Grace said. 'I just wonder what the donors would say if they knew to whom the gift had gone.'

'Don't worry about it. You have enough challenges up ahead without borrowing trouble.'

Just at that moment, Alex walked into the foyer of the babies' home. He had Irene with him. Grace saw Irene smile at her the moment she saw her.

'Hello, Irene,' she said.

'Miss Shore. I am so excited to see you again, and you have a baby sister for me.'

'Yes, darling, I do. I hope you will love her, and I know she will love you as her big sister.'

'Where is she?' Irene asked.

'I'll just pop into the nursery and get her for you,' Ivy said, and walked away.

Grace looked up at Alex. She was still feeling shy about him. They hadn't really experienced a proper courtship, and her new status of wife left her feeling uncertain.

'How are you, Grace?' Alex asked.

'Very well, now you're here.' She hoped he would come close and kiss her, but he seemed tentative. She guessed that having Irene there made things awkward. Children didn't usually witness their parents' displays of affection.

'Irene and I have a problem for you to solve,' he said.

'Oh?'

'She doesn't know what name she should use for you now.'

'What name would you like to use?' Grace asked Irene.

'I'm kind of used to calling you Miss Shore,' Irene admitted, 'but Dad says that won't fit anymore.'

'Well, no, it won't.' She gave a smile to Alex. 'You may call me Grace if you like.'

'It's a bit informal,' Alex said.

'I believe the children used to refer to their previous stepmother by her first name.'

'What about calling her mother, or mum?' Alex suggested.

'Don't force them to, Alex,' Grace said. 'I know I'm not their real mother.'

'I wouldn't mind calling you mother,' Irene said. 'I used to call my real mother "Mum".'

'I'll leave it up to you,' Grace said. 'You talk it over with Jimmy and Jean, and whatever you decide will be all right by me.'

'Except not Miss Shore,' Alex said.

'No, not Miss Shore. Not any more.'

***

Alex felt pride and pleasure as he watched Irene hover over Grace and the baby like a mother hen. Grace engaged with her easily, and the two clucked over the baby. Grace was the right fit for the children. One day, he hoped, she would realise she was the right fit for him as well. First, he had many rivers to cross before they came to a place where they could settle. Taking a tram back into the city, and another one out to Mitcham, was only a minor challenge compared to what he knew they must endure before the day was out. He had enough money for the train fare for the entire family to travel back to Victoria, but the next train didn't leave until tomorrow. They were going to have to stay another night, but he didn't have money for a hotel as well as the train. He was already calculating how difficult it would be to camp the night under the bridge in the park with a newborn baby.

'Irene, could you run along and tell Jimmy and Jean to come out and meet us, please?' Alex asked.

Irene took a moment to kiss her sister on the forehead, smiled at Grace, and then took off up the road towards her grandparents' house.

'I need to warn you, the Johnsons have been very antagonistic about you and the baby,' Alex said.

Grace dropped her chin and let out a sigh.

'I don't expect that they will welcome you. In fact, I think we will be lucky if we get away with them not abusing you to your face.'

He watched Grace's face for a response. She looked miserable.

'I'm sorry,' he said. 'I don't know what else to do.'

'Unfortunately, I expect we will receive the same reception when we get back home.'

'From your parents?' Alex asked. 'Surely not!'

'Meg wrote to me, and told me Dad was very upset. She hopes he will calm down and at least allow us to stay, but at this stage, he doesn't want to recognise the baby.'

'I'm sorry, Grace. You must feel awful.'

'I guess you feel pretty bad too.'

Alex gave a wry smile. 'There are degrees of awful. Today I don't feel so bad, especially having the two of you with me.'

'That might all change in a few minutes.'

Alex nodded.

The noise of chattering and laughing from up the road told him that the children were on their way to meet them. He at least hoped that with them, there would be acceptance and love.

Irene approached with confidence, and went straight to Grace. 'Here she is,' she said to her siblings. 'Our little sister, Margaret.'

'She's a beauty,' Jimmy said, following Irene's lead.

Alex noticed that Jean hung back, which was quite out of character for her.

'What's the matter, Jeanie?' he asked. 'Don't you want to see your new baby sister?'

Jean shook her head, and kicked a stone along the ground, as if she wasn't interested at all.

'Jeanie,' Alex injected a sternness into his tone. 'You need to say hello to Miss Shore … I mean, you need to say hello to your new step-mother.'

'I don't need a new step-mother, or silly baby either,' Jean said.

Alex was winding himself up to another level of firmness when Grace stepped in between them.

'Hello, Jean,' she said. 'I guess you are feeling a bit horrible, now that you're no longer the baby in the family.'

Jean didn't lift her sulking head, but kicked another stone.

'That's exactly how I felt when my mother had my baby brother, CJ. All of a sudden, nobody seemed interested in me anymore.'

Jean lifted her eyes and gave Grace a quick glance.

'And I know it must be hard having someone new step into the mother role in your family. I hope we can be friends—but I especially hope you can take your position as big sister soon. I know Margaret will need someone to teach her things, and to help keep her out of trouble.'

'Grandma says she isn't really my sister,' Jean said.

'Not your full sister, but she is your half-sister. Your daddy and her daddy is the same.'

'Grandma says that you're a bad person.'

'Jean,' Alex growled, but stopped when Grace held up her hand.

'Sometimes we make mistakes in life, but God forgives us. I hope you will forgive me too. I need your help very much.'

Jean appeared to accept the explanation and took a look at the baby.

'She hasn't got much hair,' she said.

'It will grow, as she gets bigger.'

'Can we call her Maggie?'

Grace looked up for Alex's response. He shrugged his shoulders.

'I guess so, if you like,' Grace said.

'Good. I'm hungry. Tea is nearly ready.'

Jean turned around and headed back along the footpath towards the Johnson's house. Irene and Jimmy followed.

'Jimmy,' Alex called after him, and waited for him to come back. 'Do you think Grandma and Grandpa will let us in the house?'

'They're pretty mad about it all. It would be better if you came and talked to them first.'

Alex looked to Grace. 'I'm sorry,' he said. 'There's a garden seat out the side of the house. Would you mind waiting there for a few minutes while I see how the land lies?'

Grace nodded. Alex could see by the slump of her shoulders that she felt discouraged. He took her bags in one hand, and her elbow in the other.

'One way or the other, we will get through this together.'

***

Grace sat on the seat in the garden. There was a beautiful view of the valley, leading down to the creek. The Johnsons' gardens were well kept with flowers in bloom, and trees laden with late summer fruit. She tried not to worry, but the fact that Alex had already taken so long indicated the Johnsons weren't waiting with open arms. She hadn't really expected they would be, although she had hoped. Margaret began to fuss, and Grace knew it was time for her feed. She felt her milk come down, and knew that she needed to find a private place to see to the task of nursing the baby. She got up from the garden bench and tried to placate the baby by putting her over her shoulder and rocking her up and down.

'Hush now, sweet thing. Your daddy is doing his best. We need to be patient.'

Margaret was not impressed by this information, and continued to wail in protest. Grace took to walking up and down the garden path, which seemed to quieten her a bit. As she passed under a shady oak tree, she saw an old carving, a heart shape with the letters AM L NJ. She knew what it meant and who had carved it. Here was a permanent memorial to Alex's young love. They had risked her parents' displeasure by carving their initials into the tree.

Grace felt a wave of sadness. Alex had told her how much he'd loved Nancy; how the promise of marrying her had kept his courage alive during the war. Now all he had left of her was the children and her parents. And right at this moment, she suspected that Nancy's parents were being as difficult as they had promised they would be. They wanted nothing to do with her, the mistress and the home-wrecker. Grace felt awful.

***

By the time Alex entered the dining room, all the children were seated ready to eat. Alex saw that no other place had been set. He felt a stab of hurt, not only for Grace's sake, but for his own. It was a clear statement of rejection.

'Well?' Doris said, in an icy tone. 'It's our tea time, Alex. It is not really convenient for you to be here now.'

Alex toyed with the idea of just leaving quietly, without any fuss, but he was hurt by what was presented before him.

'The children will be coming with me right now,' he said. 'I had hoped to stay for another night, but since you have no sense of decency or hospitality …'

'Decency? You are the fine one to talk!' Samuel said. 'I do not want this discussion here and now. If you don't mind.'

'I do mind, actually. Jimmy, Irene, Jean, please get up and go pack your clothes. We will be leaving directly.'

'Don't be ridiculous, Alex,' Doris said. 'It's their tea time. They need to eat.'

'So do I. So does my wife, and I know you'd like to pretend you can't hear it, but my baby, Margaret, is ready for her feed as well. Since we are not welcome here, and can't tend to our needs in this house, I will take the children, and we will find another place.'

Alex saw the three children nervously watch the tense exchange of words. They hadn't moved from their places at the table, and had not dared to take a bite to eat.

'Go and pack your things,' Alex said again.

'Stay where you are.' Doris glared at Irene first, then the others. 'You're not going anywhere.'

'But what about Dad and Mother and Maggie?' Irene asked, her large brown eyes begging for peace.

'Mother! How dare you?' Doris stared at Alex. 'How dare you allow your children to refer to that individual as their mother?'

'Please go and pack your things,' Alex said again, trying to inject more firmness in his tone.

Jimmy and Jean got up from their places and began to move out of the dining room, but Irene stood up and faced her grandparents. Suddenly Alex saw what Norma must have seen when Irene decided to take Jimmy's part in defence.

'I'm very disappointed in you,' Irene said. 'You are being nasty and cruel. It is not Maggie's fault. She is only a baby. And Mother has always been very kind to us, and loving too. I don't like the way you are behaving.'

'Don't you be impertinent, child,' Doris snapped. 'You have no business speaking out of turn.'

'This is my business. My poor little sister needs to eat, and Mother too.'

'All right, Irene.' Alex stepped in. 'You've said your piece. Go along and pack your things.'

Irene left the room, but Alex saw thunder in her expression. He knew he should scold her for speaking disrespectfully to her grandparents, but she had stood up for what was right. He was impressed, and realised she must have been an avenging angel when she took Norma to task. No wonder Norma had taken the whip to her. She would never have endured such insolence from a child. Alex was proud of her, but was sure he shouldn't be. Was this just another proof of his sinful character?

'I am truly sorry that we are not able to part on amicable terms,' Alex said instead. 'I am more sorry that the children have witnessed that act of meanness on your part. They have held you in great esteem, and this will be a huge disappointment to them.'

'You are responsible for this,' Samuel said. 'Don't you be laying blame at our door.'

'I am responsible for many things,' Alex said, 'but your lack of grace and kindness is not one of them.'

He waited for almost a minute, watching to see if they would relent, apologise, or say anything at all, but it was like a standoff. Meanwhile, he could hear Margaret wailing outside in the garden, and he knew he had no choice. It was time to leave and find somewhere for them all to stay the night.

Alex turned to leave the dining room, and headed towards the bedrooms where the children had been sleeping. 'Are you ready?' he asked.

'No, Dad. It's going to take longer than two minutes to find everything and get it all packed.' Alex couldn't be annoyed with Jimmy. What he said was the truth. He gave a huge sigh.

'Just stop what you're doing for a minute and listen.' Once he had their attention he went on. 'I'm sorry Grandma and Grandpa are so angry with me and Grace. I can't do anything to make them happy, unfortunately. You go back and eat your tea with them. I'll try to find somewhere for Grace and Margaret to rest for the night. Tomorrow morning, I'll come back, and hopefully by then, you will have all your things packed. Our train will leave tomorrow about eight o'clock. Be ready early.'

***

Grace knew Alex was upset, but that was only her second worry. Margaret was hungry and impatient. Alex had set a fast pace away from the Johnsons, and wasn't talking at this stage. She understood why he was upset. He didn't need to tell her.

After walking for about ten minutes, they came to the public park. There were benches there, and he guided her to one of them. Grace wanted to protest that she had no privacy to nurse the baby, but she knew that Alex was out of options. She sat down and balanced Margaret on her knee while she undid the buttons on her blouse. She knew that Alex was watching her, and she felt self-conscious, but Margaret's impatient crying urged her to continue. She was glad for the silence when the baby attached and began to hungrily draw the milk.

'That is the most beautiful thing I have ever seen,' Alex said.

Grace flushed.

'I'm sorry you're embarrassed by it. Nancy was never keen on me watching her nurse the children, either.'

'Then would you kindly find a nappy I may drape over my shoulder, so that I might retain some dignity.'

Alex rummaged through her bags and found a nappy. He unfolded it and carefully draped it over the feeding baby's head and the exposed breast.

'I still think it is beautiful,' Alex said, 'and you are beautiful.'

'Alexander Moreland, I do believe that sort of attitude was what got us into this fix in the first place.'

He smiled at her. 'Only we're married now. I have a licence.'

She smiled back. 'And you have no place to go, and all the world against us.'

'Not all the world,' he said. 'It's not too far to the manse. If you're all right for twenty minutes or so, I'll run up to Matthew's and see if they will offer us a place to rest for the night.'

Grace knew that the Deckers would be hospitable; she just hated to be left alone.

'You won't take too long, will you?' she asked. 'I'm alone in a strange town.'

'You're not alone. I'll be back in a jiffy.'

Chapter Twenty

Grace had only just finished buttoning her blouse when she noticed someone approaching. She was anxious for a moment, until she realised it was Jimmy.

'Miss Shore?' He was tentative as he approached.

'Is everything all right, Jimmy?' she asked.

'Where's my dad?'

'He went to see if we might stay with Reverend Decker.'

Jimmy cast his eyes in the direction his father would have taken.

'I would imagine he will be back fairly shortly,' Grace said. 'He said he'd only be about twenty minutes, and it is about that now.'

'Do you mind if I wait here for him?'

'I'd be relieved, actually,' Grace replied. 'I don't much like being left alone in a strange city on my own.'

Jimmy didn't sit down, but stood nearby, shuffling his feet. Grace wasn't sure what to say to him, so she went about laying a baby blanket on the grass and changing Margaret's nappy.

'I feel kind of funny about this being my sister,' Jimmy finally confessed.

'Yes, I guess that would only be natural. I'm sorry your Dad couldn't tell you about her earlier.'

'It's all been a major mess up, hasn't it?'

'I'm afraid so, Jimmy. Your dad and I made a mistake, but once it was done, we couldn't change the way it would turn out. Do you understand?'

'A bit. Dad hasn't talked to me about … that … yet, but I know some fellas at school talk about things, and ...'

'I think you need to ask your Dad about it,' Grace said, a bit flustered to be discussing a delicate subject with a teenage boy.

'I'm not sure we're going to have the chance,' Jimmy said.

'Of course you'll have the chance. Once we get back to Green Valley, there will be plenty of time.'

'I don't think I am going to come with you.'

Grace was stunned by this announcement. Her stomach clenched with anxiety, just knowing how this would hurt Alex.

'All of you?' she asked in a small voice.

'No, just me. Grandma wants Irene to stay and look after her too, but Irene doesn't want to.'

Grace nodded.

'I know Dad is going to be disappointed,' Jimmy said. 'I sort of wish he could stay, as I will miss him and the girls, but ... well, Grandpa wants me to learn how to manage the store. I like working there, and one day I'll have to manage it. Uncle Frank can't really do it, you know.'

'I know,' Grace said. 'I understand.'

'Do you think Dad will understand?'

Grace paused for a moment. 'I think he will be a bit disappointed, Jimmy. He really loves you all. But I think he will understand, eventually.'

'Do you think he would stay?' Jimmy asked.

'We can't,' Grace said. 'Your grandparents won't accept us.'

Jimmy hung his head, and Grace felt the wave of guilt, all over again. If it weren't for her—if she and Margaret would just disappear—then the family could stay together and not be split up.

'I'm sorry,' she said. 'If I didn't have Margaret, I would just leave, but she needs her dad too.'

Jimmy nodded.

Just then, Grace looked up to see Alex walking across the grass toward them.

'Jimmy,' he called. 'Everything OK?'

Jimmy turned towards his father, shoved his hands in his pockets and waited for him to come close.

'Are you all right?' Alex asked.

'I need to talk to you,' Jimmy said.

'Are the girls all right?'

'Alex,' Grace interrupted. 'Jimmy needs to ask you about staying with his grandparents.' She couldn't bear to see the boy squirming with his fear of telling his father.

Alex turned his full attention on his son. 'Is this what you want?' Alex asked. 'What about going to school? What about your sisters?'

'I wish you could all just stay,' Jimmy said.

'You know we can't.'

Jimmy nodded.

'Grandpa says he will pay for me to go to Scotch College if I stay.'

'Scotch College?' Alex said. 'That is a very prestigious school, son. It costs a lot of money.'

'I know, I've seen the college boys around the store. They are always dressed fancy, and have loads of money to spend.'

'I gather you've been thinking about this for a long time. Are you sure it's what you want?'

'I want to stay, but I want to come with you too,' he said. 'I have to choose, and I'm not sure what is right. Grandpa seems to need me. It would mean one less mouth for you to feed.'

'Don't stay because of that, Jimmy. I'd prefer to have you with me, than the savings it might mean.'

'Are you angry with me for wanting to stay?'

Alex was quiet for a moment, and hung his head.

'Not angry,' he said, 'just disappointed. You're my son, and I want to do the best for you. But I know your grandpa has better opportunities for you than I can give.'

'If you really want me to, I will come with you tomorrow, but …'

'Can we think about it for a little while?' Alex said. 'Help me carry Grace's things over to the manse, and after we will talk about it some more. Is that all right?'

Jimmy nodded, and turned to pick up the suitcase.

***

Alex knew he had to see the Johnsons one last time. Now that he knew Jimmy was considering staying, he decided he'd have to see them tonight. Tomorrow morning would be too late. Once Grace and the baby were settled with Rosie Decker fussing over them, he felt at ease to walk back to the Johnson's with his son.

'Please don't be angry with them,' Jimmy said. 'They're just lonely for Mum.'

Alex nodded. 'I know. I'm lonely for her too, but I have you.'

'You have Grace now too.'

Alex smiled. He was glad that Jimmy had accepted the fact that Grace was now part of the family, even though he wasn't sure that it was just to take care of the baby.

'I like her,' Jimmy said. 'She's always been kind to us.'

'I'm glad you like her,' Alex replied. 'I kind of like her too.'

Alex saw Jimmy blush.

'You're fourteen, Jimmy,' Alex said. 'I guess I really should talk to you about girls, huh?'

'I've heard bits and pieces. And there's all the stuff that Grandma and Grandpa say. I don't like the way they say they won't forgive you. Is what you did so wrong?'

'I won't lie to you,' Alex said. 'It was wrong, and got Grace into terrible trouble.'

'But you're sorry, right?'

Alex was quiet for a minute. If this was his last opportunity to share with his son, he realised he'd better tell him some of the hard facts of life.

'Sooner or later, you will notice girls, Jimmy. And you'll probably be attracted to one or maybe more than one. The thing is, close intimacy with a woman is something God created for one man and one woman to share within marriage. When we fool around with that outside marriage, it will only lead to trouble.'

'Like with you and Grace.'

'You can see how it is. Grandma and Grandpa won't forgive us, and we're a little worried that her parents won't forgive us either.'

'But God forgives you, right?'

'So Reverend Decker says. It's just that even with forgiveness, there are still consequences that have to be sorted out.'

'Like Maggie.'

'Like Maggie. I love her, and want the very best for her, but sometimes people can be pretty mean, and might call her names.'

'Not now that you're married.'

'Hopefully not. Still, it has been a very difficult time for both Grace and me, but I can't blame anybody except myself.'

Jimmy nodded.

'Son, if this is the last thing you remember me saying: respect girls, and don't use them physically. Unless you are prepared to marry the one special girl, and look after her, keep your hands off, do you hear me?'

Jimmy blushed again.

'I'm sorry to be so frank, son, but this is very important, and I just want you to remember what Grace and I are going through at the moment.'

'OK, Dad. I'll remember.'

'Have you ever noticed girls?' Alex asked.

'Like Evie Shore?' Jimmy replied.

Alex smiled. He was his father's son. Evie Shore was a beauty, even at twelve years old. Alex was kind of glad that Jimmy had decided not to return to Green Valley. He was still too young for that sort of thing.

***

Alex was not sure what he hoped to achieve through this last interview. *Some sort of peace between us, perhaps?* But Doris and Samuel were not in a peacemaking mood.

'I don't want you taking the children away,' Doris said. 'I need Irene here.'

'I told you before, she is not staying to become a housemaid and nurse to an invalid. She isn't even thirteen years old yet. She will be coming with her family. Perhaps we can reconsider when she is older and can make her own choices.'

'You have lost the right to have a say in this,' Doris persisted.

'How?' Alex asked, exasperated.

'You know how, by your immorality.'

Alex shook his head. 'Look, I'm not going to argue about this again. Jimmy may stay on two conditions: firstly he will make the decision himself, not because you demand it, and if he ever changes his mind, I will pay for him to join us wherever we may be.'

'And your other condition?' Samuel asked.

'He will go to the ordinary state school at Mitcham. You can save the private school tuition fees and hire proper household help for your wife.'

'I don't see it's any of your business,' Samuel said.

'You are wanting to use my daughter to nurse her, and you are wanting to place my son in a school where he will be bullied mercilessly because his old man is a swagman. I won't have it, Samuel. Those are my conditions, and if you're not prepared to agree to them, then Jimmy will come with the rest of us.'

There was tension for a few more moments, then Samuel nodded his head.

'I said I want Irene here,' Doris said.

'Leave it, Doris,' Samuel growled. 'Alex is right. Irene is too young to become an invalid nurse.'

Alex was surprised to see Doris's eyes fill with tears.

'I won't have anyone left,' she said.

'You have Frank and Jimmy. You need to be thankful,' Samuel said. 'I'll pay for proper help.'

'What, like that Norma woman?'

There it was. Finally she acknowledged Norma was bad news— had been bad news for all of them, right from the start.

'I don't want us to leave on bad terms like this,' Alex said. 'For Nancy's sake, couldn't we just call a truce?'

Tears overflowed from Doris's eyes, and Alex's own throat tightened at the memory of his much-loved first wife.

'I'll bring the girls down to the station in the morning,' Samuel said.

'And Jimmy too, please,' Alex asked. 'I want to say goodbye to him.'

Samuel nodded, and then they all cried.

***

Grace was seated in the carriage. She felt sick as she watched what was happening on the platform. The girls were crying as they hugged the older man, who must have been their grandfather, then again as they hugged Jimmy. Even Jimmy swiped away tears. Then Grace's own eyes flooded with tears as she watched Alex take his son in a strong embrace and hold on fiercely. Grace felt the ripping apart they must be feeling. It was all her fault. Alex wouldn't split the family apart like this if it hadn't been for Margaret.

She hung her head in misery, unable to watch any more. Even when Alex and the girls shuffled into the railway car and took their seats beside and opposite her, she found it difficult to look at them. Eventually when she did, Grace saw the sadness and tears still evident in the girls' eyes. She was too afraid to meet Alex's gaze in case she saw the same. She wasn't sure she could endure the guilt she was feeling. The train pulled away from the platform and Jean burst into a fresh round of tears and turned her head into her sister's shoulder.

'Why couldn't we stay?' she wailed. 'I don't want to leave.'

Grace forced a glance to her husband seated stoically beside her. His face was granite and it was as if he had hardened to avoid the emotion.

Jean didn't appear to need her father's reassurance, happy enough to accept Irene's comfort. The train gathered speed, even though it was beginning its ascent into the Adelaide Hills, and it wasn't going very fast. Still they were moving, and Grace turned her gaze out the window to watch the passing bush that rushed past the window. She couldn't find anything comforting to say to any of them. As far as she knew, there was no promise of anything better in Green Valley. The knowledge of this twisted her insides up with fresh worry. The only thing she was thankful for was that Margaret was asleep, unaware her entire family were going through turmoil.

They had been underway for only about forty minutes before Margaret began to stir. Grace looked at her fob watch and saw that it was nearly her feed time. Alex hadn't been able to afford a first class compartment, they were all seated in third class, folks dotted throughout the carriage. As much as there was some safety in the silence that had been upon them, Grace knew that Margaret would force them to face the ordinary details of life.

'Could you find a cloth for me, please?' she whispered to Alex. 'I will need to feed her.'

Alex didn't make any comment, just got up from his seat and pulled the baby's bag down from the overhead rack. He pulled out two nappies, unfolded one and handed it to Grace to use as a modesty covering. He gave the other to Irene to hold, along with a wash cloth and a waterproof bag.

'What are these for?' Irene asked.

'After Margaret has had her dinner, she will need her nappy changed,' Grace explained.

'Why?' Jean asked, finally distracted from her misery.

'Because babies don't know how to use the toilet yet, and the nappy will be dirty.'

Jean screwed up her face in a picture of disgust.

'That's what babies do,' Irene said to her sister. 'Don't be silly.'

Grace was glad the girls were distracted while she tucked the nappy in her collar, and then went about untucking her blouse and getting ready to feed the baby. Even though they couldn't see exactly what was happening, Jeans eyes widened. Grace could see the questions beginning to form.

'Do you want me to take the girls to the cafeteria car for a little while?' Alex asked.

'No,' Grace replied. 'What I think might be helpful is if you went to the cafeteria car and left me with the girls to have a chat.'

'A chat! About what?'

'The birds and the bees.'

Alex gave a nervous laugh. 'They're too young for that,' he said.

'How old are you girls?' Grace asked.

'Twelve and a half!'

'Nearly eleven.' They both answered at once.

'Given our situation, Alex, I think they are old enough. We can't dance around the subject forever.'

'But right here?' Alex lowered his voice, almost to a whisper.

'There's nobody in the immediate vicinity. I'll keep my voice down.'

'I'm not sure it's a good idea.'

Grace shrugged her shoulders without disturbing the feeding baby.

'What is she doing?' Jean asked, her eyes fixed on the draped nappy.

'She's having her dinner,' Grace answered.

'How?'

Alex got up from his seat. 'I'm going to the cafeteria car. Do you girls want to come?'

Irene and Jean shook their heads. 'We'll stay here and help Mother,' Irene said. She moved across and sat next to Grace as she spoke.

Grace gave Alex a weak smile. 'This is girl business, Alex. Go and have a cup of tea.'

***

Alex didn't want to waste his few pennies on tea. He got a glass of water and sat at a table on his own. He'd found it difficult to say goodbye to Jimmy. One part of him wanted to be upset with Grace, but he knew this course was set because of the decision he'd made a little over nine months ago. If it came down to it, he'd prefer to say goodbye to Jimmy for a little while, knowing they could write to each other and visit eventually, than to have given Margaret away to strangers—to never hear of her again. The situation was hard.

The promise of the future didn't bring much cheer either. He fully expected to be met with hostility when he came face-to-face with Grace's parents. Charlie would help them find accommodation and work, and that was something. But he wasn't sure of Grace. Yes, she would be faithful, and an attentive and loving mother. She would even be a good companion. But would she be his lover, in the way she had been the night Margaret was conceived? Or had the whole fiasco stolen that chance away from them? The guilt she felt—guilt that was bound to be exacerbated once she faced her parents—stood as a barrier between them. And Alex didn't have an argument that would ever assuage that guilt. It was a depressing thought.

***

'When your Dad gets back,' Grace said, 'he won't want to know what we've talked about.'

'Why not?' Jean asked.

'Because it's not a subject that is discussed in polite company.'

'But it's very interesting.'

'And if we don't understand about it, we might get into trouble too, like you did,' Irene added.

'That is why I've told you,' Grace said. 'Still, your Dad won't want you to discuss it, and you should remember it is something you shouldn't just talk about willy-nilly. If you ever have any questions, you can come to me, and we will discuss it privately. All right?'

Grace could see by Jean's screwed-up mouth that she wanted to persist, but Alex was making his way through the carriage towards them, and it was time the conversation ceased.

'That's enough now, Jean,' she said. 'I'm going to teach you how to change Margaret's nappy.'

'I thought you said we could call her Maggie.'

'If you'd like.'

'How did you girls get on?' Alex asked, as he slipped into the seat beside Jean.

'We're not allowed to talk about it,' she said, her voice sullen.

'Right. That seems very wise.' Grace saw him trying to suppress a smile.

'Jean, would you like to go to the washroom and get our washcloth wet, ready for changing Maggie's nappy?'

'I'll come with you,' Irene said.

'How did it go?' Alex asked Grace, once the girls had set off down the aisle.

'We're not allowed to talk about it.' She smiled at him. 'They needed to know, Alex. With all the talk, and the way things happened, just shushing them up and pretending they don't understand is just plain silly. Besides, I'm feeding the baby. I can't just pretend it's not happening.'

Alex nodded. 'I'm glad you're here. I don't think I could parent the girls through these growing-up years on my own. It's a bit of a foreign language for me.'

'Are you all right?' Grace changed pace. 'I saw you and Jimmy on the platform.'

Alex pursed his lips and blinked away sudden moisture.

'It's hard,' he said.

Grace nodded. 'I'm sorry. I feel as if it is my fault.'

Alex shrugged. 'What's done is done, and we both made the decision.'

Grace swallowed a lump in her throat.

Margaret began to squirm and Grace sat her up to burp her.

'She is the happiest one out of all of us,' Alex said.

'And yet, if we'd given her away, she would have been the most miserable. I'm not sorry we kept her. Are you?'

'No. I love her.'

Grace wished he'd say he loved her too, but she wasn't going to push it. Not when she was afraid he might resent having had to leave Jimmy behind.

Chapter Twenty-One

Nearly thirteen hours being jostled about by the train, a fractious baby, squabbling girls, and various nappy incidents, left Grace frazzled by the time the conductor announced they were approaching Brinsford station. Perhaps her worn patience and extreme tiredness was a blessing in disguise, as it meant she hadn't had time to dwell on the reception they were likely to receive once home in Green Valley. It wasn't until she'd stepped foot on the platform, with Alex by her side, Margaret in her arms, and Irene and Jean helping with the hand bags, that she considered just how her brother must have felt seeing them emerge as a family. Grace was somewhat relieved by his warm smile. She had been single and completely unattached for their entire lives, and she knew this new arrangement must seem odd to him.

'How are you, mate?' Charlie said as he shook Alex's hand. 'How was the trip?'

'Long.' All the tension and frustration was clearly expressed in Alex's tone.

'I can imagine.' Charlie took the baggage tickets from Alex and headed towards the baggage car.

'Hello to you too,' Grace said, without intending to be heard.

'Give him time to adjust, Grace,' Alex said.

'He adjusted to you all right.'

'You're his sister. He hasn't seen you like this before. He'll get used to it.'

It hurt, but Grace didn't say anything more. Instead she ushered the girls through the station to the ladies waiting room to freshen up before embarking on the next hour in whatever transport Charlie had brought along.

After having attended to their immediate needs, Grace brought the girls outside to the car park. Charlie and Alex had loaded their luggage, even having to tie a few things onto the roof. Charlie turned as they approached.

'Well, let me see my new niece,' he said in the tone he'd always used as a brother. Not particularly affectionate. 'She's a beauty all right. Has she settled yet?'

'Being as I was discharged from the hospital, spent one night in someone's guest room, and then the next day on the train, I couldn't say. To be honest, Charlie, I feel all at sea.'

'I dare say. Well once you've got home, there'll be plenty of time to settle.'

'Where's home?' Grace couldn't help asking the question. It was going to have to be asked sooner or later.

'Not now, Grace,' Alex said.

'Where will you take us, Charlie?'

'You're coming back to our place for the night.'

'You managed to resurrect the shearer's quarters?'

He laughed. 'Not likely. No, I've left our kids over with Mum and Dad for the night and borrowed his car. We'll swap the car for the kids tomorrow. In the meantime, we can sit down and have a good chat about the future.'

'So Mum and Dad know you've borrowed the car to fetch us from the station?'

'No. Not yet.'

'Grace, just leave it for now. We need to get back to Green Valley and rest first, before we embark on this confrontation,' Alex said.

'And it will be a confrontation, won't it, Charlie?' she asked.

'I guess. Let's just get you home … back to my place.'

Another hour was spent being jostled about in the back of her father's Model T Ford. Margaret was unsettled, naturally. At least Jean and Irene sat quietly. Alex sat in the front with Charlie and they chatted about the farm, the reconstructions following the flood, the likelihood of rain, all carefully avoiding the one subject Grace wanted to discuss. Finally, they pulled up outside Charlie and Meg's home. The dog barked and ran out to greet the car, and within moments, Meg was on the veranda, then running down the garden path. By the time Charlie pulled the handbrake on, Meg had the back door open and was reaching into the car to help Grace emerge.

'I'm so glad to have you back,' Meg said. She had taken Margaret and immediately began to cluck over her.

'We named her after you,' Grace said as she straightened the kinks out of her body.

Meg threw her other arm around Grace's neck and kissed her cheek. 'I love you, Grace, and this little one is going to be such a blessing.'

Grace swallowed her thoughts. *Blessing? Really? How can something started so wrong be a blessing?*

'Now let's get you inside. I have the kettle on. You'll feel like your old self in no time.'

Grace followed Meg, who had commandeered the baby. She was thankful for her optimism, but couldn't see it herself. Before she made it to the gate, Alex called to her.

'Wait a minute, please.'

Grace turned back and waited while he undid the ropes holding the large suitcase on the roof of the car. Charlie had taken two cases, and the girls had picked up a bag each, leaving only one case for Alex. He stepped over and took her arm in his. 'Can we walk in together?' he asked. 'We are husband and wife now.'

Grace nodded. It was hard to think of this relationship. He had saved her from abandoning their child; he was going to provide for them all. He had lost so much by the choices he had made. But in it all, she couldn't see how they would be like Meg and Charlie, for instance. If things had been different from the start, she would love to think of him in intimate terms, to look forward to the time when they could be alone. She let out a long sigh. It couldn't work, could it?

***

The conversation over tea had been censored. None of the adults wanted to discuss the challenges that existed while the girls were in the room. Alex didn't want to send them out of the room on their own, either. They were already feeling upset and insecure, having been torn away from their grandparents and brother. If Charlie's children had been at home, he might have suggested they go into the other room and play.

'Meg, I'm really sorry,' Grace said. 'I'm nearly dead on my feet. I'm going to have to turn in early tonight.'

'Of course,' Meg said. 'The girls can sleep in Evie and Aimee's room, and you and Alex can sleep in the boys' room.'

Grace nodded and slipped out with the baby.

'Irene, would you go and see if Grace needs a hand please,' Alex said.

Irene stood up from the table.

'Can I go too?' Jean asked.

Alex nodded. 'If she wants to go to sleep, you leave her alone and perhaps you can get ready for bed too.'

Irene nodded. The two began to leave the lounge room, but he heard what she said as they left.

'They want to talk grown-up talk,' Irene said to Jean.

'Like what Miss Shore told us on the train?' Jean asked.

Alex didn't hear Irene's reply. They were smarter than he gave them credit for. He took a deep breath and turned his focus back on his brother and sister-in-law. 'So …'

'It will work out, Alex,' Meg said. 'It may take a little time, that's all.'

'Don't water it down, Meg.' Charlie shook his head. 'They're hopping mad, and you know it.'

'Both of them?' Alex asked.

'Dad is,' Meg said. 'Mum understands, but she is so terribly worried about what everyone will say.'

'Do you think we should just move on and find somewhere else to live?' Alex asked.

'Like where?' Charlie asked.

'And do you have the money to set up somewhere else?' Meg asked.

Alex shook his head.

'And your people back in South Australia?'

Alex shook his head again and gave an unamused laugh. 'Worse than here,' he said.

'I'm sorry, Alex,' Meg said. 'I'm sure Mum and Dad will come around eventually.'

'It's the pain of it now that's the real problem,' Alex said. 'Grace is so overwhelmed with guilt she can hardly stand upright.'

'That can't be good for the baby,' Meg said.

'Or her,' Alex said.

'Or you,' Charlie added.

'How far off are you from restoring the shearer's quarters?' Alex changed the subject.

'The last thing on the list, mate. Sorry, I've had to start with all the work sheds first.'

Alex felt awful. He didn't really want to have to face the wrath of Colin Shore, but there was little choice.

'Listen, I'm feeling quite done in myself. I think things might seem better after a night's sleep.'

'Don't forget the baby,' Meg said. 'She'll be waking up several times in the night for a feed.'

Alex had only spent the one night with them, and it had been punctuated by several night-time feeds. He didn't admit he'd barely woken up for any of them. A stray thought of his past life with Nancy swept over him. She used to complain bitterly that he never woke to the children at night. He would like to have smiled at the memory, but the heaviness of the present prevented it.

'Goodnight,' he said as he got up. 'Thank you for having us.'

'Our pleasure,' Meg said. 'I wouldn't have missed it for the world.'

Grace was asleep in one of the single beds when he came into the boy's room. She'd left the bed lamp burning. She had Margaret tucked up in her suitcase between the two beds. He was at least glad they were asleep and comfortable. It had been a difficult day, and tomorrow would no doubt be just as difficult.

***

Wallace Hill was a grand property, an imposing three-storey home surrounded by extensive gardens like a softening garland. Alex had been used to the Johnsons as people of property and good standing in the community, but Grace's parents were on another level again. Colin was on close talking terms with members of parliament and a circle of people who considered themselves the landed gentry. Grace had told him of her father's much more humble beginnings, and Alex knew that Colin wasn't a snob—but he was her father, and Alex had taken his daughter outside of marriage and got her pregnant. This was not a way to get on the good side of an influential man. But all was done now. All that could be done to make it right had been done. There was nothing else that he could do but beg his forgiveness. Meg believed he would forgive them—eventually—but what about right now?

Meg had stayed home with Irene and Jean, while Charlie had brought them across to Wallace Hill in the motor car.

'Do you want me to come in with you?' Charlie asked.

'No, thanks mate,' Alex said. 'I think this is a conversation I need to have alone.'

'Alone with me,' Grace said.

'No, I think I should start alone.'

'They are my parents,' Grace objected.

'I know. I mean just me and your father,' Alex said. 'You go with your mother and show her the baby. There will be time for us all to talk later.'

Charlie shrugged his shoulders and got out of the car. 'I'll keep the children out of the way,' he said, before walking inside.

Alex took a deep breath. 'Are you ready?' He turned in his seat and looked deep into Grace's eyes.

'No. I'll never be ready for this, but it has to be done.'

Alex helped her out of the car and put his arm around her waist as they walked up the steps into the main entrance hall.

'Auntie Grace!' Aimee bounced out of the front sitting room and raced up to them. She threw her arms about Grace's neck and kissed her, then she kissed the top of Margaret's head. 'Now, who do we have here?' she said.

'Your parents have told you, haven't they?' Grace asked.

Aimee put a finger to her lips in a shushing action. 'I'm not supposed to know anything, you realise. At least, that's what Grandma thinks. It's hard to tell her I'm interested in a man myself.'

'Aimee, please. Not now.'

'Oh, I know. I know. It's all a whole lot of controversy. My job is to usher the children outside and pretend to catch butterflies.'

'Please, if you would, that would really help.'

'Well, I think it is wonderful.' She kissed Grace on the cheek again. 'I told her,' Aimee turned and spoke to Alex. 'Right from the start, I said, that Mr Moreland is a man worth looking at.'

'Aimee!' Grace scolded.

She just smiled, kissed her again and bounced towards the back of the house, where Alex assumed the other children must be.

Just then Charlie emerged from the sitting room. 'Mum is going to freshen up. She will meet you in the formal lounge, Grace. Dad is ready to see you, if you like,' he said to Alex.

Alex nodded. He gave Grace's hand a squeeze and then left her. This was her childhood home. She would manage.

He walked into the sitting room and saw Colin Shore standing at the bay window, looking out across the garden. Alex cleared his throat.

'Mr Moreland.' Colin spoke without turning towards him.

'Mr Shore.'

'Well? What have you to say for yourself?' On this question, he turned a dark look upon Alex.

'I have done you and your family wrong, and I wish to ask for your forgiveness.'

'Is that how you see it? So easily fixed with a small apology?'

'I don't see it that way at all, believe me. If you imagine that I have not been aware right from the very start how much trouble this has caused, then you are mistaken.'

'I hope it has caused trouble. I hope that you have suffered for your actions.'

'I have. My life has been a mass of misery, as has Grace's.'

'I'm still not prepared for you to even mention her name. I cannot conceive how you could have betrayed our trust in such a manner.' Colin's eyes were ablaze with undisguised fury.

Alex didn't say anything.

'Do you know what this will do to her mother? To our family? Our reputation in this district, and amongst our friends in the city? Well, young man, I think you should have something to say.'

'There is nothing I can say that will make it right, is there?'

'Damn right, there's not. And you bring her and the child back here, as if you are a happy family. Well, my neighbours are not fools, man. They can count. Everyone will know.'

Alex was without any defence. He'd always known that this would be how it would turn out. From the beginning. He didn't have a leg to stand on.

'Well?' Colin demanded.

'I can only ask for forgiveness. I have nothing else.'

'And you think it's that easy?'

'For heaven's sake, man. I know it's not easy. Do you think it has been easy facing the idea of abandoning a child to some orphanage where she might have been abused, or sold into service, simply because her mother and I made a mistake? I chose to keep her for her sake, and I've paid for it with my own reputation, and my own property, and my own son. Yes, I've had to leave my son behind. If you want me to suffer, don't worry, I am. Both of us are. And if you will not forgive us, we will continue to suffer. I may even take them all on the road and sleep in ditches if we cannot find a home here.'

Colin swore and turned his back on Alex.

Alex's own breathing was heavy. There were things he would like to have said, but he had no right, so he kept quiet. The silence hung heavy in the room for a couple of minutes. Alex began to feel uncomfortable. He wasn't about to scuttle out of the room, chastened and guilty. He wanted to resolve this, one way or the other. Eventually, without turning around, Colin spoke.

'You can stay in the servants' quarters until you can find another place somewhere else.'

'Thank you, sir. I appreciate your hospitality.'

Neither said anything else. Alex knew this wasn't hospitality, or even forgiveness. It was the very least thing Grace's father could do so that they wouldn't be on the roads with three children. That was all. But it was all that Alex needed for now. He'd have to face the rest of it later.

***

Grace hated seeing her mother's painful expression. She didn't have to say anything for Grace to know how disappointed she was. They had barely spoken until Aimee had come inside with the younger children.

'Here she is,' Aimee said, joy in her voice.

'Auntie Grace,' Evie said. 'Is it true? Is this a new cousin for us?'

'Yes, dear,' Grace answered the twelve-year-old. The young girl's face was a picture of delight, and Grace smiled. Aimee came across and took Margaret from Grace, then she found a chair and settled herself down. Evie went with her and the two girls began to coo over the baby.

'How are you, Johnny, Joey?' Grace spoke to the boys. 'Joey, you look like you've grown an inch while I was away.'

'I'm eleven, Auntie Grace. Dad says I can try out for the junior colts football team.'

'Really?' Grace allowed her tension to drop. These children had been her constant charges for many years. She knew and loved them as if they were her own.'

'So, what about you, Johnny?'

'I've decided that I want to be called John,' he said. 'I'm leaving school at the end of the year, and coming home to work on the farm with Dad.'

That was unexpected. 'What does your father have to say about that?'

'He wants me to continue with my education and go to university.'

'That's what I thought.'

'But I don't want to. I can't see the point.'

Grace took a deep breath. She had enough troubles of her own without buying into an argument between Charlie and his fifteen-year-old son.

'So you and Mr Moreland are married?' Joey asked. 'I'd always thought he didn't like you much.'

Grace smiled.

'Mr Moreland had a change of heart,' she said.

'All right, children.' Emily Shore finally spoke up. 'That's enough. Why don't you go outside for a while?'

'We only just came in, Grandma,' Aimee complained. 'Don't be chasing us away. We are all excited to see the new baby.'

Grace looked across to her mother. She hadn't been excited. She hadn't asked to hold her, or even come across to look at her. It was hurtful, and more so as Grace watched Aimee and Evie begin to fuss.

'We can take the baby with us.' Aimee said. 'If you and Grandma want to talk alone.'

'No,' Emily said. 'I haven't had a chance to meet her properly yet.'

Grace looked up to her mother. Emily was looking at her, and had tears in her eyes.

'Take the others outside for another half hour please, Aimee,' Grace said. 'Grandma and I need a little time alone.'

Aimee gave an exaggerated huff. 'Honestly, I don't know why everything has to be so dramatic.'

Grace couldn't bring herself to scold anymore. She just came across and took Margaret from her.

'Half an hour, and then we're coming in for morning tea,' Aimee warned, as she herded the others out.

Grace turned to Emily once the children had left the room. 'Do you want to hold her?'

'I do. I'm sorry that I have been so ... it's hard for us to deal with Grace. Really hard. You understand that, don't you?'

'I understand. But Margaret hasn't got anything to do with it. She is just an innocent child. She needs her grandparents as much as she needed her parents, no matter how wrong the start was.'

Emily came across and took Margaret in her arms.

Grace watched through a sheen of tears. Her mother was also teary-eyed. Eventually Emily spoke again.

'I had lost hope that your mother would ever marry, little one,' she said to the baby, hugging her close. 'It's not quite how I had hoped it would be, but you are a darling child, and I'm glad you're here.'

'Her name is Margaret Emily,' Grace said. 'After Alex's mother and you.'

Chapter Twenty-Two

'How are you, old friend? And how are Grace and her family settling in at Wallace Hill?'

Colin was met with this question the moment he stepped into the manse sitting room. The Reverend John Laslett had been his close friend for nearly forty-five years. He knew straight away that the question was carefully designed to provoke a discussion. This was not why he had come to visit.

'I'd heard you weren't well.' Colin avoided answering.

'I'm staring down the barrel at old-age, my friend, and as much as I don't want to admit it, things aren't as easy as they used to be when we were young.'

'Well, I've just dropped in to see how you are.'

'And I'm ignoring your avoidance and coming straight to the point.'

Colin rolled his eyes. He might have known John Laslett wouldn't let things go.

'I'm not just going to pretend that everything is all right.' Colin's tone rose with intensity. 'He's done irreparable damage to the family, and I'm not just going to welcome them with open arms.'

'Irreparable damage? How?'

'Don't you start.'

'Colin Shore, you were always a hard-headed fool, and I might as well call a spade a spade. You are still a hard-headed fool.'

'What do you expect that I should do?'

'Well, let's just review the facts first, shall we?'

'Moreland took advantage of our trust, betrayed us all, and lured Grace to her shame and disgrace.'

'Yes, and ...?'

'And what? That's all there is to it.'

'So he hasn't done anything to try to make reparation?'

Colin was annoyed, and didn't answer.

'Let me tell you the facts as I know them.' John said. 'Grace is miserable. Alex, from all accounts, has dangerously low spirits, his two daughters are showing signs of insecurity—probably from living in a hostile environment—and the new baby hasn't been christened.'

'Christened! How can she be christened?'

'Easily enough. Her mother and father and family bring her to the church, we present her to the Lord, pray a blessing on her, and celebrate with a party afterward.'

'You talk nonsense, John. I won't listen to it.'

'What problem do you see?'

'How can I invite my friends and neighbours to witness our family's disgrace, and pretend to bless it?'

John took a deep breath and pursed his lips.

'Well, it isn't just as easy as that,' Colin excused.

'So the young Mr Moreland hasn't repented in any way at all. He's just marched in and taken your kindness for granted, and just expects you to overlook his mistake?'

Colin didn't answer.

'And Grace marches about your house, as if nothing has happened, expecting you to make way for them as if it is her right?'

Still Colin didn't answer for a moment.

'Has she been over here to tell tales?' Colin asked after a long pause.

'Not at all, I assure you. In fact, I haven't seen any of them since they've been back in the valley, and I believe they returned over six weeks ago.'

'Then how is it that you seem to know everything?'

'They are part of my flock, Colin. Meg has paid several pastoral visits, and she is very concerned for them all.'

Colin shuffled his feet, uncomfortable with what he was hearing. He knew Meg came to see Grace as her sister-in-law. He didn't pay it any mind. He had ignored all of them. They hadn't eaten with the family, and he hadn't even taken a moment to meet his granddaughter. He could barely accept that she was his granddaughter.

'Well?' John wouldn't let the matter drop.

'What do you think I should do?' Colin asked.

'I think you should help them organise a christening, but before that, I believe it would be useful to have a private blessing with them for their marriage.'

Colin almost choked. 'You can't be serious.'

'You haven't forgiven them, have you?'

'Why should I forgive them?'

'If I wasn't getting so old, Colin Shore, I'd like to give you a good rattling. I know you really aren't that stupid.'

'Now I'm stupid?'

'I said, I know you aren't that stupid. Stubborn, on the other hand …'

Colin shook his head.

'I fail to see why I should forgive the man who has ruined my family.'

'As it stands, you are the man who is ruining your family. Alex Moreland succumbed to temptation in a very difficult situation, something I'm sure you probably faced more than once in your life …'

'I never succumbed to it. I had more self-control than that.'

'Did you? Well, you are the righteous one then. However, now you are going directly against God's Word with your attitude.'

'I have my pride, John.'

'Yes, I can see that. But it's your unwillingness to forgive that will see you separated from God.'

'That's a fairly harsh call.'

'Do you want to refresh your memory of the Scripture?'

Colin made no response.

'In the Gospel of Matthew: If you don't forgive others, God won't forgive you.'

Colin blew out a breath of frustration.

'If your family falls apart, it is your fault, Colin. No one else's. You are the head of the household, and it is you who can forgive and bless the young couple and their children. You are the one who can release them from the burden of shame that they are carrying.'

'I've got you there. The Bible says that it is Christ who carries our sin and shame.'

'Christ has done His part, but you won't let them rest in it, because you feel as if it is your right to make them suffer, to remind them every day of their sins.'

'And you seem determined to remind me of mine.'

John shrugged his shoulders. 'Well, I've said what I'm going to say. Shall we have a cup of tea?'

Colin drank tea with his friend, and the minister didn't say another word on the subject. That didn't mean that his words weren't ringing in Colin's ears the whole drive back to Wallace Hill. John was right—he wasn't stupid, but he was stubborn. That attitude had nearly cost him his chance with Emily, right at the beginning. And he knew he'd been hard to get on with when Charlie went through his troubles, years ago.

But it was a bitter pill to swallow now—to have his daughter bring her adulterous lover and illegitimate child into the house. Now John wanted him to hold a private blessing for it, and a public celebration. It didn't sit right with him, no matter if they did have a genuine marriage certificate. Hearing Meg's report repeated to him wasn't a pleasant thing to face either. He had avoided the lot of them, so hadn't watched to see how any of them were faring. John's words made him feel small and mean-spirited.

As he swung the car around the circular drive, along the side of the house, he swerved to avoid hitting the two Moreland children. They had obviously been caught by surprise, as he had, and had rushed to get out of the way of the car; however, the younger one had tripped and fallen on the rocks along the edge of the drive. He pulled the car into the shed and then went out to see if she was all right. Having John's voice nagging in the back of his head helped him swallow his pride.

'Are you all right?' he asked, his tone gruff, even while he was making the effort to attempt to be kind.

'I'm sorry, sir,' the older girl said. She sounded frightened. 'We were trying to get out of your way, but Jean has fallen. She can't seem to stand up.'

'Let me see.' Colin came over to them. His heart felt sore as he noted the tears running down the smaller girl's face.

'I'll be all right. I don't want to be a bother to you,' she said. He noticed the forced bravery in her expression, and at the same time, he could see she was in pain.

'Let me look. Is it your ankle that you've twisted?'

Jean nodded. Colin knelt next to her and carefully rolled down the sock. Already the ankle had started to swell.

'Go into the house and fetch Grace. I mean … your step-mother.'

He saw the older girl go. He should at least know her name, but he didn't.

'I'm really sorry, sir,' Jean said again. 'Don't you worry about me. Irene will fetch some help.'

Colin didn't move, but waited until Grace came out the back door by the laundry.

'What's happened?' She sounded anxious.

'She's twisted her ankle. I hope she hasn't broken it.' Colin wanted to feel a sense of pride in showing concern, but he just felt worse and worse, realising that none of them really trusted him. All he had shown to them was a barking, nasty old man.

'I'll take care of it, Dad,' Grace said. 'You go inside.'

'I think you should take her into the town, to the clinic. Doctor Roberts holds clinic in Green Valley on Tuesday afternoons.'

'Yes, I know,' Grace said. 'I'll put a cold compress on and wait and see if the swelling goes down.'

'Nonsense! The girl needs to have her ankle looked at to make sure it isn't broken.'

'Dad, thank you for your concern, but Alex and I can't afford medical bills at the moment.'

'I'll pay for it.'

Grace looked at him, and he felt that stab of guilt again.

'Don't dither, Grace,' he said. 'Take the girl into the clinic.'

'I don't have a car,' she said, 'and I'll need to wait for Alex to hitch up the sulky to help me, if I am going to go.'

'Take my car, and don't be silly.' Colin stood up and looked firmly at his daughter. 'Just do it, Grace.'

He knew he sounded brusque, but didn't know how to say he was sorry for being proud and cruel and selfish. Grace still stared at him.

'Oh, for goodness sake.' He prepared himself to pick the girl up from the ground to carry her to the car himself.

'Dad, are you sure?'

Colin just shook his head. 'Go and tell your mother that you're going into town. She can watch the baby while you're out.'

***

Colin watched Grace drive the motorcar away with Moreland's youngest daughter in the back seat. He had a flash of realisation, which led to yet another stab of guilt: Moreland's youngest daughter wasn't in the car—she was in the house. The eight-week-old baby was also his youngest grandchild, and he had refused to acknowledge her. He hadn't so much as taken a look at her. He let out a huff of resignation. There'd never been a confrontation between him and John Laslett, where he'd come out the winner. Just once in his life, he would like to be right—but pretending to be right didn't make him right.

'Blast it all,' he said as he went in the back entrance of the house and found Emily in the sitting room. 'Where's this baby?'

'What?' Emily looked alarmed. 'What baby?'

'Grace's baby. Who else?'

Emily stood up and faced her husband. 'Why are you barking at me?'

'Because John has given me a lecture about my pride and unforgiveness, and I'm not happy.'

'And you want to go and frighten the children as a way to make penance.'

'I'm not going to frighten the children. I just packed the younger one off in the car to the doctor.'

'Well, Irene certainly sounded anxious when she came and reported it to me.'

'Where's the baby?' Colin brushed her off. 'It's time I had a look at her.'

'Past time, Colin Shore.'

'Don't you start on me too.'

Emily gave a smile, squeezed his arm as she walked past and led the way.

Colin didn't think he could feel any worse than he already had, but then Emily led them downstairs into the servants' area, down the long corridor to the bedrooms out the back. How on earth could he have abandoned his daughter to such inadequate accommodations? They weren't the only ones living down here. In fact, the four of them—five including the baby—were crammed into one of the five bedrooms they offered the estate workers.

The room Emily showed him into usually housed two servants. There were the two single beds, and two mattresses made up on the floor at the end of each bed. The old family cradle Emily used to keep up in the nursery was squeezed between the beds. The older girl, Irene, was sitting on one of the beds watching the baby. When she saw the door open, her face lit with panic, but she didn't say anything.

'It's all right, Irene,' Emily whispered. 'Mr Shore just wants to take a peek at Maggie.'

Maggie! What sort of name is that? There wasn't much room for him to stand in, but he came up to the cradle and took a look at the sleeping infant.

'Can we pick her up?' he asked.

'Shh!' Emily held her finger to her lips and went on, whispering. 'She is sleeping now. If you wake her up, she will want Grace, and Grace isn't here to tend to her at the moment. Come away now. When she wakes up, Irene will bring her to us, won't you Irene?'

Irene nodded, but still had that look of terror on her face.

This is all nonsense. Why should the child be afraid of me?

But even as he thought it, he knew exactly why she was afraid. His rejection and nastiness had been real. He knew it, and wished it was as easy to fix as offering a simple apology. Perhaps it was.

Chapter Twenty-Three

Alex was working in the orchard at the back of the big house at Wallace Hill. It was the end of the apple season, and he was picking the last of the fruit to take up to the house for the cook to stew and preserve. He was up a ladder, getting the fruit that was right out of reach, when he heard Irene's voice below.

'Dad, Mother says you are to come up to the house. You're needed.'

'What's wrong?' He was never needed at the house. Usually he worked as hard as he could, either here or at Charlie's place, then he ate in the kitchen with Grace and the girls, before they turned in. There wasn't time for socialising. There wasn't any welcome for socialising. He worked hard, and hoped that one day, he'd have enough money to get the family away and into more suitable accommodation.

'Come on, Dad. Stop dawdling.'

Alex climbed down the wooden ladder. 'What's wrong up at the house, Irene?' he asked again.

'Mother says that you're to wash up. Mr and Mrs Shore want to see you in the formal lounge room.'

'That sounds ominous.'

'What?'

'Nothing. Where's your sister?'

'Which one?' Irene smiled at him.

'Where's Jean?'

'It's Saturday, and we were invited to go over to spend the day with Evie.'

'So why haven't you gone?'

'We're getting ready to go. Mr Charlie Shore is here and will take us back with him when he goes home.'

Alex took a deep breath. Charlie was here; Grace said he had to wash up because her parents wanted to see him. That only meant one thing—another confrontation. He hoped they weren't about to tip them out on the road.

Alex didn't have a good shirt to put on. With all the expenses for the baby and keeping Irene and Jean clothed and fed, he didn't have extra money to spend on himself. Besides, he didn't have need of a Sunday best shirt. He knew he wasn't welcome in the church, so there wasn't any need to go.

'Hurry up, Alex,' Grace said to him, once she found him combing his hair in the servant's washroom.

'What's going on?' he asked.

'Mum and Dad want to see us.'

'I see they have visitors.'

'Meg and Charlie, and Meg's parents.'

'The Reverend?' Alex sounded surprised. 'Shouldn't we wait until they leave?'

'It's a party, and apparently we're invited.'

'I'm not going to a party, Grace. Look at me.'

She gave a small laugh. 'Let me rephrase. It's a gathering, and we're invited.'

'I don't see why.'

'Does it matter? Dad is not going to huff and puff while Reverend Laslett is here. Let's just go and have a cup of tea with some friends, and see what happens.'

Alex sighed. 'I don't know how much longer I can take this.'

'This? Living here at Wallace Hill?'

'That, and just working myself into exhaustion every day, just so I don't have time to think about real life, and what a family should really be like.'

'I'm sorry, Alex. I wish it were different.'

He sighed again, straightened his waist coat and began to walk up the steps into the main part of the house.

'Come in Alex, Grace,' Emily said in response to his knock on the door of the lounge room. 'Come in and sit down.'

Alex felt ill at ease. Everyone else was sitting down, dressed nicely, if not in their Sunday best. He was scruffy and dirty in comparison.

'I've still got a lot of work to do,' he said. 'Is there something you need me for here?'

'Yes,' Colin said. 'There is. Please come in and sit down.'

Alex swallowed a lump of anxiety. He and Colin Shore had barely communicated since their return, and though it was civil, the hostility was evident beneath the surface.

'What is it, Dad?' Grace asked.

There was a pause and all eyes focussed on the head of the house.

Eventually he cleared his throat. 'I have an announcement to make.' He paused to swallow. If Alex hadn't known better, he would have thought he was nervous.

'Spit it out, Dad,' Charlie said.

Colin gave his son an angry glare, then swallowed again.

'I need to apologise to you Alex, and Grace. I have treated you shamefully, and I would now like to take the opportunity to offer you my blessing.'

Alex found that he was holding his breath, but when there was the sound of clapping and congratulations from Meg, Emily, and Mrs Laslett, he was forced to exhale and review what he'd just heard.

'I'm sorry. I don't understand.'

'I've invited Reverend Laslett here today to conduct a small blessing ceremony. None of us were able to be present at your marriage, and we missed the opportunity to wish you well, and to pray for your prosperity and success. My friend, the reverend, has pointed out to me that this could cause damage to your relationship and to ours, and so I'm trying to make amends.'

'Really, Dad?' Alex didn't have to see Grace's face to know she was smiling, but he looked to her anyway. She also had tears running down her face.

'That is, if you are prepared to forgive me for my pride.' Colin held Alex's gaze. Colin was asking for forgiveness. Alex's thoughts whirled. He had been so caught up with the burden of the situation that when it was suddenly released, he was taken by surprise.

'The appropriate answer is, yes, I forgive you.' Charlie had stepped next to him and spoken in his ear. 'I'll be the best man you were missing.'

Alex turned his gaze on his friend, his confusion still evident from the frown creasing his brow.

'It isn't that hard, Alex,' Charlie said. 'Please don't get all stubborn now.'

'I'm sorry,' Alex said. 'I just wasn't expecting …' Then he was chagrined to find his throat tightening, his jaw wobbling, and tears pouring out of his eyes. He couldn't make a sensible answer. To have been carrying the burden of rejection—knowing it was because of his own actions, knowing it affected all his children and Grace, knowing there was nothing he could do to make it better—and then, to suddenly have that weight lifted. It was too much to process in two minutes.

'Excuse me,' he said, and then fled from the lounge room.

'Alex.' Grace called after him, and he knew she would follow. He paused near the entrance to the kitchen and waited for her to catch up.

'Alex?' Her tone was kind, and her hand on his shoulder was comforting. He turned to look at her and then broke down, sobbing. Grace was crying too. Somehow they'd found each other's embrace and they clung together until the storm passed.

'It's all right!' Alex heard Charlie's voice echoing in the hall way. 'They're just … just getting used to the idea.'

'I think we'd better go back,' Alex said to Grace, fumbling in his pocket for a handkerchief.

'When something as wonderful as forgiveness and blessing is held out as a gift? Yes, we'd better go back.'

'I'm sorry I don't know what to say,' he said.

'I guess "thank you" would probably do.'

'It seems inadequate.'

'One step at a time.' She blew her nose on her own handkerchief she'd found in her sleeve.

He gave her another hug. 'Perhaps it's not hopeless after all.'

***

Meg found her eldest daughter, Aimee, sitting on the lawn under a shady tree, reading a book, with the pram next to her. Aimee must have heard her mother's approach because she put a finger to her lips.

'Shh!' she said in a stage whisper. 'Maggie's asleep.'

'Yes, I know.' Meg kept her voice down. 'However, she is needed in the formal lounge.'

'Why?' Aimee had never been one to just act without knowing the reason why.

'Just because,' Meg said.

Aimee stood up, but Meg didn't think she would let it go, not for a minute. She positioned herself behind the pram and began to roll it back toward the house. As she moved along the footpath to the side of the house, she saw another car in the driveway.

'Why are Grandpa and Grandma Laslett here?' she asked.

'They've come to visit,' Meg said, hoping to put her off.

'Well, why didn't you call me?

Meg could see it was useless trying to evade Aimee's questions, so she decided to speak frankly.

'Your two grandfathers have had a long heart-to-heart, and apparently, Grandpa Laslett has made Grandpa Shore see the error of his ways.'

'What, you mean he's managed to get him to swallow his pride and stop ignoring this precious little beauty?'

'Aimee.' Meg wagged her finger, only half in jest. 'You shouldn't be so disrespectful.'

'He shouldn't be so cold and unloving.'

225

Meg shook her head. 'There were reasons why, you wouldn't understand.'

'Marmie! I'm nearly twenty years old, old enough to be married and have a child of my own. I know what's going on.'

'What's going on?'

'Auntie Grace and Mr Moreland. You know.'

'Yes, I do know, but I'm not sure you do.'

'I'm not a child.' Aimee objected. 'I know how this baby-making thing works. I know they weren't married, and that Grandpa Shore has been huffing and puffing about his reputation.'

'You know it wasn't right?'

'Of course. But it's done now. Maggie is a treasure. Why can't Grandpa Shore just let go of his pride and at least look at her?'

'Well, for your information, I think that is exactly what he is about to do.'

Aimee pulled up short and looked at her mother. 'Really?' Her tone was full of enthusiasm and the volume had increased dramatically. 'Oh, I am soooo glad.'

With that, the baby started crying.

'Oh, darling,' Aimee said as she scooped her out of the pram. 'I didn't men to frighten you.'

Meg just smiled. Aimee was grown up, and quite ready for motherhood.

'I'll take her in to them then,' Meg said, holding out her arms.

'No fear,' Aimee said, holding the baby closer. 'I'm not missing out on this for the world. I'll bring her in.'

Meg knew when she was beaten and allowed Aimee to lead the way. Her mother and mother-in-law would be scandalised that Aimee knew what was going on, but they had to face facts. Aimee did know, and she wanted to be part of this ceremony.

***

Grace felt nervous. The reverend had asked her and Alex to come and stand in front of him, so that he could pray for them.

'You should hold hands,' John said with a smile.

Alex cast Grace a look that seemed to say he would go along with the Reverend's suggestion. He took her hand and threaded his fingers through hers.

'And now, Colin and Emily, would you come and stand with your children to give them your blessing as I pray.'

Grace felt the tears form and then begin to run from her eyes as her parents stood next to them, Colin with his hand on Alex's shoulder, and Emily's hand on her shoulder. Then John began to pray.

'Father, we your children often get lost and make mistakes, but when we return to you with open hearts, we know you accept us, and we are forgiven through the work of your son, Jesus Christ. Today, we ask you to bless this union between Grace and Alex, that they would find joy and fruitfulness in their marriage and in their family.'

Grace almost couldn't believe what she was hearing, and that her father seemed to be adding his own affirmation just by his presence in the room. After John finished praying, Aimee stepped forward, holding the baby.

'Hello, dear.' Kate Laslett smiled at her granddaughter. 'Let's have a look at the little darling.'

Grace watched as the Lasletts fussed over her child, but then became aware of her father, still standing behind them. He suddenly cleared his throat.

'All right,' he said, his voice gruff. 'It's my turn. Pass her to me.'

Aimee retrieved the baby from her grandmother and brought her over to Colin. 'There you are, Grandpa, and what a beauty she is too.'

'Now then, none of your nonsense,' Colin said, but he took the baby anyway and cradled her in his arms.

Eventually he looked up to meet Grace's anxious gaze.

'She's a beauty all right,' he said. 'Congratulations to you both.'

Grace smiled from ear to ear, with tears all over her cheeks that didn't seem to fit her smile. Then Alex put his arm around her and pulled her close. She looked up at him and it seemed the most natural thing in the world. He kissed her. Not too quickly, so that it looked as if he hadn't thought about it, but not too long either, so as not to alarm the parents in the house. Just long enough to communicate love, relief, hope and gratitude.

<h1 style="text-align:center">Chapter Twenty-Four</h1>

Meg was helping Grace make up the bedrooms upstairs. They had housemaids, but Grace insisted that as she and the family were moving upstairs, she would make up the rooms. Wallace Hill had five large rooms upstairs. Colin had insisted that Alex take two of them for his family. Alex hadn't said anything to Colin, but had confided in Grace that he felt funny moving from being cramped in a small servants' room to being spread out into the two large upstairs rooms filled with fine furnishings.

'Do you want to stay below stairs?' she asked.

Alex had merely looked at her with a hungry look. She'd seen that look before, the night of the flood. Since Margaret's arrival and their marriage, they'd not had opportunity to be alone. Grace wondered that even if they had, how she would respond to the intimacy of true marriage. She still had reservations and doubts.

'I remember this is the room where Charlie and I started our marriage together,' Meg said, as she tucked sheets under the mattress, insisting on using the nurses' corners she'd been trained to use.

'It is a beautiful room,' Grace said. 'It was the guest room when I was a child.'

'Not tonight, though.' Meg gave her a wink. 'I assume you haven't had much opportunity to be alone since you married.'

Grace blushed and shook her head.

'Looking forward to it?'

'Meg!' Grace put on her scolding voice.

'It's marriage, Grace. Husbands can be nice, sometimes.'

Grace swallowed the lump in her throat.

'What is that look of worry all about?' Meg asked. 'It's not like you haven't done it before.'

Grace frowned at her. 'Honestly, Meg. This is very modern of you, to be talking about marriage like this.'

'Well, we live in modern times, and besides, I'm excited that you've found love at last, especially now your father has decided to bless it.'

'Please, Meg. I don't want to talk about it. Really.'

'All right. I understand. You just want it to be between you and your man.'

Grace didn't realise she was still frowning, until Meg spoke again.

'What is the matter, Grace?'

Grace finished straightening the pillows with their starched laced pillow cases, and then sat down in the chair by the window, letting out a sigh.

'Tell me,' Meg said.

'I still feel as if I'm doing the wrong thing.'

'What? By making love to your husband?'

'Well, he was divorced, and the Bible …'

'Grace Shore!'

'Moreland.'

'Grace Moreland! You really are the giddy limit. You and Alex have repented of your mistake. Given the consequences, any decision you made was going to hurt someone, and you chose to protect and love Margaret. Christ has taken care of sin, and yet you still think you have to earn your salvation by this ridiculous idea of abstinence or penance or something.'

'Well, I don't know—'

'Do you accept the forgiveness of God for your sin or not?'

'Well, yes, but …'

'But what?'

'I still feel guilty.'

'Read Romans Eight. That guilt you feel is condemnation, and it doesn't come from God. You need to pull yourself together and accept the freedom Christ offers, instead of wallowing around like some sort of miserable martyr, intent upon saving yourself.'

Grace looked at Meg for a moment, and smiled.

'Why don't you say what you really feel?'

Meg held her gaze for a moment, and then they both laughed.

'You're being an idiot,' Meg said.

'You're right, I know.'

'Then let's get this room made up, and move your things up, and tonight …'

'You're incorrigible!'

'Ooh, and I love it!'

***

Grace found it difficult, but she read Romans Eight, and decided she needed to take the guilt in hand. She and Alex had a chance at a proper relationship, and she wasn't going to stand in the way. Still, she wasn't *that* confident she wanted to be forward. They still had Margaret's cradle in the bedroom by the bed.

Grace hadn't felt so light-hearted in a long time. Her father had announced he would host a christening party. He'd even offered to pay for Jimmy to travel across for a couple of weeks' holiday, so he could attend the celebration as well. Emily and Meg had begun to make plans with Grace for the happy event. Colin wasn't the sort to become all soft and mushy, but Grace had seen how he looked when he finally took Margaret in his arms. He couldn't hide the love that welled up, even if he had tried. Now that the barrier had been broken down, the relationships within the household had begun to flow like old times. Grace felt genuine happiness.

The only fly in the ointment was that Alex was still tentative for some reason. He was talking to her parents at least, and their conversation was more than civil. Irene and Jean had begun to laugh, and were coming home from school happy each day. They were forming friendships with Charlie's children and other children from the valley. Yet Alex was still holding back and she worried about the reasons why.

She was feeding Margaret in the rocking chair by the window in their new room when Alex came in. Grace looked up and offered him a smile. She didn't have a cloth over the baby, as she was in the privacy of her own room, but Alex's steamy look made her wish she did have. She didn't say anything, but continued with the task.

'How are you feeling?' Grace asked to divert her thoughts.

'About what?'

'About life. How are you feeling now that we have this ... this acceptance? Now the load has been lifted?'

'Good.' Alex's reply was without any great enthusiasm.

'Good?'

Alex shrugged. 'What did you want me to say?'

'Like, how are you feeling?'

'Lonely.'

'Really? Why?'

Alex caught her gaze and held it. 'I'm lonely for you.'

'But I'm right here.'

'You know what I mean, Grace.'

She swallowed hard. 'Could you spell it out for me?'

'We haven't been together since that night, and ... well ... I want you.'

Grace nodded. 'Me too.'

'Good.' Alex gave a smile. He stood up and went over to the cradle and picked it up.

'What are you doing?'

'I'm moving the cradle in with the girls.'

'Wait, what about when Maggie wakes up?'

'She hasn't woken up in the night for nearly a week now.'

'How do you know? You never wake up.'

'I do, I just pretend I don't.'

Grace gave him a stern stare.

'Anyway, I know Irene is more than capable of tending to our little Maggie in the night if she wakes up.'

'Do you think so?'

Alex just shook his head and opened the door. He hefted the cradle out of the room, and suddenly Grace felt nervous. She sat the baby up and burped her, and by the time she'd finished, Alex had come back into the room. He walked over to her and took the baby from her.

'What are you doing now?' she asked.

'Changing the baby for you, and settling her in with her sisters.'

'What am I supposed to do?'

Alex gave her another look that encompassed her from head to toe, and back up again.

'Perhaps you can find something a little more elegant than your everyday work skirt. I won't be more than ten minutes.'

Grace blushed.

'Do you even know how to change a baby's nappy?'

'I'll figure it out.'

Grace watched the door close, and a forest full of butterflies released in her stomach.

By the time he returned, she had donned a graceful satin negligee Meg had insisted she borrow, turned out the lights, and lit a candle. She wasn't that brave. Shucking his braces and casting off his shirt, Alex met her half way across the room.

He took her face in his hands and kissed her deeply. Grace felt the passion rise up like it had the first time they'd been together, and for a split second she felt that worry.

'This is right, Grace. You are my wife, and I love you.'

Grace nodded and allowed her arms to go around his neck.

'Yes, this is right,' she whispered back, 'and I love you too.'

About the Author

Author Page Amazon:
http://tinyurl.com/pvkyb3m
Author Facebook Page:
https://www.facebook.com/MeredithResceAuthor
Website: www.meredithresce.com

Thank you for taking the time to get to know Alex and Grace in *Echoes in the Valley*. I hope you enjoyed their story. 2017 marks the twentieth anniversary of the first release of the full version of *The Manse*, #1 in the *Heart of Green Valley* series. Look out for the new editions of all five previous titles in this series, due for eBook release soon. If you follow me on my FaceBook author page, you will keep in touch with each one as it comes out. Also, I'd love for you to read some of my other titles that are available from Christian Bookstores or online. See my website for details. The Heart of Green Valley series

    Book 1 – *The Manse*

    Book 2 – *Green Valley*

    Book 3 – *Through the Valley of Shadows*

    Book 4 – *Wallace Hill*

    Book 5 – *Beyond the Valley*

    Book 6 – *Echoes in the Valley*

Lastly, I'd love your opinion: I have the story idea for Aimee Shore's story all mapped out. Would you like to see it released. Post your answer on my FaceBook page.